To Jack,

It has been m[y] pleasure to know [&] work with you. I[']ll never forget the tim[e] hung out in the massage and you got me laid cause I... HaHaHa Just broke that day.

Jade
7/29/14

An Endless Journey

An Endless Journey

Jade Dean Krieman

Copyright © 2011 by Jade Dean Krieman.

Library of Congress Control Number: 2011902522
ISBN: Hardcover   978-1-4568-7014-0
              Softcover   978-1-4568-7013-3
              Ebook   978-1-4568-7015-7

All rights reserved. No part of this book may be reproduced or transmitted in any form or by any means, electronic or mechanical, including photocopying, recording, or by any information storage and retrieval system, without permission in writing from the copyright owner.

This is a work of fiction. Names, characters, places and incidents either are the product of the author's imagination or are used fictitiously, and any resemblance to any actual persons, living or dead, events, or locales is entirely coincidental.

This book was printed in the United States of America.

To order additional copies of this book, contact:
Xlibris Corporation
1-888-795-4274
www.Xlibris.com
Orders@Xlibris.com

To Julie W.,

    From the first moment I gazed into your eyes I knew you were special. You captivated me with those Blue Topaz eyes of yours, and that smirk was priceless. I wish at the time I could of surrendered my Heart to you, I know now that with you my heart would have been safe. I have thought of you during this endless journey, during the quiet moments I was allowed to have. Do you believe in love at first site Julie? I believe, I fell in love with you at first sight, and never fell out of love, it was just hiding when I was lost for so long. You were my first love. We never shared a first kiss. We never shared holding hands. What we did share was just as strong, you were and are now a light in the darkness. You are the calm in the storm. Fate has given me a second chance in life, and allowed me to open my heart and soul to you. You know my secrets, you know my pains, you know only the truth. You are my best friend and I now surrender to you my heart, your love warms it, your kindness protects it, your smile fills it with joy. You are a real princess Julie, and I am forever your knight.

With the deepest love and admiration for you,

Jade Dean Krieman

Chapter I

STANDING IN THE blistering snow shower, he could feel the arthritic bones in his finger aching, swelling with each pass of the wind. Not wanting to wear gloves, he wanted to feel the delicate hair trigger on his finger. He would suffer this brutal icing to make sure the shot was perfect – the fatal shot, as in the past, one bullet, one kill. Deciding to sit on the park bench, figuring he had about an hour until the cell phone should ring if everything went according to his plan. It has been such a long time since he designed his plan, his guide for the journey he had been on, and now the journey was coming to its conclusion, and he would finally rest.

Ah, the target is special – more personal; death will come fast. *How long has it been?* the killer thought. *Twenty years?* Twenty years since the day they set up his friend, his best friend, who also was as much his older brother, his mentor, and the only one who was able to refrain him from releasing the murderous beast within.

He admitted to himself that the plan those motherfuckers had created and devised was a brilliant one, almost perfect – almost. They didn't factor in him though. The pain of his friend's death was a constant reminder that he was human – well, some of him; the rest was the beast, a terrible part of him that felt no remorse and knew no mercy, thirsting for the blood of his enemies. Also was the list, the thing that kept him going – that too was at its end. He had made the amends with all he had harmed, except one, but that too would be settled soon.

He still can remember that day the letter came to him. He thought back to the early memories of his childhood, the days he tried so hard to erase, the pain, the abuse, and the suffering. With sixty minutes to kill, so to speak, he remembered the story from the beginning to relive his happiest days, to relive the bond they shared, and to relive the feelings on anguish he felt when the letter touched his hands and the tears scorched his heart as he realized the contents of that letter. As the tears now touched his cheek, he remembered – everything!

Jaden was born in Chicago, a city known for its corrupt nature and unlawful ways. His father an alcoholic and his mother a drug abuser, he had no chance once released from the womb. His family was dirt poor, just had enough to pay some bills but nothing more. The furniture he grew up with were things like a milk crate for a TV table and maybe a couch handed down from someone, not much else. Whenever they did get some nice thing, it would be broken soon after. The rage of a drunken father destroys all around him.

They say it falls on the parents to raise a child and to teach the child what would be needed to be successful in life – the tools to build a good life. Jaden's parents gave him broken tools. They moved around a lot, never staying in the same apartment more than a year, always moving, with him always being the new kid and always starting new. His whole family had roots in Rogers Park, the far north side of Chicago. There they had stayed most of his childhood.

The year is 1970-ish, and chance has set the scenario for the two boys to meet – a very familiar scenario: poverty, abusive parents, and the attraction of hanging in the streets, exploring the unknown. That's the scenario, and then they met and the path was chosen for the both of them. The younger boy, Jaden, had met the kid who lived upstairs in the building, David, and they were hanging out in the alley. David's friend, Jimmy, happened to show up, and David introduced them.

"So what we gonna do today?" asked Jaden. Eyeing the new kid with a feeling of uncertainty, Jimmy suggested they go hunt for snakes on the railroad tracks, testing to see if Jaden would have the balls to go. Jaden thought about the suggestion, and his mind was excited. Hunting snakes was new to him and he was game. David wasn't allowed to leave the alley, so he declined as the other two left for the hunt. As they walked to the hunting grounds, the conversation was a get-to-know-you session, both young boys feeling each other out and both having a familiarity with each other.

Jaden, eleven years old, was about five feet two, stocky build, and not fat but not skinny. His skin wasn't white, more olive color, reflecting the Jewish side of him. He was half Jewish and half German, with long wavy brown hair and light brown eyes that have a kinda orangish tint to them. Jaden was a handsome young boy, and his personality was magnetic and enjoyable to be around. He had a great sense of humor, and away from his home, he was more relaxed, more free to be who he was, and a wild, free spirit always looking for adventure.

Jaden saw Jimmy as a companion in his search for adventure and a partner, someone who would meet the challenges and continue on with the journey. It was fair to say that Jaden liked Jimmy the moment they met and that they would be friends a very long time. He never had a good friend or a best friend for that matter. Maybe Jimmy would be just that, a best friend. As they walked he kept that thought in mind, willing to give Jimmy that chance, letting him fit into that role in his life, but only time will tell.

"Okay, here's the plan. We walk until we see the garden snakes sunbathing on the tracks, and we run to catch them," said Jimmy.

"Do they bite?" asked Jaden.

"Yep, but they ain't poisonous though," replied Jimmy, knowing that this important piece of information reassured Jaden, who was having a great time today – a lot more interesting and exciting than hanging with David.

"I might as well tell you the story of Old Moe," came the voice up ahead.

"Old Moe, what the fuck is Old Moe?" replied Jade. The response was quick, almost as if planned by the older boy.

"Old Moe was a garden snake that has never been caught before – about six feet long and nasty as hell," Jimmy said with a smirk on his face. "Some have come close, but Old Moe has a mean bite, probably take your hand off," Jimmy had said, still with that smirk on his face and still testing Jaden, wanting to see what he was made of.

The hunt was successful; both boys caught a bunch of snakes, which alone would have solidified their new friendship, but it was the conversation that started the bond. The two boys talked about music, something Jaden wasn't up to par on. He really didn't know much about artists or which music was good or not. His only experience with music was the oldies his parents listened to. His father liked the old rock and roll, and his mother liked Motown. Jaden preferred Motown but liked both.

Movies – now that was something Jaden could relate to, and both liked the karate flicks. There were other movies also, but the karate flicks got them both excited and thus began the longest debate on which style was the greatest. Jimmy believed it was the crane, and Jaden felt it was the tiger's claw. And the two argued their points forever it seemed. They even acted out the scenes using their favorite styles. The day was perfect. By the end of the day, it was apparent they would be best friends, through thick and thin.

As Jaden was coming in the door, he knew he was about an hour late from the time he was supposed to be home. He hoped his dad was drunk and already passed out in the room. Nope, he felt the first punch as it hit the side of his head, sending him crashing into the wall next to the fridge, trapped, nowhere to run. He was fucked. Jaden lay on the floor, curling up, trying to protect his head and body, but his dad always found a vulnerable spot. The belt his father used was a thick leather one, with a large metal buckle. With a violent drunk rage, his father swung that belt at his son. Each swing hit its mark, stinging the young boy, hot, searing pain racing through him, numbing the spot that was hit until hit once more. The time seemed to pause for these beatings, and Jaden knew he would have to endure the pain.

He could hear his father's yelling, the drunken slurs that came out his mouth each time he swung that belt. "Ya fuckin' piece a shit," his father kept saying, "don't wanna listen." Another swing, more pain. "I'll show you," he heard right before the buckle of the belt hit him on his head. Jaden cried out in pain, "Stop, you're killing me," but the next blow came right after. Jaden was in terrible pain, his head was throbbing from the first two blows of the buckle, covering his head now, leaving the rest of his body as a sacrifice. His father took the sacrifice and continued to violently beat him until Jaden lay there, unconscious, no longer aware of the pain. There was no dreaming in this type of sleep. This was where you go to avoid life, pain, and death.

Jaden woke up the next morning in pain, his body sore and aching from last night's beatings. He tried to open his eyes, but they both were bruised shut. He just lay there, the tears stinging the wounds. He hated his father, wishing his father was dead. No matter what, he knew every night there would be a beating. Whether it was him or his mom was anyone's guess, but there would be a beating just the same. His father had tried to do that to Jaden's younger sister, Angie, but Jaden got in front of her, taking the blow and incurring the wrath of his father but saving his sister from this maniac's abuse – small sacrifice to make. Jaden loved his sister, and he would take ten beatings a day to protect her from what his father could and would do.

Angie was a year and a half younger than Jaden. She was petite, with long brown hair, which was past her shoulders down her back. She was about five inches at least shorter than Jaden. Angie was a good girl, tough for her age. The two of them were close. Angie knew what her brother was going through – the beatings, the verbal abuse. She could hear it every night from her room, from under the bed where she hid, always fearful she would be next. Jaden had protected her a couple times, and he paid an awful price each time, but he sacrificed himself for her, and she loved him for that.

Angie would get their other younger brother and sister, Tony and Rebecca, and bring them to her hiding place under the bed, protecting them when the horror would start. Jaden protected her; she protected the other two. That was their unspoken agreement. She wished her father was dead. Tony was three years old; Rebecca was one. No motherfuckin' way would Jaden and Angie let their father get to the two youngest; they would die first. Their mother was unable to help; she was usually the first one to get beaten unconscious, unable to protect her children.

I know the people who read this and figure out who they are will then understand things they didn't know back then – all those school days missed and the bruises they showed up to school with. To the cops who would come to their apartment, see the terrible things that had happened to them, and leave, leaving their father there with them, shame on all of you. One day you will have to atone for your part in this story. You stood by and did nothing, and they lived with the horror and the torture of a drunken madman. Don't worry, they won't be coming after you; there are too many of you. Instead I'll just finish the book and let you know how shameful and wrong you all were.

As they spent every day of the summer hanging out together, the bond was being forged between the two. Jimmy, the older of the two, was thirteen, taller, and light skinned. His mother was white, and his father was black. Jimmy lived with his mother; two brothers, one older and one younger; and his mother's boyfriend. He lived about two blocks away from Jaden, making their daily hanging out easy. Jaden lived with both parents and two younger sisters and a younger brother. He was the oldest at eleven years of age. Every day away from his apartment was a good day – away from the beatings he took on a nightly basis by his drunk asshole father.

Jaden looked forward to meeting up with Jimmy, hangin' out and getting into all kinds of mischief. The two of them were both bad influences, not so much on each other, that they could do all on their own, but they fueled each other, supported the ideas each would come up with.

By the end of the summer, the two had decided to form their own street gang, the Deadly Demons. All their friends had joined, of course, and why not? They all hung out together anyways, and it was something cool to do. The gang grew to about fifteen members. Jimmy – he was the leader. Jaden was second in command. This wasn't a real gang though, just hanging out together, doing what kids do. Of course, there was the criminal activity that kids that age do: stealing pop bottles, stealing from stores, and other little bullshit like that. That was what filled their day up.

Walking the railroad tracks and hanging out there was cool too. The cops couldn't see them, and it was the craziest place to play catch-one-catch-all. If you don't know that game, well, it's simple. Set the boundary lines. One person is it and attempts to catch the others. As each person is caught, they help catch the remaining players. The first one caught is it for the next round. Jimmy was usually the last one caught. He was always the prize catch, always chased first but got away just about every time.

Their other favorite game was pom-pom tackle – same as catch-one-catch-all, except that it was played with two goal lines, usually fifty yards across from each other and the goal was to tackle someone instead of tag. That was Jade's favorite game. It was definitely a rough boy's game, and he liked playing rough and showed how tough he was, and he was tough.

Each day, the boys would take daily excursions to several of the local stores, in which they would practice using their stealing skills. That too was a competition among them, and that drove the store workers crazy. The workers couldn't watch them all, and if they tried to stop the boys, they would run out of the store. The pure adrenaline rush was worth it; it was what they lived for and sought each day. Jaden was very adept at theft. He didn't give a fuck about the consequences; he stole because he could and because he needed what he took. Otherwise, he would never be able to have it. Jaden was dirt poor, and shit that he stole was out of his financial reach.

He knew that the other boys knew he was poor, and they really never said anything about it, unless they were talking shit about each other, then it was an optional target for them, not knowing that each time it was brought up, he felt shameful about it, but he never let them know it. He buried that feeling deep within his self, locking it away from himself and others. Jimmy never used that against Jaden though. He knew the feelings Jaden hid from the others, and he would never betray Jaden that way.

Jimmy knew firsthand how bad Jaden had it at home. He was there one night for a sleepover when Jade's father went into another drunken rage. The two boys were in the room when the shouting began, and then they could hear things smashing against the floor and wall. Jimmy had never been through this shit before, and he was scared. He looked at Jaden, and Jaden motioned him to get under the bed and to be quiet. Jaden stayed by the door, pushing against it, attempting to barricade it with his body, offering himself as the only thing that would stand between his father and his best friend. His father tried to open the door, but felt the resistance.

"Open the fuckin' door, you little motherfucker," his father commanded. "No," Jaden replied, pushing against the door harder, awaiting the next move from his father. The door flung open violently, knocking Jaden to the floor. His father was in the room, standing there with a cowboy boot, looking for Jaden – looking for Jimmy. Jaden's father was a racist; he didn't want some black kid in his home, eating his food. He would show that nigger kid just who he was. Blinded by his hate, fueled by the alcohol, his father found Jaden on the floor and started to beat him with the cowboy boot. Jaden wanted to cry out, but he didn't want his best friend to see it. Jimmy saw everything from under the bed. He could see Jade's father's hand with the boot every time it hit Jaden. Jimmy could see the pain Jaden was taking. He could see the god-awful sorrow in Jaden's eyes. Jimmy was crying the silent cry for his friend.

Once the beatings were over, Jimmy crawled out from under the bed, went to Jade's side and tried to soothe him, but he didn't know what to say. Angie came into the room. "Shhh, my dad's asleep and we don't want to wake him." Jimmy had met Angie before. She was cool with him, as cool as a little girl could be. Angie walked into the room and closed the door, sitting next to her brother, trying to comfort him as best as she could.

Angie and Jimmy talked, Jaden just lying there, unable to move and unable to speak. The pain he felt wasn't from the beatings this time; it was the pain of shame and embarrassment. What happened in front of his friend was just too much for him to bear. He was helpless. Jimmy never told anyone ever about that night, and he never slept over at Jade's apartment again while his father lived with them. He had seen in one night enough to last him a lifetime, and he felt bad for his friend. He wished he could help, but he too was powerless.

Chapter 2

END OF SUMMER and school is starting. Jaden has been registered at the local grade school – a familiar feel being the new kid. His parents have moved around so much, it didn't matter anymore. He had the routine down to a science. But this time, he had his friends from summer to lean on, so it was not entirely new.

Fifth grade, and in Mrs. Dugan's class, where all his friends were, except Jimmy. He was in seventh grade. Same shit – make friends, become a class clown, and get them laughing with you instead of at you. Hide the truth about yourself; don't let them know. *It's so shameful*, he thought. Being very poor and raised by fucked-up parents were no joke; it destroyed his self-esteem. He had no new clothes for school and no sense of style for music or anything. Never had to because being poor, he had none of the stuff other kids had; of all his friends, he was definitely the poorest. These were the things he felt inside, and the constant feelings of embarrassment and shame weighed heavily on him. Not having good tools to deal with those emotions, he buried it deep within him, hoping it would go away. It didn't though; it became unresolved, creating other feelings that manifested itself in the form of resentment and anger.

Slowly he could feel small changes taking place within him – a feeling of danger knocking on his mind's door. He knew the change was leading to a more serious life but was unsure of the destination. There was gonna come a time, and soon, when he would need to make a decision concerning his life. Being unsure what the choices were and what they held for him is what baffled him. Something for him to worry about later, or so he thought.

The Demons hung out at Pottawanomie Park, Pott Park for short. The park was also a stronghold for the largest gang in the area, the Simon City Royals. This was a real gang. They carried knives and had gang fights with other gangs, and Jaden was fascinated by the Royals. All the members looked tough like they were warriors, and there were older girls hanging out with them – girls with big breasts, nice big breasts. Jaden was fascinated by breasts as much as he was with the Royals.

The Demons knew the Royals. Well, they were familiar with them, and the royals felt the Demons were no threat to them; they had seen the younger kids in the park many times, and they liked to see which ones could possibly be their future peewee Royals. The two the Royals took notice of was Jimmy and Jaden. Realizing the potential, the Royals invited the two into their protection and made them allies of the Royals. That was a big thing for the Demons – recognition by a real gang. Now they were real. It didn't take long for Jaden and Jimmy to realize that being allies was good, but they wanted to be Royals, even better.

Now the boys have joined the local street gang, a real gang, the Royals. Some of the boys from the Deadly Demons also joined, and together, they became peewee Royals. Their own section was Pott Park. The peewees were about fifteen strong. All of them knew each other before joining the Royals, which only strengthened the bond between them all. The older Royals all had their own favorite peewee and favored them in their own way. The one that favored Jaden was called "The Kid," and Jaden liked him a lot.

Jaden and the peewee Royals mimicked the older Royals and watched and learned from their behavior, and the training began. The older Royals would practice fighting with baseball bats, knives, and just toe-to-toe fighting, honing their skills. Jaden paid very close attention to the practice; something inside him told him these skills would come in handy someday.

As school progressed, Jaden was well aware that he was intelligent, and he did okay in school, except for homework – he hated homework. He did notice one girl, Julie – very pretty, with long brownish blond hair and a beautiful smile with those bright blue eyes that seemed to penetrate him, searing through his skin and touching the deepest part of the soul he tried desperately to protect from all others. Damn, this was a strange feeling. He found himself wanting to be next to her, talk to her, and steal moments with her whenever possible. She was shy though. It was hard to know if she liked him also. He knew there was something very special about her, something unfamiliar to him – almost pure and innocent. His heart raced when he was next to her. He was nervous; and his palms, sweaty. Every chance he got, he would just look at her and feel that thing – you know, that thing.

The classroom was made up of kids that Jaden didn't really know, except for two other peewee Royals in the class, but that's all he needed for a secure feeling. It was the other kids who were the popular ones though, but it didn't matter – he was a Royal. Being a Royal was something he wore as a badge of honor, but around Julie, he didn't feel honored to be a Royal. He felt restricted and kinda ashamed. He knew she was a good girl, innocent and shy, and smart as hell too. What would she like about him? He was a gang member and poor as dirt. He was a filthy piece of shit. Even his own father, the asshole, knew that. Jaden just couldn't understand why Julie even talked to him, but she did.

Every day after school was always the same thing – go home, get outside as soon as possible, and then hang with the Royals and have fun. Having fun consisted of stealing from stores, hanging out, and doing stupid shit like talking about each other's mothers and having spitting contests. They were safe as Royals. The royals were the largest gang in the area. The royals had six sections consisting of about twenty members from each section, but all were under the control of the main section, Farwell and Clark. The other sections were Touhy and Ridge, Damen and Fargo, Jarvis and Ashland, and Pachen Park, and of course, Pott Park.

Hanging with others from each section solidified the bonds and the friendship between all the Royals. That's how the core of the Royals was formed – the ones who would stand the test of time to become the deadliest of the Royals, and Jaden was at the front of that group. This inner core were not the leaders of the Royals, not yet. What they were was the inner circle, the ones who hung together through thick and thin, gaining experience and strengthening their bonds, especially the bond between Jimmy and Jaden.

By then, Jaden saw Jimmy as his chief, his best friend, and his role model. Jimmy had become the most important person in Jade's life, well, almost. There was that beautiful girl from school. Jaden was getting kinda close to her, talking more with her each chance he got. Even though he was on the path of destruction and danger, there was a pulling away from that life he felt when he was around her – a feeling deep inside that made him feel ashamed and dirty, not worth the attention. Jaden couldn't explain it – one side of him wanted this girl more than anything, but another side knew he would spoil her goodness if she was with him, not knowing what "with him" meant. He was only eleven years old, you know.

What was that feeling he felt in his loins? What was the nervousness he felt around her that made him unable to say what he was feeling? Nothing ever became of Jaden and that girl, but he would never forget her. He knew she was important in his life, unsure why, not knowing she would be there in the end. It's a whole lifetime to go until the end though.

Jaden and Julie would meet up at Pott Park a couple times a week. Julie was in gymnastics and also involved in other activities at the park. Jaden would find reasons to be next to her. The both of them would talk, but Jaden was reserved and Julie was shy, not a good mix when trying to discover love and let it grow. Julie could see through Jade's eyes the conflict that was in him, unsure what that conflict was though; she tried to learn more. Jaden didn't let much out though, but he was always nice to her. Maybe he wanted her to know there was a good side of him – something to care about and something to be attracted to – but he himself didn't know what that was, so how could she?

Julie was always staring into his eyes, and he loved looking into hers. She was so beautiful to him as an angel would be. She looked like an angel, with her long hair, pretty smile, and those bright, piercing blue eyes. Jaden was in love, not realizing it at that time, but in love just the same. Julie was Jade's first love.

The both of them met one day by the park fence, and the conversation was light. Jaden was especially quiet. Looking at Julie, he knew and finally accepted that the both of them could not be together. She was pure and innocent and so beautiful and perfect, and he was a piece of shit, worthless and without hope. He would only poison this girl's life if they were to be together – ruin what was so appealing to him. He accepted that fact and ended what little of a relationship they had begun. He was protecting her from himself. That is what true love is – unselfishness. As bad as he yearned for her to be in his life, he put his own desires to the side and protected her, Julie, the first girl he ever loved.

Julie didn't understand what was going on with Jaden. Their talks were usually pretty interesting. Jaden would share bits and pieces of himself, and she would do likewise. Julie had enjoyed Jade's company, the talks, and the little time they shared. Jaden was special to her; she felt a closeness to him she never felt before with a boy. She knew she liked him. She had those feelings for him. She just wanted to get to know him so much more. There was so much she wanted to express to him, but her shyness limited her – held her back.

He liked her – that's what his sister, Angie, had told her. Hmmm, that was interesting when Angie had come up to her and said she wanted to talk to her. The two had hardly ever spoken a word during gymnastics practice. Julie knew Angie hung out with Jaden a lot, and also the Royals, but the gang stuff wasn't her thing. She didn't think much about the Royals, just some kids hanging out. The day she and Angie talked though was more like a messenger giving her a letter. Angie had told her that her brother liked her, but Julie could tell Angie was disturbed by the message, as if she didn't agree with her brother's interest in Julie. Julie just thanked Angie for telling her. She had a feeling Jaden sent his sister to deliver the message and realized his sister did as she was requested to do. The two of them, Jaden and Angie, were very close. They shared some bond that went beyond brother and sister stuff. There definitely was something more stronger Julie felt.

Julie Never knew why Jaden had exited her life. All she knew was that he had began distancing himself from her, staying away and avoiding her. *Was there something I have said, done, not done*, she questioned herself. She thought things were going pretty good between them. They would meet up after school at the school and sometimes at Pott Park and just talk. Jaden would share some thoughts and things about himself, as Julie would also, but they talked of other things too. Everything seemed like they were heading in a good direction, like they would be boyfriend and girlfriend, but Jaden pulled back all of a sudden.

She had noticed the look in his eyes – that look of being torn between something. He had looked like he had made a decision and was saddened by that decision. She just didn't understand. Angie had told her that Jaden liked her, although he hadn't confirmed it himself, but still, the time spent together had to have meant something, hadn't it?

Julie was hurt by Jaden's sudden withdrawal from her, as if some unseen force was coming between them – a force she didn't know or understand. She wanted to say something to Jaden, tell him she liked him a lot and wanted to be his girlfriend, but something halted her and cautioned her to say nothing. Julie remained silent.

She remembered the last day she hung out with Jaden. She had met him at Pott Park, over by the fence that ran the length of the park property. She was wearing her favorite white coat, the one given to her by her grandmother – her grandmother's favorite coat. She liked the way she looked in this coat, and she wanted to wear it when she went to meet Jaden. She wanted to look her best, not for him though, but for herself. If Jaden liked the way she looked, then even better, she thought.

It was that day that she had really seen the conflict in his eyes and the change in his demeanor and hear the nervousness in his voice. She always had a sense about people, able to see the things others didn't see – very perceptive of her at such an early age. She knew today was gonna be a bad day but wasn't prepared for the end of the friendship between the two of them. Jaden explained some stupid thought or whatever. She didn't remember the reason why he ended it, only that he did.

She used every bit of her strength to keep from crying in front of him; she would not give him that. She would be understanding and would accept his decision without regret. Deep within herself though, she was crying and her heart was breaking and feeling an emptiness from the words he had said. She told Jaden she had to go home, turned around, and started the long walk. Unable to stop the tears as they fell from her eyes, she never looked back and she never saw his tears.

Chicago has a new mayor, a woman, and she has new ideas, ideas that will forever change Jaden's life. The mayor decided to send different kids from different hoods to different schools – not a good idea. The end result was an immediate influx of kids from the west side of Chicago – gang members of the Vice Lords. This gang was a deadly gang, familiar to the battles of gang warfare, very violent, and unmerciful. They saw this new part of Chicago as a ripe place ready for the taking. All they had to do is kill a couple of Royals, and they figured they would abandon everything. Nothing could be further from the truth; all they did was awaken the natural killers from their sleep.

By the time, Jaden was twelve years old. The battle lines were drawn; and the numbers, fortified within the gangs. The Royals lost most of their membership due to the violence. Now they numbered about thirty. The Vice Lords were about a hundred and fifty. They controlled Howard Street completely. The gangster disciples, who had become allies with the Royals, were no help. The Latin Kings, enjoying their newfound freedom from the expansion of the Vice Lords, were able to grow and expand. They now grew to three sections, with a fourth one growing, numbering about a hundred members. The Royals only had two sections now, Farwell and Clark, and Pachen Park. The other Royals in Chicago were experiencing the same problems, and the citywide Royal leadership sent word down to start doing burglaries and using the money to buy guns. They were gonna go to war with everyone in a final attempt to solidify their existence and future.

Burglary was a new crime to Jaden, one he took to very fast – fast money and good money – and the end result was guns. There were deaths, some gang related and some not. This story isn't about that though. It's about retribution. Jaden had done a burglary to the home of a dead Royal, a Royal who had owed him money and whose father had guns in the home. Needless to say, he got caught and arrested. The police sent him to the Audi home. Jaden had heard many stories of this place, this place where your manhood is put to the test.

Sure enough, he was tested. The other kids there thought he would be weak and vulnerable, maybe because he was a white kid. He didn't know for sure. What the other kids didn't know was that just about every night of Jade's life, he was beaten by that drunk asshole of a father. Beatings were nothing new to him and not something he feared. Now he got to fight back. The others soon learned he was not weak but strong, strong with hate and resentment. Each one he fought became his father, and he beat them as if they were his father. Jaden has built his reputation up as a fighter, down for the hood. He was a Royal and gonna stand on his feet.

Six months later, he was given probation and set free. Jimmy took it hard that Jaden would steal from a dead Royal, but Jaden explained they were at war and the guns were needed. Jimmy agreed and they were good. As the time passed, every day was more of the same thing – hanging out, drinking alcohol, and doing drugs. First was the weed. Jimmy and Jaden tried it for the first time together. Jimmy loved it but Jaden didn't. He felt paranoid and uncomfortable. This wouldn't be for him, but there will be other drugs that he will try and come to love and become dependent upon – addicted.

It finally happened at the age of fourteen. The Royals were now holding a large cache of handguns, and each royal had one. The time was coming, and the war was at hand. There had been small fights between the Royals and the Vice Lords in the past months, but no deaths, each gang trying to feel the other out. Then came the day when some Vice Lords had caught and killed a Royal. Steve was going home from a party and got caught by the Vice Lords. He was pushed inside a hallway and beaten to death with golf clubs. This was when Jaden and Jimmy had realized it was for real. There was no safe zone anymore.

On the way home, Jimmy and Jaden had decided to walk the railroad tracks, avoiding any unnecessary contact with Vice Lords or cops. Jimmy had the .38 revolver, and after Jaden bothered him forever, it seemed, to hold and carry the gun, Jimmy gave it to him. The feel of it was oily and heavy – awkward at first – but a feeling of power and strength overcame Jaden from that feel of the gun.

As they were almost at Pott Park, three black teenagers were coming toward them. "Vice Lords," Jimmy whispered to Jaden. "Be cool, let me do the talking," Jimmy said to Jaden, which he agreed to. "Wassup, Vice Lords," said the smaller one as he threw the three-finger gang sign up in the air. "Wassup, Royals," replied Jimmy. "We Royal killers, don't ya know?" said the tallest one. Jaden watched as the back-and-forth talking shit got louder and now these three were about fifteen feet away from him and Jimmy. "Get some bitch as hoes," said Jimmy.

The quiet one reached under his shirt, and Jaden could see the handle of the gun before the Vice Lord could pull it out. Without hesitation, Jaden pulled the gun from around his back, aimed at the Vice Lord with the gun, and fired twice. He was dead before he hit the rails on the tracks. The other two Vice Lords were frozen when Jaden heard Jimmy yell, "Smoke those other two bitches," which Jaden obeyed, emptying the revolver. Within five seconds, all three were dead.

Jaden just stared at them, unsure of what just happened and unsure if he actually was the one who pulled the trigger, but the murder weapon was in his hand, the hand that was as still as the wind. Jimmy grabbed the gun and pulled Jaden away from the site, Jaden moving but not fully aware of moving. He was stunned in his mind as he tried to understand everything that just happened.

Jimmy brought Jaden to his place and right up into his room. Jimmy took the gun and left for what seemed like forever but was only about five minutes. Jaden was in shock, not because he killed them – he knew they were gonna kill them if he didn't shoot first – but in shock at the strange feeling that was taking over him – a feeling of sureness, a feeling of power and strength, and a feeling of superiority. Jimmy knew something had changed that day within Jaden – something he respected but also feared.

There was another feeling he had – something that made him want to be sick – but he pushed that feeling down deep, locking it away. Whatever it was would not be good for him now. He had crossed a line. He was now in too deep – no room for soft, caring feelings anymore. The innocence of Jaden was slipping away, fading into some void where he wouldn't be able to reach it, held down by the other feelings he had: power, strength, respect, and fear, fear others would have of him. Now they wouldn't try to embarrass him ever again and make fun of his family life. There would be a price to pay, and he would collect from anyone who owed. He felt secure knowing he would be a force to reckon with if ya crossed his path. He held his head up higher now and walked with just a little more confidence than yesterday.

Chapter 3

THERE WAS NO word of the shooting, no extra police presence around the hood, and no questions or shakedowns. *Did they already know who did it?* Jaden questioned himself. He was nervous about the consequences. He never told a soul, and neither did Jimmy. No one was ever arrested for the murder, and there was only a small article about the killings in the paper.

Jaden never knew what happened with the gun, and that bothered him. He later found out that Jimmy brought the gun to his older brother's apartment, and he melted the gun down. Jimmy explained to the leaders of the Royal section that the gun is gone but had been used for nation business. The leaders accepted the story without question. The bond was now even stronger between Jaden and Jimmy.

Jimmy was satisfied they wouldn't get caught for that murder, but what bothered him was the way Jaden was acting – more outgoing, more reckless, and looking for something. *Maybe the next kill*, he thought. He decided he would keep an eye on Jaden – protect him from himself, so to speak. That wouldn't be easy. The change had been made. Jaden was now a warrior, craving the battle and craving the victory. Jimmy would have to join him on this quest or be left behind; he joined.

The war wasn't in the papers or on TV. Most people didn't even know it existed. The police kept that quiet. Funny how they built a police station in the district though. Wonder what was their reason?

The Royals lost no other members to the Vice Lords or the Kings for that matter. The few members who remained were the downest, the ones who were committed to the cause. Many Vice Lords and Latin Kings were killed or badly beaten in the next year and a half at the hands of the Royals, who by now were feared and respected. When the topic of gangs was brought up, the police and the insiders knew that the Royals from Farwell and Clark were the deadliest and most violent in Rogers Park.

The bodies that were left behind for the police to identify, the scenes of the shootings and the stabbings – all these were evidence to the police of what was happening, and they knew they had a gang war on their hands. The daytime was quiet usually, so the police increased the patrols at night, requesting more tactical units in their district. The new increased presence was felt by every criminal, gang related or not. It didn't matter though; the gangs owned the streets in Rogers Park – every alley, street, and gangway was theirs, and the cops were confused as to the tactics that would succeed in stopping this surge of violence.

Both Jimmy and Jaden had built up their reputations on the street. The time was spent fighting, getting laid, and partying. Jaden had built up his skills at criminal activities to include burglary and snatch and grab. These Royals were close with each other. Every day was spent on the streets, watching each other's backs, fighting for their lives, and fighting for their territory. The Kings and the Vice Lords always came with a lot of members when they came for battle, but the Royals would always unleash a hailstorm of bullets, sending the invaders back to romper room – back to their holes in the ground.

The years of burglaries and building up the arsenal had brought them a strength that didn't need membership numbers. These Royals were killers, and they had the weapons to stand strong, protecting the street names they claimed. Farwell and Clark was the nation. The throne of the nation was that corner, and none would take the throne. It had been held since the start of the Royals; it will be held forever.

The planning and tactics of the Royals were usually all defense. They rarely went into the enemies' hood to attack. Well, rarely there were some excursions, but I can't tell ya that. Can't describe what happened. No one was ever charged for it, and they won't be because of this book. The Royals became stalkers though. They would go off in groups of two, both armed and fully loaded, looking for the stragglers, unsuspecting victims who were not paying attention, and they usually breathed their last breath for it.

The Kings were the natural enemies of the Royals, but the Vice Lords were the prized kill. They had an air of arrogance to them like they were untouchable and beyond harm. They were soon brought back to reality. The Royals had the Vice Lords against a wall. The Lords were no longer coming to the Royals' hood. They were now struggling to defend their territory. The Royals didn't want that. They wanted their death; they wanted to kill them Lords, smash them into extinction, and come at them with that thought and goal.

This wasn't a game, not a fun time to live in Rogers Park. This was a fuckin' war. That's how Jaden looked at it. The area was a battleground, the streets were the battle routes, and the enemy was everywhere. His mission was to destroy the enemy at all costs, and he thrived in that endeavor. Many had fallen to his gun. The only problem was that the guns were running low. The Royals had a plan; every time a gun was used in a murder, it would be melted down to scrap metal, unable to be used against a Royal in the event one was arrested and charged for a murder. It would take an eye witness to convict them, and there were none.

Hanging out was a learning process for Jaden and everyone else. These Royals were like a pride of hyenas, each one searching for their place within the ranks of the group. Some would establish their dominance as leaders and some as killers who could not be controlled but still welcomed. Some would establish themselves as omegas, always getting tested and always getting fucked with. Nothing ever would satisfy the sadistic members of the Farwell and Clark Royals.

The membership was now thinned out. The main ones were Sinbad, Lloki, Lil Santos, Six Pack, Bandit, Stoney, Psych, Casper, and Popeye. These were the full-time Royals. There were part-time Royals. They came around when they could. They would party and help make the numbers larger, but they were not the hard-core ones; they were not the killers.

Lil Santos, half Mexican and half Cuban, was the son of a whore. We call him Santos for short. Well, he was kinda shorter than the rest of us. Santos was a fucked up kid from the time he was about ten years old. He was removed from his home and placed in different group homes on a constant basis. He would either get kicked out or run away back to the hood. His childhood was similar to Jade's. They too shared a bond. Santos was known for his extreme violent behavior and his tortuous ways to the lesser Royals, always brutalizing them and always keeping them afraid of him. He would start beating on them in a second, trying to harden them and trying to get them to commit the acts that would tear away their innocence.

Most Royals and the people who hung out with the Royals hated Santos and were terrified of him, never knowing when they would become his next target. Not Jimmy or Jaden though; the both of them had lost their innocence years ago. They had both signed on for life. Jaden and Santos met when they were fourteen. Both of them instantly got along and had much in common, but the bond between them was the fact that each one would go all the way and see the mission through, whichever mission was at hand.

Jaden didn't especially like Santos's methods, but he did get the job done. The two of them had increased the peewee membership of the Royals from about seven to about thirty in just one summer. The funny thing is that Santos was also the one who ran those same peewee Royals off with his brutality.

Santos never saw the big picture and never realized the worth of the lesser Royals. He was always living in the moment. For all his brutality and hardness, Santos was by far the best ladies' man of all the Royals. He always was able to get the girl he went after. Every girl he had he controlled without remorse and without concern. He was ruthless and mindfucked each one.

Six Pack was an alcoholic who was unreliable and usually an idiot, but he was down for the hood. When shit went down, he would be there. He wasn't good for much else though. He was always too drunk to have any other worth. He was white, about the same age as Jimmy, on the fat side, and also a womanizer. He had no problem beating the woman he was with for whatever reason that struck him. He wasn't into much criminal activity and never went on the hunt but always staying in the hood, always in the bar, and always drunk.

Bandit was the sneaky motherfucker. He was Jaden's age and all-Mexican, which bothered him. He was the younger brother of older Royals, well taught in the codes of the street life. He was with Jaden and Santos every day – the three amigos as it were. The crimes these three committed were unbelievable. Burglary was their favorite though. The three of them would do a burglary in about six minutes flat.

With the routine they had, they had become so precise in their methods. Once in the home, they would split up. One would grab a bedsheet and lay it on the floor. The other would disconnect the electronics and place them on the sheet and wrap it up. The third would start the ransacking of the bedrooms. They left no piece of clothing or articles untouched and would even check the dirty clothes hamper – don't laugh. People stash shit there also.

These three had committed about two hundred burglaries in a summer's time. Once out of the home, they would make their way to the safe spot and then check each other. All three would try to stash from the others, and they all knew this reason for searching each other. The take was always about four hundred dollars once everything was sold. The three of them would do about three burglaries a day, unless the first one was a gold mine. Their friendship wasn't based on trust, on caring, or on any meaningful foundation. No, their bond was built on greed, fear, selfish need, and loneliness.

He was eventually arrested and sent to St. Charles for a year and a half. St. Charles, a teenager prison, was a tough place to go and survive. Time spent there was all about learning from other teenage criminals. Jaden had met other Royals, as well as other members of various gangs from Chicago, and learned their ways and the crimes they committed. Life at St. Charles was about routines: the waking up in the morning, the going to school, or a job assignment and then hanging out in the living unit. The place was filled with nothing but gang members, ranging from the age of twelve up to twenty.

It was in St. Charles that Jaden learned about all the different gangs from Chicago. I know you want me to list them and want to know the names of the different gangs, but I won't, not in the story part of the book but maybe in the back or something. Jaden had heard the stories of St. Charles from the older Royals, knew what to expect, and knew how to react.

After being assigned to a living unit in the general population, he was tested by a Latin count. The count had tried to size Jaden up and thought he would be weak and attempted to play him as such. He told Jaden while in the food line that he wanted Jade's tray of food. Jaden said, "Sure, let me put some more on it," barely able to contain the smile from the thought of what he was gonna do. The tray was filled now with plenty of food and hot, steaming coffee. Jaden looked at the count and smashed the fuckin' tray across the count's face, knocking him out for the count – no pun intended. That little stunt got Jaden two things: The first was thirty days in the hole; and the second, a reputation for violent behavior.

That's what St. Charles was all about – each kid testing the other, trying to determine each other's weakness and taking advantage of it. Jaden stood his ground, and each time he did, he became more violent than the last time. The more violent he became, the fewer challenges he faced. Was he scared every fuckin' time, knowing that anyone at any time could be taken down? He was always on guard.

Jaden was assigned to school, and he took to it okay. He was never very good in math and just didn't understand it until he met the teacher in St. Charles. The way this person taught had Jade's attention. The teacher was down-to-earth, very cool, and very smart, taking his time to get the lessons across to the students, making sure they had a grasp of mathematical principals.

Jaden understood the number one thing about math – all problems were solved using only four different applications, multiplication, division, addition, and subtraction. Everything else was secondary. Just know the order of what to do next. This was much simpler for Jaden to grasp, and he did. Jaden was learning math and liking it. Dealing with money was math, working a job was math – everything in life was math. Jaden had finished with his studies and completed school in St. Charles. He was set to parole in about thirty days; he couldn't wait.

At the time of his release, he was sixteen. He had become a much-hardened criminal and more determined to be a well-known royal. He liked the respect he was given but enjoyed the fear others felt of him. This was his niche. He got home and went right back to the hood where nothing really changed except Jaden, and the other Royals saw the difference in him.

The daily life was set, and they all participated. The theme was party, have sex, and gang bang. The sex came easy. The girls who hung out with the Royals made themselves a part of the Royal structure and accepted what was expected of them. Jaden took advantage of the offerings as well as the rest. They were all friends and had all become Royals for their own reasons. There were many reasons to join a gang: protection, acceptance, a sense of belonging to something, to meet boys, and to meet girls. Whatever the reason, the kids joined.

The real reason though was bad parenting most likely. I can guarantee you that each one of the kids who joined a gang was not getting the proper love and affection at home and not shown or taught what good self-esteem was. The problem always starts with the parenting. Parents usually teach what they were taught. The vicious cycle is ruthless and continuous, unless broken by counseling and therapy. All would change though, and soon.

Jaden had experimented with new drugs, and acid had found its way to Jaden. He loved it. It removed any feelings of guilt or remorse that would sneak into his mind. He was able to just enjoy the high and forget who he was and all that happened to him growing up. He could escape from reality for a while and play, so to speak. The only thing Jaden didn't like was sex on acid. He had tried that just one time, in the back of a car with one of the lady Royals – bad experience, plus the girl's older brother had caught him, but that didn't matter. What would he say to Jaden? Jaden was a Royal, but more importantly, Jaden was a bad motherfucker. The girl's older brother knew of Jade's reputation and had heard the stories of shit Jaden had done. The brother just kept his mouth shut and acted like nothing happened, so did Jaden. Please don't confuse Jaden in your mind; he may have been the victim of abuse growing up, but he was an asshole now. Jaden is not a hero and not a good person, no matter what happened in the past.

You see, Jaden never forgot the feeling he felt when he killed those three Vice Lords, and he wanted the chance to feel it some more. The only problem he had was that he didn't like the fact that someone else knew what he did, even if it was his best friend Jimmy. Jaden knew everyone had a breaking point, even the both of them. Jaden went on his own when he wanted to feel that feeling, and no one ever knew, except him.

Two parts of Jaden were at war, the good side and the evil side. The evil side won those battles just about every time. Jaden was a killer, and nothing could change that. Jimmy never fired a gun his whole life. This was the separation between the two. Jimmy liked the fist fighting. He wasn't afraid to carry the gun; he would use it if he had to but preferred not to if given the choice.

The events that happened soon after became known as the insane years for the Farwell and Clark Royals, so much so that they changed their status from almighty to insane, Insane Simon City Royals. The other sections didn't like this, but Farwell and Clark was too strong for any section to stop them. The name insane went to their head, and they acted the part. The nightly adventures into other gang hoods started to increase more frequently – not a smart thing to do, but they did it anyways.

One time, as they were driving by Armitage and Kedzie, just creeping, looking for something, they came across some Kings hanging out in the alley behind the bar at the corner. Stoney pulled the car to the T-section in the alley and waited. Jaden, Bandit, and Bubba got out and went through the gangway, looking for the two perfect points of attack. They had to be careful. This was one of the Kings' stronghold. Over a hundred Kings are from this section. There would be more around somewhere – they had to be careful.

Ski masks on, they crept up to the six Kings, unnoticed by them. The three Royals reached about thirty feet away, the Kings unaware, until the loud thunder rolled from the cannons the three were firing. Within thirty seconds, it was over. The three Royals made it to the getaway car, and they drove away untouched and unchallenged.

That night there would be mothers in agony at the moment the police notifies them their sons had been gunned down. The mothers would insist their sons were innocent and good boys, but no, they were not. They were Kings, and how many innocent people have they killed? Lesson one, join a gang and you are not innocent. Your death will be a heartbeat away.

These are the excursions these Royals took. They were a hit squad, with one goal in mind: to kill their enemies before they killed them – simple shit. Got it?

This life is fuckin' for real, and Jaden was for real about it. There was no half stepping the life – all or nothing. That was his feelings about the friends and the associates the Royals had – the ones who were kinda close to them enough to be cool from association but not willing to put in the work and not willing to have blood on their hands or soul. Jaden had disgust for these so-called friends, never the one to hang out with them. He preferred to be with the ones he knew who had his back. That in itself was a joke also 'cause they had his back in a fight, but when it came to real things, everyone was out for themselves.

Then in the summer, when Jaden was sixteen, he was at the game room where the Royals hung out, smoking some weed with another Royal when he saw her, a girl he had never seen before but stole the very breath from his lungs. He felt an old but familiar feeling; something from his past was awakened. Her name was Judy. She was about an inch shorter than him, with blue eyes and fair skin. Her hair was blond and very long. He couldn't take his eyes off her, just staring at her, remembering someone he once had loved very much – remembering Julie.

He thought it was ironic that both their names were similar, like it was destiny giving him another chance in some way, and he wouldn't pass the chance up this time. Judy was so beautiful and so enticing to Jaden. He needed to make the approach and introduce himself. He wasn't the unsure boy at eleven years old no more. He was more experienced now. He knew what to say and how to say it. He knew how to be cool. This time, the need to protect someone from him wasn't there. He was thinking only of his needs and his desires and not of the other person's.

"Hey, my name is Jaden," he said. The girl said her name and the name of the girl with her. Jaden asked if they wanted to smoke some weed. The girls replied yes. The four of them sat in the hallway to an apartment building, talking and getting high for a while till it got dark out. They decided to walk to the lakefront. While walking, Jaden was nervous. He wanted to hold this Judy's hand but didn't want her to reject him. He must have counted to ten like five different times before he got the nerve. He reached across and grabbed her hand, and she grabbed back – the beginning of a teenage romance that will have dire consequences.

Jaden was in love from that first night – well, what he felt love should be, which was a distorted form of love based on selfish desires and wants. He was never taught what true love was; he had no clue. Only once in his life had he done an unselfish act out of love, an act that he thought came from somewhere other than his own wants and desires.

Jaden had desired Julie very much, but he let her go and missed her ever since that day. He had a couple girlfriends since then. In fact, he had one now, but Jaden was a cheater. Strange how love, even distorted love, can cloud a person's thinking on one's life. And from the first night Jaden and Judy were together, Jaden's thinking and goals had become clouded. The two of them spent all their time together. They talked about a lot of things they felt were important, and some that were not. They shared inner thoughts with one another – thoughts they shared with no other person.

The bond between them was growing, and Jaden was feeling happy. They were the couple. Every guy wanted Judy, as there were plenty of girls who wanted Jaden. Judy was dedicated to the relationship, but Jaden was weak when it came to sex. He cheated and cheated often. Judy had found out about Jade's indiscretions. Torn between breaking up with him or not, she just wasn't sure what to do. She needed to confront Jaden about it and needed to know what the fuck was up.

When Jaden saw her, he knew she was told what happened and knew he was caught, and he was concerned she would break up with him, but he needed to talk to her and explain himself. She stood there as he explained, telling her that he never once attempted to have sex with her, wanting the moment that they do have sex to be special – to mean something more than satisfying some urge or feeling. He wanted her to be sure and ready when they would make love. He told her he still had urges though, and the way these girls threw themselves at him . . . they were just a fuck. She would never be just a fuck. He realized just how true this explanation was. It wasn't some good ass game he was trying to give her and some lie to escape losing her. He meant every word.

Judy realized the truth in his eyes and understood the honesty he was saying. She forgave him. That night they made love, and she had no regrets. Jaden was very gentle and loving that night, and she fell deeper in love with him, surrendering herself completely to him, loving him completely. Judy knew she would have to satisfy her man and to do the things he desired in order to keep him hers. She would satisfy his every desire.

Jaden still cheated though. There were too many other girls who wanted him and had desired his attention that he couldn't refuse. It wasn't so much the sex; it was the fact that someone wanted him and someone actually chose him. This was overwhelming since he had no real self-esteem. The sex was good though; he must admit that.

They were together for one year until Jaden was finally found guilty on an aggravated battery case. He was fighting. He had brutally smashed in the skull of some kid he thought was a Vice Lord and almost killed him. Now he was sent to St. Charles for the second time, a longer time. This was hard for Jaden 'cause he felt insecure about Judy and worried she would find another lover. The worst for Jaden was when Judy admitted she was pregnant by Jaden but had an abortion. He was crushed. The feeling of anguish and sorrow that he felt I cannot describe.

Judy knew Jaden was gonna do some time and their love would be tested, and to make matters worse, she was pregnant. She had some serious things to think about. Weighing her options, she knew what would be best. She didn't tell Jaden she was pregnant. She knew his romantic side would be a barrier when she would have the abortion, so she kept it a secret. She loved Jaden, but their future was uncertain and she was uncertain about having a child. Abortion was the best choice, not one she took lightly. She would have to eventually tell Jaden, but that could wait.

After Jaden was sentenced and sent to St. Charles for the second time, Judy received a call from him, and they talked for about five minutes. Judy felt guilty for not telling him about the abortion, but she was angry and hurt, Jaden had cheated again before he went to jail this time. He had betrayed her love and trust again, and she was very hurt, very embarrassed, and very resentful toward him – he lied to her.

She sat down at the coffee shop and began a very lengthy letter to him, revealing all she knew, the pregnancy, and the abortion. She didn't hold her feelings back; she unleashed everything she felt onto him. The paper was stained by the tears that fell on it. Jaden got the letter and reread what he thought he read, and now his heart sank. Once again he fucked up; once again he had lost a girl he had loved. He felt like there was no hope of keeping Judy and that she would leave him for good now.

He would have to serve about eighteen months on this sentence, and he wondered about all the things that would change in that time. He talked to a guard he knew, asked for a favor, and was allowed to make a direct call to Judy. He needed to talk to her. He needed to know about the baby she aborted, about why she aborted the baby, and why she would hurt him that way before she knew about the cheating. He just had too many questions and a whole bunch of feelings, unsure of what his future held.

He was angry. The decisions he had made and the actions on the street had caused him to get locked up and be separated from Judy, and now the chance of being a father was taken from him. He was more than angry. He was furious; he was gonna hurt someone. He had other things to worry about also. While out in the real world, Jaden had put more tattoos on himself, and one of the tattoo's he had was an upside-down king's crown with a pitchfork going through it, a mark of disrespect to the Kings. He wore that mark with fuckin' pride on the street, but in here, where there were many Latin Kings around him, this would cause problems for him.

Jaden was well known among the Royal nation. Inside the jail as well as outside, he was well respected by all the Royals and even other gang members. The first month of being in St. Charles, he had become the first C of the joint. The joints rank system for most gangs goes like this in the juvenile system, from top to bottom: first C (captain) and second C (these two controlled the whole joint).

Then there were the first lieutenants (they controlled each housing unit), second lieutenant, chief enforcer, enforcers, and then membership. Jaden knew many of the gang members in St. Charles, most because they were there from the last time he was in. The place is a revolving door for most offenders.

The Kings had sent word to the Royals and the gangster disciples that they wanted the upside down crown removed from Jade's arm or they would come after him. Jaden sent a message back, "Come get it." The Kings started the planning and waited for their chance.

About the same time, on the streets, his sister, Angie, was dating some guy who lived outside the hood. She had found out he was a King and decided to break up with him. He tried to beat her down. She stabbed him in the heart and killed him. (The rest is her story. I'll let her tell that story; I'll tell mine.) The Kings were now even more furious. They knew about the murder, they knew Jade's sister did it, and they knew Jaden killed Kings on the street, so they were gonna kill him. There was gonna be a war in the joint. This would be the first war ever.

About three weeks later, Jaden was working in the dining room of the kitchen, mopping floors. The first chow lines were coming through, and the Kings were in the first lines, maybe about twenty of them. Jaden kept his eye on them, watching for any little sign, something that would give him a hint as to their intent, and he noticed it. They were staring at him. They had the look, the look of purpose and intent. He prepared himself.

Jaden started to twist the mop handle slowly, releasing it from the mop head but keeping that fact hidden, waiting patiently for the first wave of the attack. Then they came, about six of them, running at him screaming, "Royal killer," announcing to all their intent. Jaden took the mop handle and broke it in half, each piece about three feet long, and held both pieces like swords, and he entered the battle, swung with precision and strength, and with anger and fear, and put the first wave down. He was standing there untouched – the victor.

Then with a motion of some unseen signal, every single King charged at him. He was ready but never got the chance. He was tackled from behind by a staff member and protected by his body, and about thirty staff members rushed into the dining area and subdued the charging Kings and placed them in handcuffs. The battle was finished – well, the first part of the battle was. Jaden would get even and show them bitches how to conduct an attack.

The staff had all the Kings from the dining hall transported to the confinement building's holding cell, and Jaden also. All of the Kings were in the holding area. Jaden was in a chair outside the holding cell for his own protection. As he was sitting there, he had seen Joker, a Royal who worked in the confinement building. He signaled to Joker and gave him the orders. Joker acknowledged and then informed the staff he was gonna go to lunch. Joker was walking to the chow hall, saw the Royals from Lincoln and Adam cottage, about thirty of them, and gave them the signal. They acknowledged, and went into the chow hall prepared for the battle.

They got their food and sat at the tables waiting, waiting for a Peewee to come to chow. Peewee was the first C for the Kings; Peewee was the only target. Pierce Cottage was now entering the chow lines, and Peewee was unaware of the orders against him. As the Royals were getting up to empty their trays and exit the chow hall, they positioned themselves next to Peewee and then attacked him. Those Royals had about two minutes with Peewee before the staff could interfere. They had fucked him up very bad that peewee needed to be transported to a hospital in the town of St. Charles.

The warden of St. Charles put the facility on lockdown. This shit had to end and end now. The warden called a meeting with the chief of security and discussed the problem. They then had a meeting with the leaders of each gang together in the warden's office to enlighten these little fucks as to what was gonna happen, and they would follow the directions or life would be hell for each of them. The gang leaders agreed; the war was over. Ever since that day, there would be a heavy presence of staff members in the dining hall during chow time.

Judy would visit Jaden in jail from time to time and that was nice, but he had a problem. The state of Illinois had notified him that he would not be allowed to parole to Illinois and would have to leave the state. Would Judy go with him? He didn't know. He thought about how he would tell her and ask her. He had two months left before release. Judy had said she would go with him to Florida for a week. That was fine. He thought if he could have her for one week, she would stay, but he didn't know there were changes in her life too, but he would soon find out.

They arrived in Fort Lauderdale and were met by Jaden's mom at the bus stop. Judy and Jade's mom got along very well from before, so this was nothing new. They spent all their time together, hanging at the beach, shopping, and just chillin' in the trailer. Jaden was feeling reassured that all was going well.

On the fifth day there, Judy went with Jade's sister, Amy, to the flea market, but Jaden stayed home. He was talkin' with his mom when the phone rang. It was Judy's best friend, Lori. "Hey, Jaden, how you feeling?" she asked. Jaden replied fine and that Judy was out. Lori asked if Judy had told him. "Told me what?" he said. Lori explained that Judy was now sharing an apartment with Jimmy. They were lovers and had been for the past seven months. Jaden dropped the phone and was in shock. The evil part was growing, and resentment was the fuel.

He told his mom and decided it was time for Judy to leave. She had gotten her revenge on him for breaking her heart each time he cheated. Now it was his turn to feel that pain. And he did. When Judy returned with his sister, he asked her about Jimmy, and she admitted it with sadness in her eyes. Jaden had his mom take her to the bus station that day, and she went back to Chicago, free from the past, but not Jaden though. His heart was hardened with each tear he shed. His mind and soul were tormented over the betrayal from his friend, his best motherfuckin' friend, Jimmy.

What was left of his humanity was now dead and buried so deep behind a wall of protection that he would never let another touch him. He would use everyone to his advantage and never think twice about it. Revenge though – it burned in his eyes. He wanted revenge on Jimmy, that weak motherfucker who never used a gun. At that moment he knew he would kill Jimmy one day, and he accepted that.

Chapter 4

JADEN WAS FUCKED up in the head. The agonizing pain of Judy's revenge was something he wasn't prepared for. The double betrayal had left him an emotional wreck, and his family knew it, but what could they do? Jaden was never taught how to process these emotions – how to feel them and resolve them. No. What he was taught was to harbor the anger, allow the resentments to fester, and blame others for his pain. He knew who was to blame – Jimmy. How could he? Was he wrong about their friendship? Was everything a fuckin' lie? All these thoughts ran wild in his mind, but the one thing that bothered him most, the icing on the cake, was whether they were laughing at him. Goddamn, he was gonna make him pay.

Every day was this same mind fuck and emotional roller coaster. Maybe it was because it was easier to focus on the anger toward Jimmy than the betrayal from Judy. Damn, he loved her his way for so long, it was ripping him apart. There were only so many tears.

Jaden ended up living in Florida for four years. He ended up meeting an old girlfriend, the very first girl he ever had sex with back years ago when he had visited his grandparents in Florida. Jaden started dating Sandra for a while, and they got married at the age of nineteen, not because he wanted to but because Sandra pressured him.

Sandra was in love with Jaden. Jaden was always someone exciting to her, not like the other boys. He had a hardness to him that cautioned you and made you wary to approach him and a certain confidence. He was also fun and willing to do anything without caution, and that was attractive to her. Jaden had revealed some of his past to Sandra – the gang life and the jail time – but not much more. Some things are best left unsaid.

Julie was nineteen now, and high school was over with and college was right around the corner. All those years of studying, following the rules, and making the right choices in life were paying off. She had applied at five different top colleges and had been accepted at each one. Her options were open, and her path was very clear. At least she thought it was clear until she met David. David was five feet eight and stocky built, with long brown hair. He had a certain hippy way about him, and Julie was attracted to him at first sight.

Julie had also grown up, was now very attractive, and had a certain sex appeal about her. She was very easygoing and a sociable person, easing out of that young girl shyness. She had learned she would need to speak up for what she wanted in life and what she desired. It was okay to speak her thoughts – something she had learned when Jaden had exited her life. She thought about Jaden from time to time. She wondered what ever happened to that young handsome boy, the one with the internal conflict. The eyes had shown her that.

The two of them had started dating, and eventually Julie moved into David's apartment. She had felt a love for David, something familiar from her past but not quite certain what it was, just familiar.

Julie had decided on attending the University of Virginia. The psychology program was excellent and well established in the science field. This would give her more options once she graduated.

Being in this relationship with David was a strain after a while. He was starting to show other character flaws that he had hidden from her in the beginning. He started acting rude and uncaring about the small things – a sign she decided not to heed. She was gonna give her relationship and school everything she had.

The same thing that attracted Sandra to Jaden was also the same thing she hated. She couldn't control him or his constant search for something, something she had no idea about. The truth was that Jaden was yearning for his past life – the Royals, the parties, the danger, and most of all, his revenge. The sting never went away; it just festered. The marriage lasted exactly one year. On their one-year anniversary, Jaden left for work but instead went to the Miami airport and went back home to Chicago. He could stay away no longer. Whatever force was pulling him back was too strong to ignore anymore. He would succumb to the urge.

Jaden had spent the last six months slowly detaching from Sandra and his marriage, slowly preparing for the inevitable decision he would make. On his one-year anniversary, the choice had been made. He grabbed his personal belongings, well, just his clothes and left. He was going back to Chicago, with no good-byes, no letter – no nothing for his wife, only abandonment and heartbreak.

Julie was reaching her limits with David. He was becoming a burden, and his uncaring attitude was beyond her tolerance. She saw herself as a good young woman, capable of love and companionship, intelligent and fun to be with, a good lover, and an outgoing personality. She felt and knew she was a good catch for any man, not perfect – no one ever is – but she was damn close. And if David or any man couldn't see that, well, the hell with them. She left David, left his apartment, and continued with her life. She had given that relationship every chance to succeed, but David wasn't a willing participant, so it was time for her to move on. Good-bye David.

Julie didn't see the past year as a waste but more as a learning experience in life and a chance to deal with different situations that life could throw at her, and she dealt with it, maybe making a couple mistakes here and there, but for the most part, she had dealt with it in a mature way.

Stepping out of the O'Hare terminal, the cold November breeze slapped him hard in the face. He smiled. He was ready to put his plan into action, looking at the world through his new eyes, the eyes of a person unrestrained and with a mission. They would pay – the both of them and anyone else that crossed his path. He would no longer be caught off guard, unaware, or helpless. This is a cold world, and he would be colder.

He made a decision that nothing mattered except him and his desires. He would never again let his guard down and never again trust a friend or woman. He would not allow someone to ever get that close to him, not even his family. He loved his family, but they were fucked up like him. They were all a bunch of pit bulls, so to speak.

He had enough money to start his plan: Buy the drugs, and sell the drugs. That was the first step of the plan. He was thinking back to the time he was in St. Charles, trying to remember the hood that Scooby was from. Scooby was Jaden's cellmate for seven months. During that time, they shared war stories, ideas, and a sort of criminal friendship. Find Scooby and buy the drugs – crack to be more accurate. Jaden had a firsthand look at the powerful drug's effect on the addicts while in Florida and referenced that information away in his head for a later recall.

Crack was new to Chicago, and he would get his foot in the door. At least that was step one of the plan. It seems fate would have something to say about that decision. Standing in the bathroom at his mother's apartment in Chicago, Jaden looked at himself in the mirror. He was no longer skinny. He was now five feet six inches, weighing about 195 lb., and with many tattoos on both his arms and back. He looked the part; this was his part in life. Still, he was a little nervous. He hardly ever traveled out of his hood, and to go to Scooby's hood . . . well, that was just crazy, but still he went.

At the west side of Chicago, Jaden got off the bus and found himself smack-dab on the corner of the hood that belonged to the traveling Vice Lords, his enemies for so many years. How many had he shot and killed? The number he knew but kept to himself. What if he was known here? What if they had a hit on him for what he'd done? The chance he had to take but still cautious.

He'd seen the group of Vice Lords by the store, and with one final convincing, he walked up to them and said, "I'm Lloki, looking for Scooby. Said to look for him here." The Vice Lords looked at this white boy, trying to size him up, wondering what would possess a white boy to come to their hood, but the fact that he asked for Scooby gave them an idea to the purpose of the white boy's visit. Scooby had been released and went back to selling drugs, not like he had a choice. It was his family's business.

Living in the projects of Chicago is no joke, there are no do-overs when you make a mistake; there is only death and a funeral. Scooby had seen many deaths of friends and had been to many funerals, but this story isn't about Scooby. It's about retribution. The dark-skinned Vice Lord stepped up, "Gonna holler at him. Wait over by the Laundromat, Lloki," he said with a look of do-I-know-this-mutherfucka'. "Bet," Jaden replied and made his way to the laundromat.

Damn, he was nervous. All it would take is one of these bitches to know him and what he's done and they were gonna hold court in the street. That's okay with him. To go out like that would be glorious, but the plan of his was the main concern and main goal. *Stick to the plan*, he thought.

A bright gold Chevy pulled up and Jaden could see Scooby in the driver's seat. Scooby double-parked and met Jaden in the laundromat. They talked, reminisced a bit, and then got down to business. Scooby took Jaden to one of his apartments, deep in the heart of the Vice Lord stronghold, to complete the deal. Jaden memorized the layout of their hood – where the lookouts were, how many, and where the vulnerable spots were. All this was a habit of his, something put away for future reference, as was his way.

Scooby brought the product to the table – an ounce of cooked up cocaine, crack, the drug of choice. Jaden inspected, tested, and paid for the shit. "Where's the other thing I asked for?" he asked Scooby. "Relax, it's coming," he replied.

There was a knock at the door five times, and Scooby opened it, letting in some girl who looked to be about sixteen. She entered pushing in a baby buggy. He kissed the girl and told her it's all good. She reached underneath the baby and pulled out the object that Jaden had really come for – long and shiny, the silent death, the silencer. This was the key to the plan that took four years to create. The plan is the goal.

As Scooby handed the silencer to Jaden, he looked at him and said, "Your word that this will not be used on any Vice Lords." His stare was just as hardened as Jaden's. They both knew each other for what they both were, and Jaden looked back into Scooby's eyes and said, "My word, I never will" came from his mouth – a lie, of course. He knew it to be a lie, as did Scooby, but still it satisfied Scooby enough to clear his conscience.

The deal is done, and Scooby drove Jaden out of the Vice Lord hood for Jaden's safety and his. Oh yes, those Vice Lords knew Jaden as soon as he approached. But the way the streets work with the Vice Lords is that business always comes first.

Money allows their families to live well, so they never interrupt a business deal. Jaden knew their ways; he counted on it. As Jaden was getting out of the car, he told Scooby later and Scooby replied back to him, "Page me next time, and I'll meet you somewhere else. My brothers wanted me to tell you the next time they see you, it'll be roll call." Jaden took the warning as it was: Okay to do business but not in their hood. He understood the logic of that.

Time to complete the first step of the plan. The Royals still did not know Jaden was back. It has only been two days, but he figured he would be the director of the show. He would set the stage and decide who would know what and when. To carry out his plan would mean an all-out war with his own gang. The royals would not accept one of theirs killing one of theirs. There would be a price to pay, but in Jaden's eyes, they would be the one paying it.

Jaden had no clue that Jimmy and Judy were not together. The whole thing didn't last long at all. Judy was not from the hood; she was from a whole other life, just a visitor in theirs. Even though Jimmy wasn't a killer and never shot anyone, he was a Royal, and he was down for the hood, or at least most of him was.

Chapter 5

JIMMY HAD NOTICED the small changes in Jaden from the very start of his thing with Judy. Jaden wasn't in the hood every day like before, and when he did show up, it was with her, Judy, the one who was changing Jaden. At least that's how he saw it. He never saw Jaden act this way toward one girl, so he was confused. What was it that she said or did that would distract him?

Jimmy didn't hate Judy. Truthfully she was very cool – got along with all the Royals. Well, they all wanted to fuck the shit out of her, but they knew the consequence of that, especially after Jaden put the gun under Greg's chin when he thought Greg was trying to flirt with her. That was a fucked up moment 'cause it caused half the Royals to take Greg's side and the other half to take Jade's. Jimmy tried to resolve the issue, but what could he do? Jaden was actively fighting to keep the Royals alive, and Greg was somewhat of a part-time Royal and really couldn't be counted on. That's how the split happened, so to speak.

At the meeting, there were about thirty Royals, the older ones who held leadership status and the younger ones who were hard core and way more dangerous and committed to the nation. This was obvious to all. When the matter came up to find a solution to what Jaden did to Greg, the older Royals felt a three-minute head-to-toe violation would be best, but Jaden was strapped, as was Nitty and Lucifer, Jaden's two crime buddies.

Jaden walked to the middle of the group and said it plain as day, "Ain't no muthafucka' touchin' me." Looking at Jimmy, he said, "Sinbad now runs it for Farwell and Clark, and if it's a problem, step up to the plate," as he pulled out the nine millimeter. Lucifer and Nitty took their cue and upped their straps also, showing support for the new royal leader. "For too long, you muthafuckas been holdin' us back, talkin' shit 'bout we makin' the hood hot, fuckin' up your money. Well, we ain't seen a dime of it so it done," Jaden commanded.

Who was gonna stop him? They all thought they knew what he had become, although no one there knew for sure, except one, Jimmy. Jimmy stepped to the middle and explained the new situation to the older Royals. Their time was over; they were now ex-Royals with full respect but no longer allowed to represent. They knew the play and walked. The new Farwell and Clark was established but not for the better. But who could have known?

The following months was open season on Kings and Vice Lords, and the damage was mounting. Jimmy knew that with Jaden supporting him, he would have full control and they would flourish. Those were pipe dreams though. He thought Jaden was back, back from whatever vacation he had taken, but that was not how it played out. Jaden had helped establish Jimmy as the leader for only one reason. He knew Jimmy would always favor him above the others and allow him leeway in his endeavors.

That summer was fun for everyone. Jaden was hangin' in the hood again every day because Judy was there with him. Jimmy was managing the crew well, and all the Royals were making small amounts of money from their criminal activity. Jaden's court case was coming up for trial soon, and he finally told her, which she didn't take well. That made Jimmy happy; maybe she would leave then.

He couldn't help notice her though. Every time she came around, he would watch her, ever so carefully though. He didn't need any problems with Jaden. She was hot, her body was definitely appetizing enough, and she had a way about her. He wondered what it would be like to fuck her but pushed that thought from his mind as fast as it came to him. He didn't need that kind of problems, but still.

Then the day came when Jimmy saw Judy at the game room. She was looking sad and depressed. He knew then. "Jaden was convicted and sent to St. Charles," she told Jimmy. Jimmy reached out to hug her, to console her, and to feel her warmth finally. Something touched his heart for the first time, and he knew what the outcome would be. This was a very dangerous situation, but he would have time to figure out a plan, he hoped. He knew firsthand what Jaden was capable of but wasn't sure if Jaden would ever go that far with him. He didn't want to find out.

Jaden was still trying to stay in touch with Judy by letters and phone, and that drove Jimmy crazy. "Have you told him about us yet? He's gonna find out soon, ya know," he pressured her.

Judy hated this. She knew she was now stuck between two guys she loved, and they were best friends. One was trying to hold onto her from jail; and the other, in front of her now. "I will tell him soon. He's only been in there for two months. Give me some time," she asked.

Jimmy relented, but he was not happy. He wanted her to tell Jaden as soon as possible, figuring the time Jaden had in jail would cool his temper down, at least enough so they would only fight heads up, nothing any serious. That was a fight Jimmy did not want. Jimmy knew he was down for the hood, but he never felt or had that killer instinct Jaden did. No, best to get it over soon.

"What the fuck do you mean you haven't told him? And now you're going to fuckin' Florida with him too," screamed Jimmy. "I can't believe this shit. Don't you understand? He hasn't had time to get over what has changed. Goddamn it, bitch," and then he smacked the fuck out of Judy, knocking her to the ground. She lay there numb, crying, and feeling powerless over her life.

This was not how she envisioned her life to be. She was supposed to marry Jaden and have a family, but he went to jail. Jimmy had seduced her when she was weak, but she soon fell in love with him, not knowing the beatings she would take from him and, always about the same thing, not telling Jaden that they were together. How could she? She would also need to tell Jaden that she aborted his child before he went to jail. She never told anyone, but she knew when she found out she was pregnant that having the abortion was the best thing for both of them. That was a guilt she felt every day.

Why was Jimmy so nervous about Jaden? Sure she knew Jaden was not so nice of a gang banger, but what did Jimmy have to fear? She didn't understand. She had heard bits and pieces of rumors about Jaden, but no one knew for sure, except one, and he never told. She explained to Jimmy she was gonna go to Florida with Jaden, spend a week there, and tell him. She would explain it, so he would understand. Jimmy didn't give a fuck. He hated it that she was gonna go. He knew they would fuck. He also knew there wasn't shit he could do about it.

Judy went to Florida. They did fuck, but she never got the chance to explain shit. Her best friend told on her, and she wondered why she did that. Judy's best friend, the one who told her Jaden was cheating, had called Jaden in Florida. How she got the phone number, I don't know, but she called looking for Judy. Maybe she wanted to make sure Judy was okay, but I don't think so. I think she wanted to know what happened, as if Judy had told her what she planned on telling Jaden.

Judy didn't have to tell Jaden; her friend did that for her. She told Jaden everything from the time Jaden went to jail till then. She explained that Judy knew she was pregnant before Jaden went to jail, decided to get the abortion before Jaden went to jail, and got with Jimmy about a month after Jaden went to jail. Jaden could only say two words, "Thank you," and hung up the phone.

His mind was racing a mile a minute. He was dealing with old feelings resurfacing – the feeling of betrayal, not so much from Judy being with Jimmy but the fact that she aborted his child while he was free. Jaden understood her reasons for the abortion; it hurt just the same, but he understood. What hurt most was that she hid it from him and didn't trust him enough to share what she was going through. He was also very angry over Judy and Jimmy being together. He was feeling her revenge. He was feeling something hurting him deep inside his heart – a tightness gripping him more and more.

He had to gain control and come up with a solution. What he wanted to do was take her for a ride into the everglades and shoot her in the head and then toss her body into the alligator-infested waters. That wouldn't happen though; he couldn't harm her. She was still very special to him, and that one thing would protect her for life from his wrath.

Jimmy, on the other hand . . . Jaden could kill Jimmy. Jaden had confronted Judy. She admitted it, and Jaden told her it was time for her to leave. She was shocked. Judy didn't believe he would do that. She realized she really didn't know much about Jaden, only what he revealed, and that wasn't much for her to truly know him.

She sat alone on the bus on the way back to Chicago, alone, lonely, tired, and confused. How did he find out? He never said. She couldn't believe he had her leave two days early and didn't say good-bye. All she saw was a look in his eyes that scared her to the point that she needed to make changes in her life, and fast.

During the whole two days on that bus, she thought about her life, her future, and her choices. She got on her knees and started to cry. "Dear Jesus, please forgive me for my sins" was the start of a very long prayer, and by the end of the bus trip, she had found the strength to say enough. She ended it with Jimmy and kicked him out, stopped hanging out and drinking and doing drugs, and started going to church. This was her retribution.

Jimmy was waiting for her when she came in the door. He wanted to apologize – to say sorry for the way he acted – but he noticed a look on her face.

"Jaden found out about us from someone else" was her first statement.

"What did he say?" asked Jimmy.

She debated with herself whether to tell him about the look in Jade's eyes but thought not to. Jimmy was a tough ass, hitting girls. Let him find out for himself. "He said he understood and had no hard feelings," she lied. "Also, I want the keys back. I don't want to be with you anymore, and if you don't leave, I will call the police" was her command.

Jimmy accepted the dismissal, figuring it was some woman's emotional thing and left. What mattered to him was there was no problem between him and Jaden. Jimmy went back to the normal things a Royal does. Judy went the Christian path, and Jaden burned with resentment toward the both of them.

Chapter 6

JADEN JUST SAT in the chair. The lights were out. He was alone, contemplating the plan, always going over the plan in his head. Every moment awake was spent fine-tuning the plan and putting it into action. Each step was closer to the goal.

Once asleep – now that is a different story – his dreams betrayed him. In his dreams, he was with Judy. They were still together, and Jimmy was still his best friend. Once awake, the pain would return, only to be pushed down with anger and resentment. Tomorrow he would show up in the hood and act like it was all good. Once everything was back to normal, he would deliver the final act of the plan, and the pain would go away, he thought or hoped.

Standing on the corner of Farwell and Clark at 6:30 p.m., no one was out. Where the fuck are all the Royals? Where the fuck is Jimmy? This is not how he remembered it. There would have been at least six or seven Royals out. He walked down Clark Street toward Greenleaf. Sometimes the Royals hung out on Green Leaf and Ravenswood. Nope, no one there.

Standing there thinking, he decided to check out the bar. Walking in the front door, he noticed familiar faces immediately: Jimmy, Tank, Lucifer, Nitty, and some females with them. They hadn't noticed him yet, so he decided to announce his arrival. "King Love," he shouted. All heads turned, shocked, and then smiles greeted him. The barrage of "Wassup?" "Where ya been?" and "When did ya get back?" assaulted him, and he felt like that a fourteen-year-old kid for a moment, but only for a moment – up to the moment when Jimmy walked up and shook his hand.

"We all good, Bro?" asked Jimmy. "We never weren't, Jimmy," came his reply. Jaden could see the tenseness release from Jimmy's face and body, and relaxing signs showed now. "Don't no bitch come between Royals," Jaden announced to the whole bar, getting dirty looks from the girls who were with the Royals. Jaden would enjoy every moment he was back and remembered his promise to himself: No girl will ever touch his soul again. That was his shield.

Julie was doing very well in school. She was keeping a GPA of 3.2, which came from the long hours of studying. She was very focused on her studies but still found time to socialize here and there. She would go to Chicago on her breaks, visit with her old friends, and enjoy her time with them.

She never heard anything more of Jaden, who was on her mind still, never able to shake him out of her thoughts. She was always curious about how his life was going for him and if he ever worked out those issues that tormented him. Julie didn't get into any serious relationships after David, although she did date guys from time to time. Nothing ever came of it though. She was focused on her studies.

Julie was very close to her sister, Wendy, and they were always talking on the phone when in school, but when they were together on breaks, they shared some of the same friends. It was nice being an adult, having friends and family members in her life. She was happy. The shyness she had in her was still there, but now it was less controlling and less restricting upon her. Julie was feeling more confident in her life, and she was enjoying that freedom. Julie had also begun to form her own opinions on a great many things in life. She was a strong, independent woman, and her maturity was being established well.

She was on the liberal side of the isle and detested any violence of any kind but especially toward women and children. She believed in society being responsible to each other and helping those who were unfortunate. Julie knew she wasn't a saint in no way, but she was a good person and her heart was pure. She never meant malice to anyone, and her behavior reflected that.

She silently hoped Jaden was able to change from his path. *Why do I keep thinking of him?* she questioned herself. *He walked out of my life, not the other way around*, she answered, only that didn't satisfy her question. She pushed those thoughts of Jaden away, buried them deeper, away from her mind.

There were a couple changes in the Royals. The small ones he noticed at first, but the bigger changes he saw soon enough. Every Royal was now either an alcoholic or an addict, addicted to smoking cocaine. There were seven Royals now and no guns, and every Royal was for themselves. There was no bond like before and no trust. They each acted independently of each other when doing criminal shit and answered to no one. Jimmy was the chief still, so to speak, but the organization was gone, not only at Farwell and Clark but the other sections throughout Chicago also.

The Royals were a sinking ship, and the last members were but fixtures on that ship. They had nowhere to go, no goals in life, and no dreams to be fulfilled. That's what made them dangerous, but being crackheads made them unpredictable. *What the fuck*, thought Jaden. *How did it happen?* He had to find out, but asking these dumb fucks wouldn't produce answers. He needed to watch for the clues and allow them to reveal themselves. Until then, he should blend in, act as if, feel as if, and be as if.

Day after day, he watched his brothers do their thing, the daily habit as it was: Come to the hood, find a sting, get the money, and then get high. Day after day, this was all they did. He would walk the hood late at night, seeing what other signs there were; he didn't like what he saw. The whole Rogers Park area was fucked up. There were seven different gangs now, and the boundary lines were almost nonexistent. Except for a street corner for each gang, all other streets were up for grabs. He also noticed that the older ex-Royals had become the big drug dealers, still making money and feeding the drugs to his friends at a price though.

Most of the people who were friends of the Royals stayed away from them. They had been burned on drug deals and other things. The Royals had alienated themselves from everyone, except the police. All the hard work, all the killings, all the sacrifices – all for nothing. He had no plan to overcome this situation and didn't know where to begin and soon enough joined them. It wasn't long until Jaden was hooked on crack and acid. He followed the same routine as the others and lost himself along the way.

There was a moment – not sure when he felt it – that he had decided the plan was dead; there would be no revenge. He would deal with the pains he felt by pushing them deep within himself. There were so many disappointments in Jaden's life and so many things that went wrong. He just didn't see any hope in things anymore.

Every relationship he started went bad, each girl not worthy of him – all except one. That was so long ago; he was only eleven years old at the time. Nothing could have ever become of it, he thought. Plus, Julie was so innocent and pure. He was nothing but poison. He knew he made the right decision back then, but he thought about her from time to time, wondering how she was doing and wondering if she ever found a new love. *Go away*, he commanded those thoughts. It hurt to think about her and hurt to know he would never feel her warmth in his life ever again. *Bury those feelings deep, deeper than the rest.* There was no hope for the two of them; that was in the past childhood memories.

Jaden had committed many burglaries in the following six months – many petty crimes. He even had robbed a police captain coming out of a bar at two thirty in the morning, all to get high. He was running a couple call girls also on the side, but all the money went to drugs. This was it; this was his lot in life. He surrendered and gave up. All he could see around him were wasted souls, people not living life, just going through some routine of surviving. Each day, his memories of the past were coming back to him – the girls he cared about, the abuse he took, the people he had harmed, the killings, and the drugs. Everything was flooding his mind and weighing heavy on his heart.

Feeling more like a zombie than a human being, feeling the guilt of his past crimes, and feeling the pain of Judy, Jaden went to the lakefront one night, at Jarvis Beach. He had always had fond memories hanging out there in the early years of being a Royal, so it made sense it would end here. He didn't see any reason to continue on like this. Everything he tried to do ended in failure.

Sitting there alone, he remembered everything, allowing himself to feel those emotions that were buried for so long, so deep within him, feeling every sting and every puncture. He stared at the .38 revolver and then smiled. *How come every Royal who kills himself does it with a .38*, he wondered as he pulled the hammer back. Putting the barrel in his mouth, his final thought was *I hate you, God*, and then he pulled the trigger. Nothing. No explosion, no pain, and no death.

He quickly pulled the gun from his mouth soberly and saw what happened. The barrel had turned halfway and got stuck. "What the fuck," he said aloud, looking around to make sure no one heard. He never heard of a revolver doing this. He knew then he was destined to feel this pain forever 'cause he didn't have the balls to try that shit again. Slowly he lay on the bench and cried till sleep came.

Chapter 7

THE DREAMS WERE different this time – no nightmares, no ghostly faces of the past, and nothing of Judy and Jimmy. This was a nice dream, or did the revolver really fire and he was in heaven?

In this dream, he was much younger, maybe about eleven years old, standing at the Chicago lakefront, looking around. He sees a little girl up ahead. His attention is fully on her. She is wearing a white dress. Her hair is blondish brown and long, below her neck, but he can't see her face from the distance. He starts to walk closer to her, but the distance is not closing. Jaden stops and just looks at her, trying to see if he recognizes her. He calls out but nothing comes out of his mouth. She turns her head and stares at him, still too far to recognize her, but she is beautiful, so beautiful to him.

Then he heard some noise from behind. He turns around, but there's nothing there. He looks back toward the girl, but she is gone. Then he heard loud noises from all around him, disturbing sounds as if there was a disturbance somewhere. What the hell was it making that noise? The answer came fast as he was snatched from the dream into reality as the police pulled him from the beach bench, throwing him to the ground and placing feet on his head. Still groggy, all he knew for sure was the barrel of several guns facing him, begging him to reach for his so they may gun him down.

There was no love lost between Jaden and the police. He hated them as much as they hated him. In their eyes, he was a waste of oxygen, a scum piece of shit who preyed upon good people, and someone they would love to exterminate like a cockroach. The feeling was mutual. He had witnessed these same cops doing things that were just as criminal. Fucking hypocrites they were – all of them. He wished he could exterminate the lot of them.

As they placed those steel cuffs around his wrists, he could see their satisfaction at their conquest, but also he saw their nervousness and their relief that there wasn't a gunfight and that everyone was going home that day – well, almost everyone; Jaden was going to jail. Jaden got sloppy. The drugs had fucked him up, and he left many pieces of evidence at each crime he committed over the short time he was back in Chicago. The biggest mistake was holding onto the police captain's .38 revolver. That was stupid.

Welcome to the Cook County Jail. He had heard many stories about the county, more like a prison than a county jail. This place was very old. Many old-time Chicago gangsters had paid a visit there and died there. The jail was always overcrowded, with prisoners sleeping on floors of cells, four to a cell, a cell that was constructed to hold two. The county guards shuffled all the new prisoners to the main holding cell, about hundred of them, like sardines. That was the feeling. The prisoners consisted of bums, drug dealers, addicts, thieves, rapists, murders, and every other criminal you could imagine.

You do not get separated from violent criminals if your crime is petty. It doesn't work that way. Everyone is equally guilty and a piece of shit. The smell of the holding cell is that of urine, shit, body odor, and whatever blends of the previous night still lingered on each prisoner.

The bench in the holding cell was full. Some prisoners slept on the floor, which contained various layers of human feces, blood, and whatever else was convenient over the years to cover the surface. Jaden decided to stand. He surveyed the group; almost all of them were black and then Latino and three white guys. Not that race is much of a factor in jail, it still matters. Most criminals have a preconceived idea of white men. Jaden learned that since his days at St. Charles.

His time in jail would always consist of fighting and proving himself. There was conversation between the prisoners, mostly short details on what they got popped off for, almost like they were bragging. The guards were positioned at the large desk outside of the cell, just hanging out talking, not one of them working. This was gonna be a long processing period, Jaden thought.

"What they get you for?" asked a Hispanic male who looked about twenty years old. Jaden figured the man was nervous, looking to blend in and decided to start a conversation with him. "I don't know. They just asked me a bunch of questions, then brought me here," Jaden revealed. He really didn't know for sure, but he knew it wasn't good.

At the police station, they had questioned him about a lot of crimes, some he remembered doing and some he didn't. He definitely didn't remember doing an armed robbery/murder in a jewelry store. That wasn't his thing. When he killed, it was only gang members. They were not innocent victims in his mind. He did rob and steal from innocent people though, but that was a way of life in the city.

The cops kept asking about Rachel also. He wondered why. Rachel was a girl who hung with the Royals. She first met Jaden on the corner of Greenleaf and Clark. He introduced himself, and they got to talking, in which she revealed she wanted to be down with the Royals. Perfect, another easy piece of ass. She was about five feet four, definitely well endowed, and had a certain way about her. Rachel had told Jaden she was seventeen and lived a couple blocks away.

He ran the same game to her as he did to every girl, and about thirty minutes later, in a hallway to an apartment building, Rachel was on her knees giving head, being commanded and instructed by Jaden. The initiation was bullshit, of course, but it had its purpose. Rachel spent her time in that hallway being abused sexually. You see, at her age, a girl does not have a right to give consent, so it is not having sex. It is rape, something Jaden didn't know, but which Jaden would find out later.

Jaden walked with Rachel, and they talked and soon enough, Rachel was the newest girl out on the corner, making money for Jaden to get high – another victim to add to the list.

The processing had started now, and the guards were pulling prisoners out of the holding cell one at a time to book, take a mug shot, and fingerprint. It must have been like six hours since he first arrived. Jaden heard his name called and hurried to the cell opening. He saw what happens when you don't respond fast. A guy was brought to the emergency room not more than thirty minutes ago. The guard lifted the police photo and compared it to Jaden and then, checking the tag around his wrist with the number on his file, moved him to the desk. The sergeant behind the desk asked him a series of questions and then moved him along to the next step.

After the whole group was processed, they were strip searched, clothed in tan prison outfits, and moved to various divisions of the jail. Jaden just observed; he didn't say much to anyone. The whole process was about the guards having total control, using brutality as a means to obtain it. That is how someone presumed innocent until proven guilty is treated at Cook County Jail. Jaden realized that the normal people didn't give a shit, until they themselves were in this situation.

Arriving at the cell that would hold him, he scanned the six-by-nine cell and thought his bathroom at his mom's apartment was larger. He put his shit on the floor and proceeded to the dayroom. The gangs in Chicago were divided into two groups: folks and people. The Royals and their alliances were folks; the Kings and the Vice Lords and their alliances were the peoples. There was no division based on race. Jaden thought to himself, *How do I find out who's who, fuck it?* "Who's folks here?" asking out loud.

Jaden got acclimated to the county routine very fast. Being locked up wasn't new to him, just the different jails were. He borrowed from the folks' poor box, soap, and other essentials that other folks donate for the new folks that come in new and have nothing yet.

There were three payphones on the wall: one for folks only, one for peoples only, and the last one for anyone. He waited for his turn and then made the call to his mom. He ran the story of what happened and asked her to send him some money to pay the poor box back and so he could get the other shit he would need. He told her he loved her and said he would call her once he went to court in the morning and returned to the deck. That's what they call their holding area where they sleep, eat, and waste away the day.

Tomorrow he would find out at his preliminary hearing what his charge was and how much his bond would be. The bond wouldn't matter; he had no money. He knew he would sit here and fight his case – yes, his case. He wanted to know the charges.

Chapter 8

THE BANGING OF doors woke him from his sleep – no dreams this time. Slowly getting up from his mattress on the cold floor, Jaden wrapped what little possessions he had and shoved them in the corner out of the way. He was standing at the cell door when the guard approached, waiting to get the fuck out of this cell. The guard said his name. Jaden replied, "Yes, sir." The guard opened the cell door, and Jaden stepped out.

Standing in front of the mirror in the dayroom bathroom, he could see his reflection and it wasn't good. He needed a shave. The scruffy short beard was sticking out. His teeth were yellow like a warning sign on the street, but his eyes . . . his eyes were sunken. Lines were forming, and he realized he looked like thirty instead of twenty. God, he looked terrible.

Finished washing up, he stepped into the dayroom. Six other inmates were going to court from his deck. Not knowing the routine for the county, he followed the others, acting like this wasn't his first time. Without going through the long process the county guards take in getting inmates to the courtrooms, they found themselves in the holding cell in the back of the courtroom Jaden is going to. Waiting is the worst thing while incarcerated. Time moves at a very different schedule than in the free world. One hour in the county is one minute in the outside.

The air was stale in the holding cell, a room meant to hold twenty detainees; there were fifty-two now in this room, very cramped, with everyone on edge. There are never any fights or altercations before seeing the judge. Who would want to piss off the judge before ya see him?

Very quiet and still, each inmate was going over their story in their mind, wondering what to expect, counting their options. Jaden was no different. Finally, his name was called. Walking through the hallway, hands behind his back with two county guards behind him, he made his way to the bench. To his right was a public defender, to the left was a state's attorney, and the judge was in the middle. He thought it strange that the state's attorney would be standing so close to him, within his reach, with no barriers except the two guards behind him. He could reach the state's attorney within a second and do some serious harm before the guards could react. Hmmmmmmm, store the information in the back of his head to use later maybe.

The three started doing their legal talk. The judge was stating something called the statement of facts, reading all the charges. Holy shit, he had eight different charges. Six of them were class X felonies, one was a class 1 felony, and the last one was a class 2 felony. *What does that mean?* you wonder. All crimes are categorized into two categories, felony and misdemeanor. Misdemeanor is punishable by no more than one year in the county jail. Felonies are divided into classes also: Class X carries six to thirty years for each offense; class 1, four to fifteen years; and class 2, three to seven.

Jaden is facing over a hundred years. His knees were weakening as he was slowly realizing the consequences of his past years' activities. The charges you want to know; I feel your curiosity, but will you feel his shame? The first charge was armed robbery to the police captain, the second charge was armed robbery, the third and fourth charges were murder, the fifth charge was criminal sexual assault, the sixth charge was criminal sexual abuse, the seventh charge was residential burglary, and the last charge was aggravated battery.

I'm guessing the only charge anyone will remember is the two sexual charges. That would be what I wondered also. Remember the girl he met who wanted to be with the Royals, the one who sucked his dick in the hallway, and the one he fucked in that same hallway? It turned out that she was younger than she said she was. She was only fifteen, and he had her working the streets. Because of the thought of what he did and how he exploited that girl, he was full of shame, a shame that cripples you and holds you in contempt for life. He couldn't hold the tears back; they found their way down his cheeks, and he hung his head low, ashamed of his very existence.

He had no problem with any of the charges, but the charges against the girl were too much. He never was violent toward women his whole life, something he remembered from watching his father beat his mother for thirteen years. He would never be his father. He didn't know the law, and the law says any girl under the age of eighteen cannot give consent; thus, it is sexual assault. He never would have touched her if he knew her true age, but that doesn't matter now, he's guilty.

The judge was gonna announce the bond amount, and the state's attorney asked for a no-bond because of the violent nature of Jaden. The judge agreed. Jaden would remain in custody until the end of his trial. He figured as much; at least he knew the charges. The jewelry store robbery/double murder wasn't his doing. He didn't do those things. But he was guilty of everything else, and so much more.

Back in the holding cell, every eye of the detainees was on him. You see, there was a speaker in the holding cell, and everything that was said in the courtroom could be heard there. Jaden knew they had heard all the charges. He knew they were thinking about the sexual cases, but they were also thinking of the other violent charges, without giving anyone of them a chance to get brave, he challenged all in that cell. "Anyone got a problem, this is the time to get it off your chest," he asked. There were no takers to the challenge, and he was grateful.

Once court was over, the guards started the long process of getting the detainees back to their decks. None from the holding cell was from his deck or even the division he was in – another lucky break. He was hooked into the folks, but a sex charge is not good, even for someone affiliated with the gangs. He knew he would have to explain eventually.

In the county, all inmates go to church services, not for God but for gang business. Jaden had no use for God or religion, but he figured he would bring up his charges before someone else did. He addressed the division coordinator for the Latin folks and explained his story. To his amazement, Loco, the division coordinator, understood and explained that those charges are a common thing for gang members. He reminded him to think of all the young girls in the hoods who were sixteen and even younger who had kids already. A sex case does not always mean rape. *That may be*, thought Jaden, but it was still wrong. Fuck it, all was good as far as the folks were concerned, so he would focus on the other charges.

Every day was the same routine in the county: Wake up at five in the morning, eat breakfast, and go back to the cells. Wait for eight in the morning, and come out to the dayroom. All inmates had to exit their cells. It was a jail rule. Inmates played cards, worked out, talked on the phone, or told bullshit stories to each other until eleven o'clock. Lunch was always cold, served on compartment-style trays. There was never enough food, and they had the worst-tasting food ever. Everyone ate it though.

After lunch, it was back to the same thing as the morning until two forty-five, "Lock 'em, the fuck-up gentleman," screamed the guard. Slowly the inmates made their way to their cells. "Lock 'em up and count 'em." That's what time it was. Inmates stayed in their cells until four o'clock, back to the same routine. Dinner was served at five thirty. At seven o'clock, the showers were turned on. At nine thirty, they were turned off. Ten thirty was "lock 'em up" time again for the night. And every night was the same shit – everyone screaming and yelling in the vents, some singing songs and others rapping, never a moment of just silence, but Jaden would fall asleep quickly and sleep through the night every night.

Chapter 9

JADEN DID SPEND most his time in the legal library that the jail provided. This was between the hours of nine in the morning to ten thirty and then again at twelve noon to two thirty. All inmates may use the legal library three times a week, but those with murder charges may use it Monday through Friday, being that murder was the most serious of all criminal charges. Jaden spent not one minute researching the law as it pertained to murder. He knew he could beat those charges. He had a rock-solid alibi when that crime took place – he was locked up in detention at the Belmont and Western police department for a battery charge, and being that he was such a smart-ass to the arresting cop, the police decided to keep him seventy-two hours on hold for a fake crime.

Nope, Jaden's time was spent researching the sex case, looking at all angles of the case. What the nature of the law was, what the fruits of the crime must consist of, what an excusable defense was, and what the punishment was. He researched every day and came up with the same answer: He's fucked. Even though he didn't forcibly rape that girl, he was older than her, and that's what made it a crime since she was under eighteen. There was no defense by saying she lied to him and no defense saying he didn't know. He was fucked. He knew he would lose all the other cases, but the sex case he wanted to beat, even though he was ashamed of himself for what he did, Jaden did not want to go to prison for those charges.

His sister came to visit him a couple times while he was in the county, and she usually brought other friends from the hood. Everyone knew he was locked up and knew the charges, and they said they had his back was the message she would relay to him. "Jimmy said keep ya head up and don't fuck up in there," his sis told him. "He's gonna have the folks send a kite to the joint, letting them know the situation and that it's all good," she said. That was a good message for him; he knew prison was gonna be his next step, and the kite (a letter from the outside to the inside) would make a smooth transition for him.

The folks sent him some money, as well as his family, and he decided to not spend it; he would need it more in the prison later. After about five months, he was informed that he received a legal visitor. Fuck, legal visitors are lawyers, state's attorneys, or detectives. His visitor was a defense attorney that his mom was able to get for him. He didn't know how, and he didn't ask.

Jaden and the attorney talked for about two hours, mostly the lawyer asking questions. When they were just about through, Jaden told the lawyer, "Look, I know I'm going down on everything except the robbery and double murder. What I need you to do is negotiate a ten-year sentence to run concurrent," Jaden informed the attorney. "Can you do that?" asked Jaden. "What makes you so sure you can beat the murders/robbery?" the lawyer questioned. Jaden ran the whole scoop to the attorney and gave the attorney all the legal research he had, "I'll do my best," replied the lawyer. Jaden hoped the lawyer could come through for him 'cause the only other option was to have the girl killed, and that was something he did not want to do. He wasn't even sure he would do it if it came to it. *Wait and see*, he thought.

Back in the courtroom again for the ninth time, playing the "show me what ya got and I'll show you what we got" game with the state's attorney, neither side budging, the judge called for a recess, and Jaden went back to the holding cell. He could see his attorney talking to the state's attorney, and then he approached the holding cell and told Jaden the state's attorney has offered thirty-five years. Jaden snapped and started yelling at his attorney, making loud threats that the witness was as good as dead, knowing the state's attorney could hear him and knowing he wanted the state's attorney to hear him. It was his bargaining plan.

He then told his attorney to offer the state ten years on all cases, but as for the murder and the robbery, he would fight those cases separately. Within five minutes, the lawyer came back, saying the state attorney agreed to the deal. Both lawyers told the judge they were ready for plea bargain. The judge continued, and Jaden was sentenced to ten years for all his crimes, except the murders/robbery, all his sentences to run together. He would be out in five years.

The state's attorney thought they had Jaden lock, stock, barrel until the lawyer made a motion to dismiss the other cases due to the fact Jaden was in custody at the time of those crimes. The state's attorney objected. The defense attorney provided a validated copy from the Chicago Police Department, indicating he was in fact in custody, and the judge said, "Overruled," and dismissed the charges. Jaden would be on the morning bus to Joliet Correctional Center. He looked at the state's attorney and he smiled. He knew their game, and he played their game better than they did. He was always good at getting a bargain. This time, he bargained for his freedom, and he did well.

Back on the deck, he made three phone calls: the first to his mom, filling her in on the details; the second to Jimmy for same reason; and the third to someone he knew he could trust – someone who would gather some of his special things he left on the street and hold for him till he got released. Sorry, but none will ever know this person, not now or ever.

After finishing the phone calls, he took a shower and handed out everything he had. You couldn't take anything with you to prison except a religious book. That night he didn't sleep, instead he ran through the memories in his head concerning his life, from his earliest memories to the present day. *I should write a book*, he thought to himself and then smiled.

Three thirty in the morning and here comes the guards to get him ready for transfer to the prison. They moved him to the basement of division 1, the oldest division in the jail. This is where they kept the old gangsters from the past. This was a historic division. They processed him out and had him put on an orange jumpsuit.

Four thirty and he was stepping on one of the four buses going to prison. This was the blue light special; these buses were escorted by county sheriffs and Chicago police all the way to Joliet Prison. This special did not stop for traffic lights or pedestrians; it kept moving at sixty-five miles per hour till it reached its destination, Joliet Correctional Center, the oldest prison in Illinois. He was now home.

Julie was finishing up another semester and planning on going back to Chicago, wanting to spend the holidays with her sister. Plus, the last time she was there, she had met some guy named Michael. She remembered he was a soft-spoken man, about five feet ten and built well. He had long brown hair, almost like a hippy, but it was washed and styled better. She thought he was handsome. They had talked for a while, and she realized they had many things in common. *He had potential*, she thought. The both of them had written to each other while she was in school, and a love was blossoming through the distance.

Julie's life wasn't a fairy tale; it was very real to her. She had seen many things growing up, from the time she was much younger. Both parents got high, something everyone did back then. It was the thing to do. Because of this though, her parents never allowed her or her brother's and sister's friends to come over. That bothered her growing up, always having to tell her friends they couldn't go to her house, not knowing what her friends thought about that.

Then the physical abuse her mom suffered at the hands of her father, a drunk son of a bitch. She had witnessed some of these fights, and it took its toll on her. Then there was Jaden, the first boy she ever had strong feelings for. We all know what happened with that. Then there was David, another lesson well learned. Life didn't give her special breaks; she took what life dealt her and played the hand. She knew hard work and dedication would be her way to a better life.

Michael was very nice, and she had made sure to take her time getting to know him well before making any decisions. Now she was sure; she was ready to start a serious relationship with him.

Julie arrived in Chicago and met up with her sister, the two of them happy to see each other again. Putting her stuff away and unpacking her things, she prepared herself for seeing Michael. She hadn't told him her decision. She would ease it into the conversation. They had met up at one of their mutual friend's party, and the conversation started like it never ended. Julie told Michael her feelings, he responded the same way, and now they were a couple. Oh goody, isn't that nice? I thought you might like that part, Julie.

Chapter 10

AS THE BLUE light special rolled up to the old stone castle, the fifty-foot walls with razor Constantine wire was evident, as was the guards on the wall with rifles and mini fourteen assault rifles. The signs placed on the outside of the wall gave warning to lay down when shots are fired. This was much different than St. Charles – way different. Everything Jaden was taking in was telling him that this was for fuckin' real; there is no joke about where he is gonna be for the next five years. Time to get his head straight and prepare for whatever comes and prepared to do whatever. Jaden was concerned; truthfully he was scared.

The bus dropped the prisoners off at the annex of Joliet, the place where the officials process the new arrivals. This is again a very long and detailed process: medical evaluations, psychological evaluations, criminal history and gang affiliation, and educational background. Everything about each prisoner that the officials can gather and record, they do. All this information are then forwarded to the inmate placement department, and they decide which prison each inmate will be sent to. The stay at Joliet is only for about three weeks, unless the inmate is assigned to Joliet.

The three weeks were driving Jaden crazy. There is very minimal movement out of the cell. He needed to get the fuck out of this place and get to where he is going. There are some rules the gangs have set up for security reasons and for control of the membership. First, the gangs are in three groups: again, the folks, the peoples, and also the northsiders. The northsiders are a white supremist gang, much like the Aryan Brotherhood.

During line movements, the peoples move at the front of the line and then the northsiders, and the folks. Every line movement is done this way. It was created by the gangs and the gangs enforce it. A shank is any piece of metal or hard plastic sharpened to a point or edge. A shank is used to kill others. All gang members have shanks, and all guards know this. Jaden had two shanks. That's because he was assigned to be personal security to Kato, the unit viceroy, the main shot caller for the annex. Where Kato goes, Jaden goes. To get to Kato you will have to kill Jaden, and he had no intention of dying.

Jaden studied everything about body language that he could. He wanted to be able to read and predict when shit was going down. He learned who the main hitters (killers) were for the peoples and northsiders and what the mannerisms were for them when they were ordered to hit. Most hits Jaden witnessed were internal. Most hits are always public. It sends the message to the rest in the gang fuck up and die.

Jaden wasn't a hitter. He was security and thankful for that. Of course, that would only last until he was transferred. Because they were all there for processing, the inmates' only activities were going to chow, going to the yard or the gym, religious services, or staying in the cell. When gym or yard was called, all folks had to go. It was mandatory. The folks must always be at full strength at either one of those locations. It seems the other gangs thought the same way too.

Third week in and it is nighttime. All inmates are in there cell, and the loudspeaker came on. "Attention all inmates, please listen for your name and your correctional center assignment," cracked the voice on the loudspeaker. Every ear was pressed against the bars, waiting anxiously for their name, which was called out alphabetically. When Jaden heard his name and prison ID number called, he heard Centralia Correctional Center.

"Lucky bastard," his cellie said.

"What's Centralia like?" responded Jaden.

"Man, it's like a college campus – two-man cells with doors instead of bars and college classes," he informed him.

"What level of security is it?" Jaden asked.

"Medium security," he answered.

Jaden took all that the inmate had told him and contemplated the info and then stored it away for future reference.

Morning is here and Jaden is up and ready. The ride to Centralia was about five hours, and he was happy to see the prison. Imagine to be happy seeing a prison. Again the inmates are moved to the orientation unit. This period lasts for about thirty days. New inmates are waiting for job/school assignments and resident assignments. So everyone in orientation is in limbo, secluded from the general population, well as much as possible anyway. There are the building workers who have access, the kitchen workers, and the laundry crew.

The thirty days go by slower than fuck, but at least his money is on the inmate trust fund account, and he can buy the things he needed. Jaden came into the prison system with seven hundred and fifty dollars. He is gonna get a TV, a hotpot to cook food and coffee in, and a fan for the summer. The rest will be cigarettes, hygiene products, writing materials, and clothes. These are the basic requirements most inmates need or, should I say, desire in order to have some sort of normalcy while incarcerated.

Jaden was assigned to south four living unit. He had his shit packed, and he moved to his new cell. His cellie was some white guy, not gang related, and seemed pretty cool. They had a chat session, something inmates do with their cellies when they first meet one another, kinda like feeling each other out.

Smokey was cool and streetwise Jaden could tell and seemed straightforward. He liked that also. Smokey didn't have much possessions; his family was not helping him with money during his third time in prison. Prison has many unspoken agreements: The inmate with the most shit gets his choice of top or bottom bunk. Jaden took bottom.

Smokey and Jaden liked pretty much the same TV shows, so time in the cell was quiet and peaceful. Smokey's assignment was school; he never finished grade school and his test scores were under 8.0. Any score under 10.0, the inmate automatically gets assigned to school. Either assigned to school or work, each inmate gets paid for their participation, a nominal pay of twenty dollars a month. More skilled jobs get more pay, topping out at forty-five dollars a month.

In prison, there are what is considered premium job assignments. Working in the commissary pays forty-five dollars a month but has benefits like free shit from the commissary. Being assigned to the gym pays forty-five dollars also, but the benefits of that is a lot of movement within the prison and a lot of workout time when the gym isn't crowded. Another top job would be the prison industry program. Each prison has some sort of industry in which the goods made are sold in the free market at a lower cost, of course. The labor used is much cheaper – prison labor. That job pays anywhere from a hundred and fifty to three hundred a month. To get one of the premium jobs, an inmate must have connections – politics as it were for the job. It was not easy to get in those positions.

Julie and Michael were now dating on a regular basis, writing to each other when both were away at school and always together when they were in Chicago. Then one day, Julie felt sick with a nauseating feeling, and after spending some time in the bathroom, puking her guts out, she took the test and discovered she was pregnant. Julie was very happy to learn she would have a baby. Michael was a good man. She loved him, and now they would have a child. Michael was also very happy about being a father. He loved Julie very much and thought this was the best thing in the world.

He had borrowed some money from his parents and bought the engagement ring. Michael had taken Julie to a very nice Italian place for dinner, and once they finished eating, he got up from his chair, stepped over to Julie, got on his knee, and pulled out the ring. He then proposed to her. The tears were forming in her eyes. She was so happy. She immediately said yes, and the whole place started clapping.

They had gotten an apartment together in the suburb of Cary, a nice little place for the two of them, and started working on children. This was Julie's dream – marriage, children, and making a home. She decided college could wait; it was something she still wanted, but not her priority now. Michael finished school and had applied for a job out of state, a real good job. They wanted him. He accepted and they moved.

New Mexico was a lot different than Chicago. It was very beautiful. The land and mountain scene was breathtaking – a good place to start a family. That's exactly what they did. Julie had two children within four years – a son and then a daughter. The whole thing was picture perfect, or so it seemed. People do change after time.

Chapter 11

JADEN'S SCORES WERE very high. He topped out at 12.9, the highest score the test could give. Jaden was always smart, just didn't like homework. He was sitting in the placement office and was asked what he would like to do, work or college classes? Jaden chose work, wanting to not be trapped indoors all the time. He was assigned to the grounds crew. The grounds crew clean up the joint (term for prison) and perform various functions as a maintenance person would in the free world.

Jaden was a hustler, and from day one on the job, he hustled. He met the right inmates and made connections with them. Everything about this joint was good, and Jaden thought this wasn't a bad place to do five years. In every joint, there is always some drama going on; it can't be helped. There is a mix of inmates. Some want to do their time with no altercations; others need the drama in their life. The mixing of the two always brings problems. Jaden wanted no problems, but he realized this is not camp fun time. This was prison. He would stay on point at all times, ready for whatever came his way.

The funny thing about gang members is that the ones who act hard core are usually the scared ones, the ones who are insecure and worried about proving something. They are the troublemakers, and every gang has them. They are constantly looking to point out the issues in other members, possibly trying to deflect anyone from focusing on them. Once the pressure is on though, they always fall. They crack under pressure. The quiet ones are the ones to be concerned with and the ones who you can't figure out 'cause they don't give you enough information to form an opinion as to their character. Trying to size up everyone in the mix isn't easy but can be done. The smart ones do this; the stupid ones just assume shit.

Too bad that wouldn't happen. Some shit went down in the school between his cellie, Smokey, and a Royal named CB (Cat Burglar). It seems that the two inmates got into some argument and Smokey disrespected the Royal and the Royals, and CB didn't do a damn thing. Raven was the shot caller for the Royals. He was from Peoria and was doing seven years for aggravated battery with intent to kill. He was a decent Royal and was capable of handling business. The Latin folks' council was on the yard, talking about the situation, and a decision was made.

Raven came over by the bench the Royals were sitting on and told Jaden he needed to talk to him. As the two walked, Jaden had already predicted what was going down, but Raven confirmed it. "Since your cellie was the one who disrespected, you need to deal with him. Just fuck him up, no hit" was the order Raven gave. Jaden told him no problem and walked away.

"Fuck, goddamn pussy ass CB can't handle his own fuckin' business. Now I gotta do it," Jaden complained to no one. The yard time was over and Jaden went back to his cell. Smokey was sleeping, facing the brick wall. Jaden began wrapping up all his belongings and placed them in the corner, took out his brown jersey gloves, and put them on his hands. Jaden grabbed Smokey from his sleep and yanked him to the ground. Still half asleep, Smokey didn't have time to gather his senses, not when Jaden was throwing some hard blows at his head. The whole scenario lasted about three minutes, and Smokey was fucked up real bad.

When Jaden finished, he told Smokey that it wasn't personal, but just because CB was a punk ass bitch didn't mean the rest of the Royals were. Jaden told Smokey, "If you want to continue this, right now then. If not, then accept it as it is." Smokey told Jaden he understood and asked if this was the end of it. Jaden said yes.

Jaden came out to the dayroom and saw CB sitting in the chair, walking up to him. He told him to go to his cell. He had some shit to talk to him about. Once in the cell, Jaden unleashed mothafuckin' hell on that coward. The beating Smokey took was but a slip on the ice compared to the disfiguring punishment that CB was experiencing. Jaden never took his gang responsibilities lightly. He always handled his business with pride.

CB ran out of his cell and straight to the guards for protection. Jaden was subdued by the guards and placed in handcuffs and escorted to segregation. There he stayed for two weeks until the adjustment committee sentenced him to an extra year in prison and sent him to a maximum security prison. *Fuck, why is this shit always happening to me?* he thought. He had fucked up a good thing, but did he have a choice? He didn't think so.

Once again he packed up his shit and prepared for his next transfer, Menard Correctional Center, maximum security prison. This is the joint where the electric chair is. They don't use that anymore though; it was deemed inhumane. That's a fuckin' joke, murderers kill and destroy people's lives and society is concerned about being humane. Now Illinois uses lethal injection, a process that uses three different chemical mixtures. One mixture immobilizes the inmate, the second puts them to sleep, and the other kills.

The bus is now rolling down the steep road along the mountain. Menard was built along the side of the mountain. Well, it looked like a mountain to Jaden. The "pit" is what the nickname was for Menard. The walls were about seventy feet high, with guard towers about a hundred feet across and lining the walls. This place was a fortress; it looked like an old castle in a way. *Why would they need the walls?* Jaden thought. *Who would be able to climb the two-hundred-foot mountainside?*

Menard was known for the violence within. Every inmate heard the stories. Murder was an everyday thing just about, just like all the gang members being locked in one room with weapons and told the last one standing gets to go home. That is the feeling there.

Once off the bus, the six inmates are processed and brought to the east house receiving. The houses for inmates are long five-story buildings. Each building has five galleries or floors, but let's call them what they are – galleries. On one side of the house, the galleries are even numbered; and on the other, odd numbered. The east house odd side was new arrivals and workers' cells. The even side was general population for inmates in school. The west house was general population also, but these inmates either had a prison job or just roamed the galleries.

The cells . . . how can I describe them? Go to your bathroom and look in. Imagine four walls. On one side of the walls are two slabs of metal three feet wide and about five and a half feet long. That's the bed. From the edge of the side to the other side of the wall is about three and a half feet. At the end of the cell is a metal toilet with a sink. That's the restroom (laugh out loud). That's it. For some inmates, it's not only a cell but their coffin. See some of these inmates have sentences like triple life, double life, and life with no parole. Others have sixty-five years. Some have five years like Jaden.

There is no discrimination in sentencing and housing. You go where there is room, except for Menard. The gangs run this prison from top to bottom. The guards have no way of knowing who has double life and who has three years. They all assume every inmate is there forever and act accordingly. This prison is ran with violence. The guards are just the cleanup crew.

Jaden gets to his cell and settles in. His cellie is some older white guy who is doing ten years for fifteen burglaries. They chat and drink coffee, smoking squares (cigarette). Inmates may decorate their cells however they like and with whatever they can find. Some inmates have cats in their cell. There was no shortage of stray cats at Menard, believe or not. Cats are a good thing. They eat the roaches and mice and spiders too.

The next day, each gang sends someone to the galleries to get info on who's in what gang and to do a check on that member. They call the streets to find out about ya. Security check is more like it. You will never know what they find out; they don't tell ya.

Everything can be good and that's that, or you could have a bad name for snitching or something like that, and they make it seem like it's all good. Then one day, you feel multiple shanks penetrating your neck, back, head, legs, and every other point of entry on your body. Within one minute, you have sixty to seventy stab wounds, and bleeding cannot be stopped. Your body grows very weak at the loss of blood, and then you fall out to the floor. As your lying there in a pool of dark red blood, you realize you are dying and are alone, and soon you will know the answer to a question that has existed from the beginning of mankind: "Is there a heaven and hell, and which one will I go to?"

Chapter 12

IT'S JADEN'S THIRD night there, and he's watching TV with his cellie. They have a torn sheet that is made into a line crossing from one end of the cell to the other. Over that line is a blanket that serves as a curtain. The curtain is closed. They hear some yelling and arguing outside of the cell. Jaden goes to take a look, and his cellie warns him not to. "Fuck that," Jaden said as he eased the curtain to one side – big mistake.

As the curtain eased its way to the side, Jaden caught the murder of a New Breed (name for black gangster gang member) as it was taking place, the blood squirting on him as the victim was being stabbed by two of his own kind. Slowly the dying gangster was slipping to the floor of the gallery as his life was draining; the other two gangsters walked away. Jaden watched the gangster die. He was no stranger to death and dying, but this was something more brutal, more savage, and more surreal to him. This made him more aware of life here in the pit.

Closing the curtains, Jaden walked to the sink to wash away the blood, knowing there would be a stain. "Told ya," his cellie told him. Jaden looked at his cellie and figured what an asshole. He could have said, "Don't open the curtain 'cause there is a murder going on." Well, maybe he couldn't. *Welcome to the pit, Jaden*, he said to himself.

Lockdown! That's what happens when a murder, stabbing, or major fight takes place. Lockdown is just that. Every inmate is confined to the cell for twenty-four hours a day. No showers, no yard, and no movement at all. The administration does an investigation, trying to decide if the occurrence was internal, which they hope, or if there is gonna be a problem between the different gangs. This lockdown should only be a week long. It was an internal thing among the New Breeds. I don't know why, so don't ask me.

That was a long week, but Jaden discovered he liked lockdown, staying in his cell, watching TV, and having his meals brought to him was nice. Each day he was on lockdown was another day he survived. He thought to himself, *I could do five years like this.* But as you all know, nothing so far ever went the way Jaden would like, and neither does this. The lockdown was over in four days; he felt cheated out of the other three days.

Casino came to the cellie the day the joint came off lockdown. He introduced himself and asked for his info. He said he looked familiar, and he told him he knew his sister, Barb. He then remembered him, but that was a long time ago when he was a shorty. He asked him if he had Jimmy's phone number. He gave it to him but told him Jimmy's mom had a block on the phone. It didn't accept collect calls. He said that wasn't a problem. The gangs had direct lines out, something the gangs had killed a couple guards for when the warden refused their request. The phone lines were granted for an assurance from each gang leader that no more guards would be killed.

This was the political way at Menard. The warden was the ultimate authority for the good guy side; and the gang chiefs, for the bad guy side, and negotiations were a constant thing. When the chiefs wanted something bad enough but the warden wouldn't budge, execution orders came fast and were carried out faster. I understand the logic of both sides. The gangs are trying to make their stay as smooth and pleasurable as possible; the warden is trying to keep the guards alive. The guards are just normal people who have families and do this job because it provides for them and their families, not something to die for.

Okay, I'm gonna use leadership ranks in this story, so this is how it breaks down from the very top to the very bottom. All the gangs that are folks have what's called a board of directors. Each gang has at least one member representing them on the board. Some have more. It depends on the size of the gang. The Royals had one board member. Popeye was his name. The board was the ruling structure, what they said was law and final. They board developed a code of law for all the folks to follow, and justice was deadly and swift if broken.

Each prison has a leader called an institutional coordinator (IC). He runs the joint. The IC has what's called a viceroy who runs each cell house or cell block and then an assistant viceroy. Under the IC and the viceroys was the chief of security and then the chief enforcer, and then there was the gallery coordinator who controlled the gallery that stayed on. Below him was the law teacher (LT). He taught the prison laws to the membership and interpreted the laws for the IC. Under him was the security force (SF) and then the enforcers. Last was the membership. This was run like a corporation, and it was run well, except for the politics, and there was a lot of that.

Caisno made the call and was happy with the results. Jaden would be a strong asset to the Royals in jail. Two weeks later, Jaden was moved from the east house to the west house. I don't remember which side, sorry. Casino had pulled connections and got him moved into one of the cells on his gallery. Casino was a gallery coordinator. Jaden's new cellie was Hammer. He was a Royal from Springfield, Illinois. He has been locked up for the past eight years and only seventeen more to go. *Good luck with that,* Jaden thought.

The two of them got along from the start. Casino had already spread the word that a new Royal was there and he was a heavy hitter. Fuckin' thanks a lot, Casino, and if you ever read this book, you will know that you are a pussy ass bitch. Sorry, just thought I would get some old anger out at that asshole.

Yep, the past three years had been rough for the Royals. They didn't have a board member, so they were not represented at all. They were still folks but at the bottom of the respect barrel. Casino had been stabbed by the folks as also Hammer was. They were told they could not throw up the Royal sign since they had no board member. They did anyway, and the folks came at them. That's all old shit now. Royals have a board member, but Casino held a grudge.

Now that the Royals had seventeen members in the west house they were the largest gang in the folks beside the gangster disciples. Casino felt the sudden urge of power, especially with Jaden arriving. Casino had told Hammer and the rest of the Royals about Jaden – who he was and what his status was on the street – and then gave Jade's credentials. Jaden was accepted without question.

Joker was the next-door neighbor to Hammer and Jaden. His job was security, but his Royal job was making extra shanks that the folks didn't know about to arm the Royals even more. He got started on Jaden's sword. I like that reference, but he did make a fuckin' big a shank that resembled a sword. *Oh great, I landed right smack-dab in the middle of an internal dispute and fuckin' Bonaparte was our fuckin' leader. How do I get myself in this shit?* he wondered.

Jaden was assigned as security to Casino, so wherever Casino went Jaden went. Jaden was able to see firsthand the workings of the political bullshit that goes on, but he also learned who the key players were, not only the leadership but the businessmen, the drug dealers who made money and fed the lower brothers morsels and handouts. He quickly learned that alliances forged on the streets really didn't mean shit here. There were inner cliques within the cliques, and the streets did as they were told, if their execution orders came from the joint and were carried out without fail. They had to because eventually, every gang member could end up in jail, and if you had refused to take care of business on the streets, business would take care of you in prison. Excellent motivational tactics.

The game was on. It was very real, the characters known and ready for play, and Jaden has joined the game.

Chapter 13

THE FOLKS HAD made sure that Jaden was assigned to cell house cleaner. The job paid thirty-five dollars a month, but more importantly, he had movement from one side of the cell house to the other. This would be necessary for him to walk and protect Casino. The gangs were very clever; they created a sort of work life for all membership – something to fill their day and nights and something to keep their minds busy and not go insane.

Jaden had made many stupid mistakes and choices in his life, but he was far from stupid. He was very observant and, most of all, rarely spoke more than a few words at a time. Some liked this about Jaden, but it made others wary of him. They didn't like his quietness. Talking exposes many things about a person, what they are thinking, what they are not saying, and their personality. Jaden knew this shit, and he enjoyed playing this game. The others had years on him in this place; he was trying to catch up as quickly as possible.

In prison, there are grade statuses: A, B, and C. These grades determine certain privileges and freedoms within the prison. The C grade is restricted the most – no yard or gym time, only able to buy hygiene items and stamped envelopes. The B grade had all privileges as the A grade, except that you were restricted to a fifty-dollar spending limit at commissary but not allowed to buy electronic items. The A grade was full privileges and movement. Most inmates were on C grade. It's the grade that comes from punishment from the adjustment committee when an inmate breaks a rule and is punished. Jaden was on C grade.

Jaden had no money coming from the streets. All he had was the state pay each month, which he was gonna save up until he reached A grade status again. Other inmates would send their money home and have someone from the free world send the money to another inmate so that they could purchase commissary items for the inmate on C grade. Jaden saw the flaw with that system – easy for money to get fucked up somehow and then fights and animosity. He could wait.

Over the next couple of months, gang jobs always changed. That's the politics, and Jaden was assigned to protect the unit viceroy, which pissed Casino off. He knew the leadership was attempting to separate Jaden from the Royals and get him more involved with the alliance business than just the royal stuff. They read Casino's game plan and neutralized it. Everyone does a lot of thinking in prison, playing chess in their heads, mobilizing the pawns to set up the knight, sacrificing the bishop to attack the rook, and placing the queen in danger so the king may win. That's the game they play in their heads and in life.

Jaden liked the job change though – protect the viceroy and put him closer to the leadership, giving him a higher status in the eyes of the gang, but the eyes of the administration were on him now. He was more seen and present with the shot callers, and the prison internal investigations unit took notice and watched. The nice thing about being personal security was that you were never sent to be a hitter. And that was a plus.

Jaden watched and kept his mouth shut, observing the politics of the leadership, the cliques and inner cliques, and the unfair favoritism shown to one member but not to another. The back stabbing and the bullshit happening were opening his eyes. He was starting to see that the supposed love the membership should have for one another was not there. It was a wall of bullshit. Each member was out for themselves and would use the others to advance up the ranks. Jaden wondered where on the ladder he was.

He had made friends with some members – well, I use the word *friends* lightly. There are no real friends in prison; all are users and takers. He got along with the ones he called friends, the ones he had things and thoughts in common with. Ricky was an ambro from the south side of Chicago. He was from Eighteenth Street, young, about twenty-two, slim, and about five feet five, with dark hair and a goatee. Jaden realized Ricky was pretty intelligent and saw things clearly when it came to the happenings of the gang. They spent many hours talking with one another. Ricky was the unit viceroy. Jaden was to protect him, but Ricky told him from day one, "Don't protect me, but fight by my side." From day one, Ricky earned Jade's respect.

Oreo was the IC, and he was a fuckin' retard. He was a dirty player and corrupt beyond normal. This set the pace for the others. He would have brothers violated for some bullshit, and he was savage about it. The chief enforcer didn't like him, but he obeyed, knowing he could be replaced with a word. The chief of security didn't like Oreo either but for different reasons. They both were in different gangs, and on the street their gangs were fighting, even though both were folks whose shit doesn't matter on the streets.

There are very few leadership overthrows in prison. If done bogus, those that try are dealt with severely. Sometimes hitters are sent after their families to teach others of the consequences. The board of directors didn't like rebellious changes. It got in the way of their control and money. And that was their main concern, their money.

Prison... well, at least the maximum security joints have an air of explosiveness to it, so the population is very polite to one another. If you bump into another inmate, you say, "My fault," or war could start. No one wanted war. If an inmate was caught stealing, he would have his hand placed in between the cell bar locking mechanism and the rolling cell door, and then the door is slammed shut on his hand. Then he has no hand no more.

There are no problems in the pit with theft. Rape is not a problem either, with the folks or people that is. There are laws governing the sexual behavior of the membership. No forcible sex. You must have twenty years to do and must be over twenty-five, and it must not be seen or spoken of. Violate these laws, and you will be killed immediately. Most members refrained from this behavior. The northsiders had no rules about this. They were barbarians and preyed upon the new white inmates from day one. Either the new guy was gonna be a soldier or a bitch – no other options. The gangs all did business with each other, and there were rules governing business transactions also. A lot of work went into keeping the peace; it was always about money.

Chapter 14

FIVE MONTHS AT Menard and Jaden was a veteran with the ways and means of the daily life. Oreo had been transferred to Pontiac because of conspiracy charges, and Ricky was promoted to IC and he kept Jaden as his personal security.

Now Jaden was the most visible member, second only to Ricky. Wherever Ricky went Jaden went, and that meant dealing with the other gang leadership. The leaders only dealt with the leaders. That's their status. It would be beneath them to deal with the lower levels. Jaden met the leader of the Latin Kings inside prison, as well as outside, and other ones as well. What concerned Jaden was how easy it was to get to these leaders if someone wanted to. They truly had no idea of security and how to achieve it. It would be easy to set them up. File that one away for future reference.

The hunting season is starting, and the joint always goes on lockdown. The guards all hunt to put extra food in the deep freezers. Also it was their sport. During this lockdown, only the leaders walk around – something they worked out with the warden. Anyways, Ricky was drinking in Forehead's cell, just hanging out, and somehow the wrong thing was said and they fought. Ricky won from looks anyway. Forehead had a fucked-up face, and Ricky had none. Now we were on level 1 lockdown for a minimum of thirty days. Jaden knew that the reality of an all-out war was at hand, and the day the lockdown was over, it would happen.

Being the man next to the man meant Jaden would most likely be killed since the main target was the man he protected. *That is really fucked up*, he thought. What could he do though? Only one thing. Jaden started writing a letter to his mom. His letter was very tender, apologizing for all he had done to make her life hard and for the life he lived. He explained to her the situation he faced and then did write something that was unthinkable. He described the way he wanted his remains to be dealt with and what he would like his final clothes to be and asked if she could put a pack of cigarettes in his pocket. He said he loved her and sent the letter. His mom fainted when she read the letter. It was too much for her to take in.

About two weeks later, Jaden received a letter from his youngest sister, no doubt talking shit for the letter he sent, but that was not the case. This letter had included a newspaper article. DRUG BUY DOUBLE CROSS was the headline. He read on. Then he froze, his heart beating rapidly, unsure of what he read. He read the name again, his hands shaking and his head hurting. He was feeling sick. Jaden dropped the article and read the letter his sister wrote. "No, oh god, please no," he cried out.

Whatever strength he had was gone. His knees could not hold his weight, and he dropped to the floor as a lifeless body would. He could feel his eyes flooded with tears, his was mind blurry, his heart was racing, his stomach was knotted up. With an animalistic wail, he screamed out with agony and heartbreak. "Nooooooooooooo oooooooooooooooooooooo" was all he could get out. The cell house went quiet. All ears were now focused on the scream.

He had read that his best friend, Jimmy, was killed in a drug buy gone bad. He lay on the floor, wrapped up like a newborn baby, sobbing from the pain and the agony he felt. A part of him had died that day, and he was lost.

His cellie just lay on his bunk, with tears in his eyes. He didn't know who, but he knew someone close to Jaden had died, and like every inmate, they dreaded those types of letters. Those were the letters that caused the hidden human qualities to escape. His tears were not for Jaden; they were for his own fear.

Slowly some inmates were asking what's wrong, and Jade's cellie yelled, "Code black," and the cell house was quiet the rest of the night. Code black was the term that someone on the outside had died, and all inmates would respect a night of silence. Jaden stayed on that floor throughout the night and into the morning. When he got up, he washed his face and reread the letter and the article, searching for all the information he could gather. He hung his head down, trying to put all of it together, trying to visualize the scene, looking for the flaws.

The other people there were the killer, Jason, and Buster. Now questions started coming to him. Why would Buster be there? Why would Jimmy have the gun? He never used a gun. Why did Jason only get shot once and in the back of his arm, while Jimmy was shot six times throughout his body? So many questions but he pieced together the scene from what little info he had.

Buster must have been the middleman and came to Jason with the deal, which he told Jimmy about. They decide to do the deal but will burn the buyer instead.

The article said the gun was faulty and didn't work. And when Jimmy pulled it out, the gun wouldn't fire, and the buyer pulled out his gun and lit them up. The story sounds plausible, if you're an outsider and don't know the habits of the players. If you're someone on the inside and believe this shit, then you're a fuckin' idiot who goes through life with blinders on, unless there's more to the story that hasn't been revealed, but what?

Again, the nice thing about prison is that there are lots of time to think, and Jaden put that mind of his to work and he searched and recalled every bit of memory he had. He needed to know what really went down. The stuff he didn't know he had his two sisters try to find out, questioning a person here and there but with questions that were vague. If this was a setup, he didn't want his family in danger. Why a setup? Was there someone who wanted Jimmy's spot as chief? No, this is something else. He waited for the info from his sisters.

He barely said a word to his cellie, and his cellie was concerned, not because Jaden wasn't speaking much, but it was because he was speaking to himself. His cellie was nervous that Jaden was losing it, maybe already lost it. If Jaden was going crazy, that was a problem. The gang couldn't afford to have a loose cannon walking around, too unpredictable, especially since they didn't have the details yet of what happened, which they pressed Jade's cellie for the next day.

Jaden finally handed the article to his cellie, who read the article like a speed reader. Once finished, he was relieved the murder wasn't gang related. He told Jaden sorry for his loss and proceeded to send the info down the gallery, one cell at a time. By the time the whole gallery had the scoop, Jaden had formulated the plan to get revenge.

The article said the killer was charged with armed violence by a convicted felon, that he was also a cop's son, and that there would be no murder charges. Jaden knew this guy was going to Sheridan Correctional Center. That joint is where cops go when they come to prison. It's protective custody. Well, most of it is still a prison. He knew the killer was going there, and now he needed to get there.

He was gonna kill that muthafucka' sure as he was standing in his cell, but how to get there? The answer was simple. The leadership was always able to have inmates transferred for the right reasons. Jaden figured that since he was cool with Rick, the transfer was a sure thing. Once off this lockdown, he would . . . ah shit, the lockdown. He forgot that once off the lockdown, he could be dead like Jimmy.

He kept planning for whatever scenario would take place. He planned for the war, visualizing it and the various scenarios that could come. He memorized every scenario, every situation, and filed it for later reference, but he decided he would survive that war. He had to if he wanted to seek revenge on the asshole who killed Jimmy. Yes, he would survive at all cost, even if he had to throw Rick in front of him as a shield. He smiled. That would be fucked up for Rick, but it made sense. If the Kings wanted Rick and Rick was killed first, then maybe it would end. Nope, the momentum of the attack would continue until the guards had fired and killed a couple inmates. That's when all fighting ends – with death.

He now was in a waiting period. Waiting and planning, waiting and planning, revisiting everything in his memory. He now had a calmness about him, a resolve. The stage was set, and he was the main character. The lines were memorized, and now he waited for opening day.

Chapter 15

THE WARDEN TALKED to all the gang heads and decided lockdown was over. There was an air of uneasiness surrounding the joint as the loud speaker announced yard time. Every inmate was going to the yard, strapped with shanks and books sewn in their jackets. They twisted towels and wrapped them around their necks, also wrapping tape or bandanas around their hands. The soldiers are assembled and ready. What will the generals decide?

As Jaden walked beside Rick toward the yard entrance gates, he felt loose. He didn't load himself up with books and towels – a risk, sure, but that shit weighted you down, made attack movements awkward, and limited your vision. No, Jaden went out there as loose and light as possible. He carried two shanks with him, the two made by the Royals – his swords, if the time came, he would unleash the samurai swords and slice the fuck out of anyone who approached, friend or foe. He had a mission, and that was priority.

As they neared Forehead and his group, only Forehead and his personal security, Bam Bam, approached closer. Rick signaled for all folks to hold back, except for Jaden. "Oh goody, I get to be the one. Thanks, Rick. I don't mind getting chopped up like tuna 'cause of your drinking fights," he jokingly said in a whisper to Rick. Rick held in the laughter. That fuckin' Jaden, he didn't always try to be funny, but when he did, it was hysterical. Hold it in, Rick. To laugh now could make Forehead think you take him as a joke. Hold it in.

The four men approached each other. Jaden and Bam Bam kept their eyes upon each other, watching for any sign of attack. The guard towers were at full force, something Jaden noticed upon entering the yard. At least forty guards were surrounding the yard on the wall, mini fourteens in hand, ready to release a blaze of bullets into these fuckin' animals upon the first hint of trouble. The whole yard is silent. Every single eye is on the four men in the middle. Hearts are pounding – some scared and others hoping. Every man was ready for the battle.

Both Forehead and Rick knew this. They were not stupid, and in fact, both their superiors had sent word to fix it if possible because what would happen here would travel throughout the prison system. Internal affairs had read their letters and knew the pressure the two bosses were facing. Relaying this to the warden is what gave the warden confidence to take the joint off lockdown, but still, you never know with these fuckers.

Rick spoke first and said he apologized for his remarks. Forehead responded in kind. The two talked and it was over. Jaden would get his chance at revenge. As the crowd of soldiers started to disband and go back to the normal activities on the yard, Jaden asked Rick about the transfer. Rick answered immediately and said no. He informed Jaden that what happens on the street stays on the street and that his services would better benefit the gang if he stayed here.

Jaden masked his anger, his outrage, and his discontent for the motherfucker who stood before him. His fingers still on the shank, he contemplated driving the seven inches of steel through the fuckin' skull of Rick and the other shank through his heart. Rick's hands were close to his shanks too. He felt the condonation Jaden had for his answer and never underestimated anyone, least of all Jaden.

See, Jaden held other jobs in the folks as well, but those memories will stay hidden, for they are too brutal and violent and he was never charged with those things. No chance of this story revealing those details, sorry. Rick knew though, knew what Jaden had done and in what manner he had done it. So he took no chances now and looked Jaden in his eyes and said, "Sorry, but it's the way we do shit, and you know that. Are we good?" "I understand," Jaden replied. "Yeah, we're good." Jaden relaxed his grip as did Rick after seeing Jaden did first. Jaden followed Rick as was his duties, but whatever loyalty he had for the folks in the past was now gone. He had allowed his allegiance to them to die and now was ready to put plan B into action.

Casino had watched from a distance and saw the two talking. He noticed the tenseness between the two and had spied Jaden's readiness to strike. Casino was prepared to support Jaden in this mission, not even knowing the reasons. He saw it as a way to gain power of the joint. There's an old law within the gangs: One on one fight – you kill the boss, you become the boss. Casino had summoned all the Royals and filled them in, positioning themselves next to the closest allies of Rick. This would be a systematic revolt and would go down with precision. All they waited for was Jaden's first strike. It never came and Casino was pissed. The other Royals were bewildered as to why it hadn't gone down, but Casino knew and he smiled because he figured out Jade's game plan also and trusted that the Royals would come out ahead when the smoke cleared.

The next morning, Jaden was up at his cell door, ready to go to breakfast, which was strange 'cause he never went. As the cell doors were opened, he stepped out and followed the line to chow. Eating all on his plate, he sat there, quiet as usual, keeping to himself. As the guards called for chow to be over with, the inmates line up and proceeded back to the cell house, all except one.

Jaden motioned to the sergeant of the guard detail that he needed to talk in privacy. The sergeant knew what time it was. Things like this have happened before, and there was a protocol. The sergeant searched Jaden. Finding no weapons, he led him to the captain's office. The three of them talked behind closed doors. After telling the captain that he was ordered to kill Forehead, but in a quiet way, the captain said he needed more. Jaden laid out the location of every single weapon and which cells they were in and the method of getting rid of the weapons during a shakedown (massive search of the prison).

The captain called the internal affairs lieutenant, and they strategized according to the layout given to them by Jaden. Within ninety minutes, the lieutenant had confirmed a major success. They had recovered one hundred and seventeen shanks from the folks – the largest find in the history of the pit. This was monumental and a problem for Jaden the captain knew. The gangs would come for him with such a vengeance that he wasn't sure the prison could control. He called the warden, who called Springfield, who approved the plan, and Jaden was on a bus in two hours, heading for Sheridan Correction Center. Now time for plan C.

Chapter 16

UPON ARRIVING AT Sheridan, Jaden noticed the cottagelike buildings, the grassy yard, and the collegelike look of this joint – much nicer than the pit. He knew he had a short time until word reached Sheridan about Jaden and his crime against the folks. He needed to put plan C into effect. He had about two weeks at the longest. Jaden had seen some inmates he knew – non-gang members, just criminals, people he had done business with or known on the streets. He gave them the lowdown – how the folks tried to send him on a dumb, dumb mission and he betrayed them for it and that he was gonna get the violation and requested they watch his back just in case. They agreed. They had respect for Jaden and knew they would be good if Jaden owed them. It was nice to keep that leverage, they all thought.

Jaden went to the yard and found some Royals, and other folks said he had a message for the IC. They relayed the message, and the IC, Flaco, came to talk to him. He told Flaco the story, and Flaco agreed he deserved a violation. Giving him a three-minute head-to-toe beating with no cover-up should be perfect. This was a medium security prison, never any killings, or if there was, it was way out of the ordinary, not just beatings.

The violation occurred in the gym and was finished. Flaco sent word to Statesville, the home of the board of directors, that the violation had been carried out. The board was fuckin' livid. This stupid motherfucker, Flaco, allowed Jaden to be served in an easy way for something they were gonna send the hitters for. The law was the law; they could not proceed. To do so would show that the law did not pertain to them and could cause major problems for them. They found a better way to deal with it. They sent an order to Menard's chief enforcer to take Ricky out for improperly ordering a hit.

Taking Jaden's side of the story puts them in a better position than taking Ricky's side. If they took Ricky's side, they would look like a bunch of idiots for not seeing the play, and they couldn't have that. No, Jaden told the truth and was placed in a bad situation was the position the board took, knowing they were played though.

Jaden informed Flaco that he is taking himself off count. He would no longer be counted as a member of the folks, no longer a Royal, and no longer a gang member, and reminded Flaco that if anyone came at him, he would serve their ass with whatever he had in his arsenal. Flaco agreed, figured he wanted nothing to do with Jaden and liked the idea he wasn't his problem anymore. Jaden liked feeling the chains of gang rules released from his neck and ankles, no longer shackled by their restrictions and laws. He moved freely.

Jaden took his time. Plan D would take a while, maybe a couple of months to start. He decided to get acclimated to Sheridan's daily routines. After about six months, he finally got assigned to the legal library as a clerk. The legal clerk helps inmates with legal issues and paperwork, a prestigious job with many benefits. The job pays seventy-five dollars a month. Inmates pay you extra to do legal filings for them, and you get to make out the legal passes for inmates.

Prison passes are divided in to two categories: mandatory and nonmandatory. With a mandatory pass, an inmate must go on or face punishment. With a nonmandatory pass, an inmate may refuse. The legal library passes were mandatory. Jaden counted on that one piece of information. There is what's called the master inmate locator. It is a list of each inmate housed at Sheridan. It contains the inmate's name, prison ID number, housing unit, cell number, and grade status. All information the prison doesn't fill is top secret, so it's not hidden.

The library keeps this list available to make out passes for the inmates. Jaden needed this to locate Jimmy's killer and to arrange a mandatory pass to bring him to the law library. This he would do once he was ready, but first July Fourth was coming up and he needed to make arrangements to get some hooch (homemade alcohol). The plan would be to kill this asshole then celebrate the Fourth. Well, that was the plan.

Finding someone who would make the hooch isn't easy. If caught, it's a one-way ticket to a max joint. No one wants that, but still some take chances, the reason the prisons have inmates. We all took chances and got caught.

Richie Rich was Jaden's connect. They had done business before on some minor things Jaden needed like sandpaper, a large spool of thread, and a black electrical tape. Richie Rich thought the items were basically useless, so he didn't charge Jaden very much for them, not knowing the items were very important. First, you take your fan and take the locking nut off and remove the fan blades. Next, you place the sandpaper around the spool of thread and hold it in place with large rubber bands on each end of the spool. Place the spool of thread over the shaft of the fan where the blades normally fit, put the locking nut back on to hold the spool tight, and turn the fan on. There, you have a high-tech sander used to sharpen dull pieces of metal into a prison shank. I'm guessing that once the prison officials read this book, they will no longer allow the sale of fans – sorry guys.

Getting the metal was harder than anticipated and took a while, but finally Jaden obtained it from an inmate who worked on the grounds crew. All the pieces were in place, except for the hooch, which Richie Rich said he would get back to Jaden sometime today about it.

Jaden now was working the plan in his head – when to put the pass in, where to ambush the asshole, and how to hide the crime – working it out over and over again, finding the flaws, and trying to correct them. He saw Richie Rich at the gym later that night and was relieved he could get a liter of liquid for twenty dollars, a favorable price for a good customer like Jaden. The deal was struck, and Jaden was given the info on who to pick it up from. Of course, he could pay later. He had good credit, plus he was the legal clerk, always a good person owing you. The legal clerk was instrumental at sending mandatory passes to the inmates who conducted drug trafficking, and the only place where there were no guards was in the actual legal library. The legal clerk made friends and money easy. He picked up the hooch later the next day and placed his plan into action. July third, this motherfucker was dead.

Chapter 17

JADEN WAS UP early, barely sleeping at all through the night. His mind was playing out the way this was gonna go down. He would go to work in the library. About ten minutes before the target shows up, he would go out to smoke a cigarette and wait, hit the target, and dispose of the shank and then return to work. No witnesses means to find him guilty would require evidence, evidence that did not exist.

Jaden went through his morning ritual, made some coffee with the hot pot in the back room, turned on the copiers, and sat at his desk, waiting for the moment. Remembering that day he got the article, remembering the words he read, remembering the heartache he felt, his blood was starting to get hot now, his anger rising. And in his head, he felt this was his responsibility. Everyone on the streets would expect this of him. He was Jimmy's best friend after all.

No matter the problems of the past between them, this was his duty, regardless that he himself was gonna kill Jimmy not too long ago. *Wow*, he thought, *I really was gonna kill him.* He felt a twinge of guilt at that thought, a small point of responsibility for his death. Was it his fault? This would have never happened if he was out there. He never would have let Jimmy do the mistakes Jimmy did. No, Jaden would have been there. Jaden would have had the gun. Would Jaden have died instead ? He looked at the clock on the wall. It was time.

Jaden told the librarian staff member he was gonna go smoke one and would be back in ten minutes. "Okay, Jaden, no problem," replied the librarian. Jaden went down the hall past the guard post and informed him of his smoking break. The guard nodded, too busy reading his book. Such an easy job the guard had.

Jaden was now outside the entrance the target would be coming to, placing himself to the side and looking around. No eyes were on him. He was at the optimum spot to do the hit. Here comes the target, walking closer, closer, and closer. Now he was at the door. Jaden spoke first. "Is your name Michael Jones?" Jaden asked. The target nodded yes, and Jaden asked another question: "Do you know Jimmy Keyes?" noticing the eyes of the target were now filling with a fear he had recognized so many times before. "Well, my name is Lloki. I'm Jimmy's best friend."

As he began the ascent of the shank, something very strange happened. All time stood still. Nothing moved, and Jaden felt an overwhelming presence take him, a calming power that held him in check, and Jaden heard her voice, an unknown woman's voice that spoke in such a commanding tone but soft. He heard the words clear in his head: "You are done, Jaden. You will kill no more." Then it was gone, and Jaden looked at Michael and reassured him, "You won't have any problems. I just want to know what you know," as Jaden tossed the shank on the roof. "Go inside and sign in. We'll talk in the library."

The two talked the whole morning, and Jaden took in the information, but he was still trying to think what the fuck happened to him out there. Was that God? Did God send an angel to stop him? Why now? What was different now? Jaden didn't know the answer and probably never will as to what happened to him, but he was never gonna forget it. That was certain.

Michael confirmed what Jaden's suspicions were about the killing. Jimmy had burned the older ex-Royals on some money, and they wanted him dead. They couldn't outrightly just kill him. That would sign their death warrant, so they devised a plan to make it look like a bad drug deal gone wrong. Michael was the buyer; he contacted Buster as the middleman who went to Jimmy. Jimmy said yes to the deal and brought in Kevin as backup. Kevin got the gun – you know, the gun that didn't fire.

The plan was for Buster to pick up the buyer and search him. If no weapon is found, they continue to the buy site. Buster would give Jimmy the sign: "It's all good," reassuring Jimmy the buyer had no weapon. Jimmy would then rob the buyer at gunpoint, and it would be over with. Buster never searched Michael. Buster gave the signal, Jimmy pulled the gun out, Michael started for his gun, Jimmy tried to fire, Michael fired, and Jimmy died.

He was sick to his stomach. He told Michael it was time for him to go and reminded him of only one thing. "If I ever hear of you bragging about what you did, your family will pay" was his only warning. Michael nodded that he understood, just thankful to get the fuck away from Jaden. The whole time Michael was there, he was scared out of his mind. He saw the look in Jaden's eyes, and he saw the hurt, knowing he was one of the reasons for the hurt. All he wanted was to get back to his cell, the safety of his cell.

Jaden now sat there in his chair. He was fucked up in the head. He didn't kill the target. All he did to get to this place – the betrayal of the folks, the violation, and the preparations – everything was for nothing. He felt an overwhelming guilt building up in him, a feeling like he failed to fulfill his duties, as though he let Jimmy down. Unable to function, he left work and went back to his cell and drank till he was drunk.

The anger, the guilt, the pain – all the feelings he tried to hold in check were now uncontainable and erupted from him like a volcano, and he destroyed his cell in a fit of rage, yelling at everyone, yelling at no one. He was alone in the cell, except for the shadows of the past. The guards came to the cell and witnessed the mayhem that was taking place and called for backup. Jaden was subdued and taken to solitary confinement. He passed out and stayed that way until the next day, July 4, 1990.

Sitting in his cell, he knew he was fucked. He wasted so much time and resources and fucked his name up with the gangs, and now he knew he would get sent back to a max joint, and the board would find a way to serve him with a dirt nap (death) for the position he had put them in.

Jaden had a visitor at the door, the warden, and he looked at Jaden and could recognize the look of a man who had reached his bottom, his final recognition of defeat and failure. The warden knew the feeling and decided to reach out and to do a twelve-step call on this inmate he had come to like. He asked Jaden what happened, and Jaden told him he got drunk because he has a drinking problem – a lie, but he knew if he told the warden the truth, he would be on the first thing smoking to Pontiac prison. The warden would not allow someone like Jaden to stay here. The warden looked thoughtful and told Jaden, "I'm sending you to the gateway drug unit, where you will stay until the day of your release." Jaden agreed.

Chapter 18

THE WARDEN WAS true to his word, and after thirty days in confinement, Jaden was sent to the drug unit. Realizing the warden just saved his ass, he would play along with the game and stay cool. Anything was better than going back to a max joint. Jaden arrived at housing unit C6, the gateway drug unit. This unit was separated from the population at all costs, allowing inmates to have a chance to get sober and clean time and work on their issues without peer pressure from the general population.

As Jaden entered the unit, he was slapped in the face with the world of sobriety. The walls had painted murals on them, bright colors were all around the living unit, inmates were sitting down talking, and it was peaceful in the dayroom – what the fuck. This was new to Jaden – this peaceful look and feeling of a prison unit. He continued to observe, not realizing he was being observed. The layout was the same as the other housing units. There was the dayroom and then two wings separating off the dayroom in different directions, each wing containing nine cells. There was A wing and B wing. He was led to B wing and to his cell. The inmate who had brought him in informed him he had fifteen minutes to get settled in and report to the dayroom. Jaden complied.

As he walked into the dayroom, he grabbed a seat away from everyone else, trying to isolate himself and trying to take in what he was seeing and somehow understand the routine. The only problem was they wouldn't let him be alone. As soon as he sat down, an inmate came over to talk to him. He answered the inmate's questions with one-word answers till the inmate left – thank god. What the fuck, another one sat down. Trying to start a conversation with Jaden, again with the one-word answers. Jaden had no fuckin' clue what the fuck was going on.

This was a whole different world to him. The counselors kept observing. This shit played out for about another hour, same shit: One sat down and one left until every inmate sat down and left. Jaden didn't know what had transpired, but he felt like he was just tested, but for what?

David Spencer, the drug counselor for B wing watched with great interest as Jaden acted and behaved exactly as an addict would – standoffish when confused, isolating himself in unfamiliar settings and surroundings. He smiled at the thought of watching Jaden trying to figure out the game and the rules of gateway – a typical addict. He kind of reminded him of himself when he first came to treatment. This one was somewhat different, but he couldn't quite place it yet, but he would.

Bobby Jackson also watched; he was the counselor of A wing and also the site supervisor. He didn't like the fact that the warden had intervened and sent this new guy here. He hated when the administration interfered, but he gave way because it was this warden that had opened the doors to the unit being formed. He would keep his eye on Jaden. One major fuckup and he was gone. That was the deal the warden made. Yes, he would keep both eyes on him.

Bobby nodded at David, and David motioned to the inmate who was holding a clipboard. Then that person came to Jaden and told him David was ready to talk to him. Jaden followed him to the counselor's office, which was a cell transformed into an office. The inmate announced the Jaden was there, and David said, "Good." Now Jaden stood in David's office, and David was just staring at him, with a knowing smirk. Jaden smirked back.

Then David started to speak to him, "So you must be completely confused as to this whole treatment environment, huh, Jaden?"

"Never been to treatment," replied Jaden. Then David gave Jaden the whole rundown on gateway. The two spent two hours together, mostly David asking Jaden questions as they related to alcohol and drug use in Jade's life. Jaden answered each answer honestly. There was something Jaden trusted about David. He liked David. That was Jaden's first admission assessment into a drug unit.

Jaden was placed into orientation. This usually lasts about thirty days, a chance to get to learn the rules and the routines of the drug unit. The main thing Jaden learned was that there were three group meetings a day, and the rest of the time, the inmates spent their time having one-on-one conversations with each other, talking about shit like their drug use and feelings, fuckin' feelings. *Who the fuck wants to talk about feelings?* Jaden asked himself.

AM development was the first meeting of the day – an organized structured meeting designed to get the residents in a positive mood. Oh yeah, in gateway, inmates are called residents. AM development consisted of different topics and lasted about ninety minutes. Jaden hated AM development.

The next meeting was usually a "get to know you" session in which a resident would disclose their life in thirty minutes. This was usually a new resident giving them a chance to let the others know something about them, which was followed by questions from the other residents. The PM meeting was usually something the counselor would run and was always informative.

The gateway drug unit had structure and job functions that the residents held. Here is the structure from top to bottom: Bobby was the supervisor and counselor; David was the counselor; Jack was the house elder, the highest position for a resident; the Cornilius was the senior coordinator; there were coordinators who ran the daily routines of the unit; there were department heads who were in charge of the various functions, orientation, job functions, clerical, support team, and creative development; and then the residents. Sounds kinda like gang shit, doesn't it?

Chapter 19

JADEN WAS IN the drug unit for about two months now, and he liked it. The meetings sucked – well, most of them. There were some he liked. He liked the confrontation group. That's where a resident who wants to address something with another inmate may do so by sitting in a chair and facing the other resident sitting on a chair, both chairs in the middle of the group. Both inmates would sit on their hands. The first inmate would address his issues; the second would respond. Jaden liked this meeting. It was the drama that he liked because confrontation group was usually about something bad.

Jaden understood this group; it was about bringing an issue to another in a positive way, without personal bullshit, and it was also about responding in a constructive way also, not getting defensive, and about coming to a resolution. That seems easy until Jaden was brought to group one day.

One resident named Leroy, who Jaden and some other residents had come to call the therapeutic robot because he wrapped himself in the terminology and acted like a robot. Well, he brought Jaden to the group because he felt Jaden wasn't plugging in to the program, not talking about his emotions. Jaden thought about his response and then replied, "I've been living with my secrets for so long – livin' this lifestyle for so long. Do you seriously think I'm gonna just let it go after two months? Do you think I would trust you with my secrets? I've watched what goes on here. I understand it, and I'm trying to get to a point where I let myself open up, but I've only been here for a short time. I'm not at the growth level you are at, not yet."

Jaden has thrown some truth out there, but most of it was bullshit, and Bobby had seen it. Jaden didn't want to be in the spotlight around Bobby. There was something about him he didn't want to face and he tried to keep away from him.

Leroy started to respond back, and Bobby cut him off, "Family [that's what the residents called one another], we are all drunk right now. Everyone should be nodding out from all that dry dope Jaden just gave us," Bobby started saying. *Fuck*, Jaden thought. Bobby continued speaking, "Jaden has been here for two months, and he has watched and learned how to fit in without buying in – to walk among us but not be one of us, to take your stories and not give back." Bobby was staring at Jaden. He knew what Jaden had said was some top-notch bullshit, but it was top-notch. Bobby realized Jaden definitely was an addict, and he had some shit buried in him – secrets. Secrets keep ya sick.

Bobby looked around at the residents. He saw the men who had worked hard over the past months and years, bought into the program, and made changes in their lives and behaviors. Some were hard though, some easy. Bobby sat there quiet, thinking. He knew what was needed, but a lifeline was never done on someone so new in the program, and there were reasons for that. A lifeline is a meeting where the resident stands in front of the group and is questioned about everything concerning their life and behavior, and the meeting is ruthless. It breaks a person down in a structured way, attacking them, putting them on the defensive, attacking more, questioning more, taking the answers, and turning them around on the person until, hopefully, the person breaks down and opens up and gives up something the group can work with.

The lifeline is dangerous because it can open up something within the psyche of the person and release something no one there is trained to deal with, leaving the person wounded with no help. Bobby was concerned about what Jaden would release. He had to take this one very careful. The whole dayroom was quiet as Bobby thought, and then he looked at Jaden and said, "You need to start disclosing things about yourself. Feelings are not something that make you vulnerable once released. They make you stronger. For us to be able to help you and help ourselves, we need to know we can trust you with our feelings also."

Bobby then asked Jaden, "What is a regret you have from your life?"

"Bringing my brother into the gang," replied Jaden.

"Good. For the next thirty days, you will talk about that on one-on-one sessions. Every time we are not in a meeting, I want you talking to a different family member, at least three a day, about your feelings on that."

Group was over, and it had been a setup from the beginning. Bobby used Leroy to bring Jaden to the group, so he could see how he dealt with confrontation, but he didn't expect the response Jaden gave. It didn't matter. It opened up the door to help, which was the desired outcome.

Jaden was pissed, *What the fuck, talk to these mothafuckers about my brother? What would that help?* he thought to himself. His brother would still be in the gang, always in danger. Jaden had that guilt, the guilt of bringing Marcus into the Royals. Jaden thought it was the right thing to do at the time, but now he thought different. Marcus was nothing like Jaden. He wasn't a killer; he didn't need the gang. He would have been all right on his own, so Jaden fucked his life up. Jaden bore that responsibility and that guilt. Every day he feared for his brother, and every day he feared he would get that letter, the same one he got about Jimmy. That was something he could not bear and something he dreaded. *Fuck it, he'll talk about it. He will share it.*

The next month, Jaden had shared some of his feelings about his brother, but most importantly, he got to know some of the residents better, and there were some he liked. They shared some of their shit too, and it did feel better to talk about it. Jaden learned that they all really did share a lot in common, maybe not the same exact shit, but the feelings were common. Jaden still couldn't help himself. He judged which residents he thought were trying to change and which ones weren't. He didn't want to admit it, but deep down he wanted to change also. He was tired of the mask he wore and the costume that was wrapped around him. Change would be good.

Things went pretty much the same for the next three months, and Jaden was buying into the program more and more. One night, on a get-to-know-you, the house elder was the focus, and he opened up and shared some very deep, very creepy shit about himself, the kinda shit you don't tell anyone. He did though. He let it go and wasn't chained by that beast no more. Jaden now knew the two of them shared some real shit in common. The two would talk more, share more, and come to call each other friends in time.

Seven months into the program and Jade's behavior was not right. Things were getting to him, aggravating him. He was acting out in a way, and it caught Bobby's attention. *Seven months he lasted*, Bobby thought. Not too bad. Now the real treatment starts.

He knew Jaden was trying, but that Jaden would only be able to go so far into it if he hit that barrier, the invisible wall called "secrets." That was a wall that was built out of the strongest of emotions: guilt, shame, abandonment, betrayal, and fear. The wall was strong in each person who built it, but it wasn't invincible. It could be broken down. The way to attack that wall was to go after the fear first. Bobby knew that that's why he gave Jaden the talking exercises, helping him to realize nothing bad comes from sharing feelings.

Guilt would be much harder though. It was a feeling people placed on themselves. It's hard to get them to remove it; it takes time. Betrayal was a hard one too but not impossible. The hardest of them all was shame. Shame was a motherfucker and was hiding deep inside there, it's claws grasping at the essence of the soul, afraid to let go, afraid to release its hold. Yep, shame was a motherfucker.

Bobby knew it was time for Jaden to have a lifeline, but he needed to talk to his strongest coordinators first and needed to orchestrate this right. The plan was made, and the path was set. Jaden would be broken down tonight.

Jaden never saw it coming. The day was pleasant, with no altercations. Chow was good, and he got a good workout at the gym. Coming out to the dayroom for the PM meeting, Jaden noticed the chairs were set up all facing the wall.

"Another get-to-know-you session?" he asked the coordinator on duty.

"No, it's a lifeline," replied the coordinator on duty (COD).

Anxiety, anxiety, anxiety – that's what Jaden felt. He knew the time had come. He started thinking and preparing for the questions, but knew no matter the answers, it would be turned around on him. He was fucked and scared. *Scared of what? They don't beat you down. They don't kill you – no. But they get inside you and poke around, looking at things you don't want them to see,* he thought. There was nothing he could do to prepare himself; he was fucked.

The meeting was starting, and the COD called Jaden to the front of the group and announced the meeting was a lifeline. Everyone was ecstatic; this was the favorite meeting of all, the most intense, and the most dramatic. Expectations were high for everyone, including both counselors and the two guards in the control booth. Yep, the guards had become to the routines of gateway, had known the meetings they had, which most were boring, except the one they were gonna do now. They experienced the lifeline meetings through the three years gateway has been there. Yep, they loved this meeting.

Jaden walked to the front and stood there with his hands behind him, which was customary. He could let them hang by his side, but he was not allowed to fold them in front of himself. That was a defiance stand, which was not allowed. The COD called the first family member to start the meeting. It would be all coordinators off duty to start the barrage of questioning and attacking. They were the strengths of the family, the backbone. Each had at least a year in gateway and were accustomed to therapeutics.

Mark was the first. He read some questions from the lifeline sheet Jaden filled out when he first came there and waited for Jaden's response.

"What was your drug of choice?" was the first question.

"Cocaine," came the response.

"How often?" the next question immediately asked.

"Every day," responded Jaden.

"How did you do cocaine?"

"Smoked it."

"Where did you get the money?"

"From stealing."

"Ever steal from your family?" There was a hesitation. "What, you don't know if you stole from your family?"

"Yes, I did."

"Which ones?" again with the hesitation. "Answer the questions Jaden," barked the inquisitor.

"My mom, my brother, my sister," Jaden responded, hating to admit that.

"Do you love your family?" Mark asked.

"Yes," Jaden responded quickly.

"I don't understand. You say you love your family, yet you steal from them. Is that love, Jaden?" How could he answer that. It was a loaded question, meant to escalate the lifeline.

"It was a dysfunctional love – the only way I knew," Jaden replied. Bobby heard the answer and thought to himself, Gotcha. *Your nervous and using your defensive mechanisms to protect yourself from something. Hmmmm, family is a sore spot for Jaden.* Mental note. Bobby continued, watching, observing, and gathering info for later.

The questioning now switched to Jason, who was taking the lead of Mark.

"Did you ever hit any of your family?" Again the hesitation. The whole group yelled at once, "Answer the question." Jaden shot them a dirty look, and Jason chastised him for it. "We are here to help you. You came to us, not the other way around. If you don't want this, step down and sign out of the program." Jaden stayed where he stood. He knew he could not sign out. He knew that if he did, he was going straight to a max joint, but did they know that? Did they have some piece of information he didn't know about? Goddamn, he was fucked.

"No, I never hit my family as to cause them pain," he replied.

"What kind of answer is that? Did you hit anyone in your family?" Jason asked again.

Jaden envisioned altercations between him and his siblings, some pushing and shoving when they were little, always arguing, but he never hit them. "No, I didn't," he stated with pride.

"No, you didn't, but wasn't every time you stole from them a slap in their face, an attack of their love, a shot at their trust?" asked Jason.

"I guess you're right," Jaden replied.

"There's no guessing when you know the truth, Jaden," replied the next person to question him. This one took a softer approach, a more settling atmosphere. The questions were more of his daily habits when Jaden was free, the things he did to get high, and the feelings he felt afterward. Tony was skilled at gaining the trust of the lifeline participant, leading them into a question that would require a response that would be in depth, which would give the family more info – more ammo to attack the wall that protected . . . no, rather imprisoned his emotions, his secrets, and his bounding chains.

After the coordinators had finished, the senior coordinator came at him, ruthless with each piercing question, challenging Jaden, pushing Jaden's buttons, pissing Jaden off, sparking the anger that was within. That's the path to the emotions hiding; that's the doorway.

"Why are you here?" he asked.

"I want to change," replied Jaden.

"What have you done here to change?" The next question shot at him.

Jaden started to respond but was cut off by the house elder's question, "What scares you most?" *This was gonna be a double team*, thought Jaden. The warrior within him was rising, drawing the weapons and preparing for battle. Each question these two asked was a ladder for the warrior to climb, and the three of them were sword fighting, using swords of therapeutics and using the program concepts as shields. The battle was playing out in front of the whole group. Only the more experienced saw it for what it was, a battle to protect the secrets that lay within, the defense mechanisms of Jaden's were fighting for the trophy to keep the past and all it contained within, out of reach, buried deep beyond grasp.

Most of the group thought it was Jaden being hardheaded. They didn't have enough experience in treatment yet, but the senior coordinator and house elder knew what was taking place. The same had happened to them. They knew they were close and continued with the battle. Jaden was getting beaten up. He couldn't fend them off for long. He was getting confused and didn't know what they wanted and didn't understand why they were coming at him so harsh. It never went like this before on a lifeline. He was bewildered.

Then came the deadly questions, "Is your brother alive?" Damn brother questions again. "Are you concerned he may die? Didn't you put him in danger?" They didn't want a response. They wanted him thinking and feeling. Then came the million-dollar question: "How did it feel when Jimmy died?" The question took him by surprise. How did they know? What did they know? But the question he had were fading, the room full of residents were fading, the warrior which fought to protect him fell from his stance was gone, and old emotions were coming up, eyes watering, the knot in his stomach tightening and twisting, his breathing rapidly increasing. The whole room was quiet, everyone could see the change in his demeanor, Jaden was staring straight ahead but saw nothing. The guards had noticed too; they knew Jaden was about to do something and were ready to respond, but Bobby gave them a sign that indicated it was okay. They eased back. They trusted bobby and knew he had it under control.

Bobby knew the moment was close at hand, not too much longer, just a little more pushing. Bobby started the questions now, and the family remained silent. The rule was when the counselor talked no one interrupted, and Bobby was the boss. "How did Jimmy die, Jaden?" Bobby asked. Jaden couldn't catch the words. His nose was running, and the tears were now flowing down his cheeks. He couldn't focus. "How was your friend killed?" Bobby asked again.

"I killed him!" Jaden screamed out, falling to the floor. He was reliving and refeeling the moment when he read the letter. The pain as strong as it was then still sent him to his knees. He hadn't the strength to stand. All he felt was sorrow, guilt, and shame. And those emotions stood on his heart and soul as if they were conquering him, subduing him, and killing him.

Bobby was fast to respond. "Every one to your rooms, now," he commanded. "And the house is on silence until further notice." Being on silence meant no talking whatsoever, unless in your cell. Bobby approached Jaden and helped him up to the chair. He looked at him and knew Jaden didn't kill his friend. Bobby was from the streets also. He had friends who knew shit, and Bobby reached out to them for the info he needed. It took a while, but eventually, he found out the story, some from his friends on the street and some from the guards. No one person had the whole story, only parts, but bobby had most of the pieces and was able to put the story together – well, almost all of it. He still wasn't sure what made Jaden turn on the gang in Menard. In time perhaps he would find out.

Bobby refocused on Jaden, helping him up and leading him to his office. Jaden was still crying as he limped to where the counselor led him. He felt exhausted, confused, and helpless to what was killing him. And now he was gonna sit in the office of the man he tried to avoid for seven months. Jaden surrendered to Bobby.

Chapter 20

JADEN FELT WEAKENED from the whole ordeal as he sat for the first time in Bobby's office, head held low, feeling embarrassed over crying in front of the whole gateway group. Jaden hated showing this side of himself, something from way back in his childhood memories, ever since the daily beatings he took from his father. Those feelings are still there, still fresh in his mind and in his heart. He never forgot.

Jaden's earliest memory of the abuse was about the time he was around nine years old, driving with his dad in the cab his father worked. His father had been drinking and driving, another daily activity, and his father had the same routine when he drank. Jaden had learned the routine. While driving, his father started with the talking to himself, just garbled words here and there. Mutherfucker this, cock sucker that, Jew bitch – that was Jade's mother. Little bastard – that's Jaden. These were all the precursors to the brutality that would follow.

Jaden kept his head down as his father would continue, getting more angry, more aggravated. Jaden was terrified of his father and rightfully so. *Whack*. He felt the pain of his father's right hand as it smacked the fuck out of his face. Jaden started to tear up, trying to hold them back. *Please don't cry. Please don't cry*, he begged himself, *Dad hates when I cry*. *Whack*, another brutal hit upside Jaden's head. "Shut that sissy cryin' of yours," yelled his father. "You fuckin' little bastard, you know I'm not even sure you're my son. The fuckin' Jew mother of yours, just a whore she is," he informed Jaden – something that he informed Jaden about every day.

He fought to hold the crying back; sniffling was just as bad and usually brought another *whack*. Yep, there it was. His head was killing him. He was feeling punch drunk now, unable to see clearly, just numb. He hated his father. He secretly wished his father was dead.

Jaden reached in the fridge, grabbing the beer his father sent him to get, wiped the can off, opened it, and brought it to him. That was Jade's job at home – Jade's routine or the beginning of it. Jaden brought his father the beer and then went to sit at the other end of the couch, as far away as possible, out of reach, a somewhat safe distance. Being in that apartment though, no distance was safe. All Jaden wanted to do was go in his room and play with his army men and escape into the world of imagination, a place where he could be safe, at least for a while. Then came the start of another night of violence, his father talking, more like yelling to himself, the anger again rising.

Removing any hope that Jaden would be okay tonight. Jaden tried to brace himself for what was coming, trying to position himself to be able to run to his room before . . . *whack*, his head bleeding and burning from the cut the can of beer just sliced open. The beer spilling out onto the floor, the blood trickling down the back of his neck, warm liquid slowly moving, he was trying to stay focused, but he was dizzy, trying to get off the couch, trying to escape. *Whack* came the next blow, a fist from his father's rage. Jaden was lying on the floor. He was half awake and half in la-la land. He lay still, pretending to be knocked out, secretly hoping his father would stop and secretly hoping his father would direct his anger toward someone else, his mother. He felt ashamed; he felt guilty; he was only trying to survive.

The abuse Jaden was dealt with had taken its toll, hardening Jaden, forging his body into an armor, able to withstand any punishment a human being could dish out. He no longer felt the pain of a whack, a beer can, a belt, a cowboy boot, or even the dresser his father flipped over on him. Jaden knew one day his father was gonna kill him, and one day he would hit him one time too many, hit him in the right spot and darkness would be eternal. This Jaden realized at the experienced age of ten years old.

All the beatings, all the verbal attacks, and all the anger and resentment had done their job. Jaden was completely fucked up in his head, pushed off the road of sanity and moral sturdiness and off the road of good decisions and common sense. He was on the road of dysfunctionality, the road of insecurity and inadequacies, and the road to suffering and shame. Jaden was relaxed, steadily breathing. It was time to awaken from the trance.

Bobby just stared at Jaden, with tears in his eyes. He felt the pain of this nine-year-old child Jaden. He listened and felt what Jaden had revealed while in hypnosis, and he shuttered. Jaden was having a hard time composing himself, so Bobby decided to attempt hypnosis on Jaden and was successful. He finally had a good sense of the beginning of the pain and emotions that held Jaden bondage, but that was Jaden's recollection of his earliest memories of his father and the abuse he had taken.

Bobby had, over the years, heard just about every story he could from the many clients he had helped. Many forms of abuse and terror had shown their ugly face, and he never really got accustomed to it. Each new story touched him deeply as the first one did. Jaden's story wasn't new to him, but it touched his heart, brought tears to his eyes, and made him angry, so very angry. How can people do this to a child? He questioned no one. How can a child have a chance in life when this is what is done and taught to them? The daily terror of physical abuse, emotional abuse, and even sexual abuse. What kind of world does the child see, and what kind of hope could they possess for tomorrow?

He wanted to call his mother and father and tell them thank you for never doing these things to him, for always being good parents and showing him love and compassion, and for making him feel safe as a child growing up, but that couldn't happen. Both Bobby's parents had passed away a couple years ago, but he whispered it to them and then slowly brought Jaden out of hypnosis but not before he placed a couple suggestions into Jaden's self-consciousness, something to aid him in the healing process. He prayed it would work, or Jaden was gonna be lost forever.

Jaden raised his head, a feeling of calm and easiness relaxed his mind and body. He looked at Bobby and apologized for falling asleep. Bobby said, "That's okay," and gave Jaden a work assignment and then let him leave from his office. Jaden walked to his cell, still feeling somewhat embarrassed from earlier. *Fuck it. It is what it is*, he thought and locked up for the night.

The next morning, Jaden awoke and got ready for the morning meeting and washed up. Feeling refreshed and drinking his coffee, Jaden took a seat at the front of the group and waited for the meeting to start. For some reason, he was waiting for the meeting with a new look and a new feeling for the meeting he once hated. The meeting began, and so did the healing. Jaden's eyes and ears were open now. The healing benefits of the meeting were finally reaching the addict, penetrating what once was the impregnable wall. If even just a small amount, it was getting through, enough to take hold and enough to give a small glimmer of hope. Jaden finally participated.

Julie's life was as she imagines it would be – married, two children, a nice home, and her family close. She was involved in many family functions. Her children's sports activities were always going on, and she was always there. Julie didn't hound her kids. She gave them the room they needed but was always within reach. She truly enjoyed watching them, seeing how they interacted with their friends and how they conducted themselves. They were her priority in life, and she was satisfied with where they were as a family.

She instilled in them a sense of tradition like the gingerbread/caroling time. This was about bringing family and friends together, making different gingerbread houses, eating, and having fun, and then going out caroling. Some would think it kinda corny. What do they know? This was a great way for family and friends to spend quality time together.

Julie was a wiz in the kitchen, always baking or cooking something new, something very tasty. Every kid wanted to be there when those ovens were on, wishing they could just stay there and eat their lives away. She really appreciated the affection the kids had for her cooking. Cooking was also like her therapy time, along with swimming. Oh, how she loved to swim.

The life she was living was just about complete, but there was something in her that wasn't totally fulfilled. She couldn't place her finger on it, but the feeling was there. She often wondered what, often examining her life, past and present, but not aware of what was causing that one feeling. She didn't share that with her husband; there were a few other things she didn't share with him also. It seems Julie and her husband were doing great as parents, but the love between them was subsiding and they were growing apart very slowly. She cared for him, but the love wasn't being sustained, and she understood that love does that sometimes. Sometimes we fall out of love, and she was with her husband and felt he was too with her. She still continued on with the marriage for the sake of the family.

Chapter 21

JADEN WAS PLUGGING in to the program, talking in meetings, sharing something of himself with others during one-on-one sessions, and applying himself to the program. He had started reading the *Big Book* of Alcoholics Anonymous (AA) and learned to work the twelve steps of AA.

There was one problem though. Jaden never truly believed in a god, heaven or hell, and angels or demons but not from lack of trying; it just never took. He didn't have the faith it took to believe in any religion, and faking it wasn't an option. He was tired of faking it. He wanted it to be real. He did believe there was something out there. It had touched him not so long ago and stopped him from killing Jimmy's killer, so he knew there was something, but what it was, he had no idea.

Jaden also liked the fact that Bobby had become his counselor instead of David and looked forward to their weekly sessions, but he really never remembered what they talked about. All he knew was he felt good afterward.

Bobby was fascinated how easily Jaden could go under hypnosis, maybe because sleep always came easy for Jaden. Bobby never before had this kind of success in the past with hypnosis, and he liked the fact that he was putting it to excellent use, helping Jaden to build softeners to the emotional volcano that lived within Jaden. He had suggested little quirks and stress relaxers for Jaden – little things he could do when the volcano would start to erupt. The eruption was the cause of his behaviors, his defense mechanisms his soul had created to protect him. Protect him was so bullshit. The defense mechanisms actually kept him in bondage, suffocating him from feeling what needed to be felt, giving him a chance to deal with the pain and all the other issues that had taken refuge within his self.

He knew he had seen parts of Jaden that no other person had ever seen. Jaden would never allow it to be seen, but Jaden's eyes could not hide what was buried within, the torment and the pain were visible through his eyes. Maybe that's what made Bobby pay attention to Jaden in the beginning. Maybe that's why Bobby had a fear of what Jaden was or could do if it ever came to the surface in one final eruption. Bobby continued with the therapy, listening and feeling what was revealed.

Jaden was fourteen and now in the gang. He loved being a Royal. He felt accepted, like he was actually wanted and like he belonged to a family. This was a strong feeling for Jaden – to be a part of a family and to be accepted. He had a lot of friends, and they hung out all the time. He still took beatings from his father but not nearly as much as when he was younger, maybe because Jaden was rarely home, always out on the street with his real family, the Royals. He needed to be with them. He needed the reassurance he felt when they were all together, and they all had taken new roles in his life. Jimmy had become his older brother. One or two of the lady Royals he was close to were his new sisters, even though his real sister was a lady Royal and hung with him.

Yep, the Royals were more than a gang; they were his family. Jaden felt okay, like everything was all right for the first time in his life until that day. That was the day the world came to an end for Jaden.

"They got a gun," he heard his friend call out, but Jaden had his gun already out, aimed at the enemy who was reaching for the gun, and he unloaded without even realizing it, hitting the mark and ending the threat. "Oh my god, what did I do?" Jaden said, still in the trance, his stomach knotting up, a feeling of dread coming over him. When he realized he had taken another person's life and seen the body lying there in a pool of blood, dead, lifeless, a corpse, he felt a sickness in his heart and soul. This wasn't what he wanted. Killing someone was not his plan; he wasn't a killer. He felt like he was gonna vomit, wanting and wishing he could have a do-over, but do-overs are not a part of this life, not once you're dead, and that vice lord was dead, that young boy not more than seventeen, dead now. His mother, his family, and the grief they would feel – all Jade's fault.

Jaden had a sudden urge to run, run somewhere, anywhere, just get away and forget what happened, but before he could, he heard his friend, his brother, his role model, his chief, give the order to kill the other two, and he obeyed, and the other two lay dead within a few seconds, each bullet hitting the mark. Jaden was crying. He didn't cry when it happened. He had suppressed that feeling, used another emotion to mask his regret, but now, in a cell converted to an office, he cried, cried for the loss of three teenagers, cried at the feeling of despair, and cried at the loss of his humanity. That day, a part of his soul had become damaged and corrupt, and he knew it, felt the change within him, and he cried.

"Holy shit," Bobby had whispered. He had just heard the confession of a murder. He couldn't believe Jaden revealed it, exposing a secret that was so intense and damaging – a secret that could get Jaden locked up for the rest of his life. Was it Jaden's fault though? He wondered who was really to blame. Sure Jaden pulled the trigger, but who put the gun in his hand? Jimmy, the Royals – no, he knew who put that gun there. Jaden's father did. He put it there throughout the years of abuse. Each time Jade's father beat him and degraded him and each time he didn't love him, he put that gun there.

Bobby knew this was a secret he would hold to his chest forever. He would never reveal what he had just learned. There was hope for Jaden, and he knew Jaden had a chance to recover and change – yep, Bobby knew this was going to the grave with him – he wanted Jaden to have a chance, a chance he was not given as a child growing up. Bobby slowly brought Jaden out of the trance, smiled, and told Jaden he would see him next week. Jaden smiled back and left the office, feeling good but still not remembering what they talked about.

Chapter 22

TIME WENT BY and Jaden was becoming more and more engulfed in the twelve steps of recovery. He was always involved in the meetings, always talking about feelings and sharing things about his experience out there, and always one of the first to talk to the new guys, wanting to help them get plugged into the program. He wasn't robotic and wasn't just rehashing program slogans and innuendos – no. Jaden was a strength in gateway, a positive role model, a family member. His transformation wasn't unnoticed by the other family members, the ones who were there when he first arrived. They had seen the program work in others and helped many people change their lives around, and now they were witnessing it change Jaden, which was no small miracle.

Every one of them thought Jaden wouldn't make it. They all had their reasons. Some thought he was too far gone; others were jealous of him. Jaden always had a way about him, was always very direct when he dealt with people, could take charge when needed, and removed himself when the situation called for. Jaden was also very intelligent, always learning from something and always expanding his knowledge. Some were jealous, and they tried to hinder Jaden at times, resist here and there, but the change he made was real. The newfound hope was strong. They couldn't compete with that. They lost every time.

One year of sobriety, one year anniversary in gateway, Jaden was feeling top of the world. A year has passed and he's doing well. He was the support team leader, a decent job function in gateway. The position was a respected one, and he had held it for four months now. He liked the job, but secretly, he wanted to be a coordinator, support team coordinator to be exact. That was his desire, but he kept that quiet. He knew how it worked. If you wanted something bad, you never got it.

And this was a treatment center; it was all about therapeutics. Everything that happens is about treatment, a learning experience, something to help you grow, to deal with issues, to learn to accept the things you could not change, have the courage to change the things you can, and the wisdom to know the difference. Yet still he desired that coordinator spot. Bobby knew this and knew for a while, and he withheld it from Jaden. Bobby knew Jaden would have no problems carrying out the functions of the position. Being in charge was nothing new to Jaden, but he still wasn't ready for it – the real purpose of the coordinator and the true meaning of a leader. Nope, Jaden still had some things to learn and deal with.

The therapy sessions were going well with Jaden, slowly decreasing each month. They had served their purpose. What Jaden couldn't talk about on his own, the things he couldn't share in the open, he was able to share under hypnosis, able to relive and refeel, slowly releasing what was hidden within, slowly healing, slowly venting the volcano, removing the threat of an eruption.

Jaden had made real progress, and Bobby was satisfied that the sessions could come to an end soon. What to do about Jade's one-year anniversary? He knows he wants that coordinator spot, but what would be best for Jaden, he thought.

Jaden was in good spirits all day, and when it came time for PM meeting, job changes meeting, he was anxious, hoping he would get the job he desired, and why shouldn't he? He had worked hard for it, done all that was asked and expected of him, and then some. This would be a just reward, an earned reward. He would get it, he thought. It made sense.

Oh, to be so young in recovery, Jaden had no clue. He was still a baby in this life, still learning. If the life of recovery could be compared to a human's progress in life, then Jaden was at the age where he would just be getting out of diapers, the point where he finally stopped shitting on himself. He would learn though that the recovery life had some requirements and unspoken truths about it, and that being "nothing is constant but change."

Time for the meeting. The family is taking their seats, and everyone is in good spirits. This is an upbeat and fun meeting. Well, for most members it is. Everyone is sitting, drinking coffee, and smoking cigarettes. This is the only meeting you may smoke in at gateway. And waiting for the counselors, Jaden noticed that the house elder and the senior coordinator were in Bobby's office before the meeting. *Hmmmmm, that's different*, Jaden thought. *Who cares? Tonight is the night, baby. Coordinator.* He could hardly contain himself. He would act surprised, act like he wasn't deserving of the job, and he would act humble.

Come on, start the fuckin' meeting already, he anxiously thought. Talk about time standing still or moving slow, every time he wanted or waited for something, it always seemed like time was his enemy. *Tick, tock, a broken clock*. He smiled after thinking that in his head. He was trying to calm himself down. Finally, the meeting was starting, and he was ready. They always start off with the lowest ranked jobs in the house, promotions of new members completing orientation, and shit like that.

Get to the coordinators, he just about was begging, and they did. They announced no changes to the coordinators function. *What the fuck*, he cried within his mind. Could they be making him a senior coordinator? Why not? He had showed tremendous growth within the program. Maybe that was the plan. *Happy one-year anniversary*, he thought to himself.

No more job changes. The meeting was over with, and he had no job function – no mention of him at all. Jaden felt hurt, left out, and forgotten. He wanted to stand up and ask, "What about me? You forgot me," but his pride kept him still, trying to mask the disappointment he felt, the crushing blow to his ego. *What was going on?* he wondered.

The COD came to him after the meeting and told him he was needed down the hallway for a therapeutic peer reprimand (TPR). He nodded and went down the hall. Maybe they were gonna surprise him, maybe they were just fuckin' with him, maybe the promotion would be coming still, maybe . . .

"Jaden, I need you to stand at attention during this TPR. Please keep eye-to-eye contact with the person giving you the TPR at all times, and do not respond to what is being said," ordered the coordinator, who was standing with three other coordinators, two on each side of each other, and then it started.

"Jaden, what makes you think you have what it takes to be a coordinator? One year in the program and you think you're recovered completely, walking around this house like you were never sick in the first place?" the first coordinator screamed at the top of his lungs, the whole house in silence, everyone hearing what was being said, everyone witnessing Jade's feeling of shame. The yelling continued, "Listen, family, here he is, Mr. 'Look at me doing everything right – where's my reward.' I deserve the coordinator position 'cause I'm Jaden. I'm a special addict. I got special needs. I need attention. I need recognition from others 'cause I have no clue how to be humble."

The next coordinator started along the same lines. Jaden barely heard what they were saying. Jaden was crushed and deep in thought, far away from this hallway, far away from the yelling coordinators. He was in his mind, his escape. He didn't understand, but he was angry, resentful, outraged at the counselors, and at Bobby. Why did he do this to him? What reason could he have? Didn't he see how hard Jaden had worked? Didn't he see the growth in Jaden? Why was he doing this? Jaden couldn't find the answer to his question, but if he would have listened to what the coordinators were saying, he would have known. He would have realized he was filled with false pride, not humility. He wasn't humble, which meant he wasn't deserving of the coordinator position, but he didn't hear that. All he heard was laughter in his head, the laughter of the family, laughing at him. They were making fun of him, belittling him in a way, pushing him aside. Well, that's how it felt.

He could feel the defense mechanisms rising, trying to show themselves, trying to encase him, but he fought back, reached somewhere in his memories for the real strength, the thing that was right. The serenity prayer . . . he kept repeating it over and over in his head. "God, grant me the serenity to accept the things I cannot change, the courage to change the things I can, and the wisdom to know the difference."

The TPR was over with. Now the main coordinator was letting him know he was busted down from a job function and placed on a learning experience to consist of a seven-to-seven work contract until further notice. He was also placed on ban from the family, not allowed to speak to anyone but the coordinators, the senior coordinators, and the house elder. He would clean the unit from 7:00 a.m. through 7:00 p.m., with ten-minute breaks each hour, no gym or yard privileges, and no television privileges in the dayroom. This would be until further notice. Jaden was devastated! Yet he surrendered.

Chapter 23

IT WAS A gamble, Bobby thought to himself, but he had to take that chance. He knew the progress Jaden was making in the program was legitimate. The hypnosis sessions had helped also, but the only way to truly observe Jaden's growth and coping skills was to deny him what he wanted, the coordinator position. Bobby saw the look on Jade's face and knew there was great disappointment, but the seven-to-seven learning experience would be the first test on Jaden's acceptance capabilities.

Was he for real? Did Jaden want this way of life? How far was he willing to go? Jaden had put many years and entrenched himself within the sickness of addiction. He would need to face many challenges to stay sober and to stay free from that bondage. The seven-to-seven was unfair. Jaden didn't deserve that, but sometimes in life, things are unfair. Sometimes they are harsh and brutal. How we cope with and accept those moments is what separates success from failure.

Jaden accepted the TPR from the coordinators, and they tore into him and hit every key point, and that wasn't easy for them. They liked Jaden a lot and felt his realness and his honesty, but they did what they were told because they had faith in the process, but most of all, they wanted to be an instrument in helping Jaden get healthy, stay sober, and continue to make progress. They truly cared for Jaden. These were the thoughts Jaden tried to keep in focus each day of the seven-to-seven.

He would scrub the floors of the dayroom, the hallways, the showers, and the toilet, all with a toothbrush. Jaden thought a lot while working, mostly about the program – from when he first came to gateway to now. He smiled when he thought about the different times his sickness would manifest itself and he would act up. Usually he was brought to the confrontation group to answer for this, and the learning experience he would receive was always creative. Once he had to spend three days walking around the unit with a bedsheet on him made to look like a diaper and carry a baby bottle in his mouth and a rattle in his hand while wearing a sign that read King Baby. He smiled at this memory. Oh, he was pissed at first, was ready to say "Fuck it" and sign out of the program, but he accepted this, along with many others.

He was given exercises like mandatory speaking in certain meetings where he had to explain to the family why he felt the need to be heard but not listen or the time he would have to stand in front of the family every morning and act out the little teapot song as he sang it. "I'm a little teapot short and stout. Here is my handle. Here is my spout. When I get all filled up, watch me shout. Tip me over and pour me out" was the song. That was a great one. That one he received for constantly holding on to his feelings and not talking about them and then blowing up from some little thing, which was really a compilation of a lot of shit he was feeling. Kinda like too much pressure will burst a pipe.

He had done every learning experience he was given and learned from each one. This one though bothered him. Jaden didn't see the reason or logic for it; he just accepted it. The hardest part of this was he couldn't smoke a cigarette until he was on his break period. Oh, the agony of it all. He smiled.

Monday came around. It had been ten days since Jaden was put on the seven-to-seven, and now he was tired, but he continued on with the learning experience but wondered how much longer he could do this? He missed being able to talk to family members one-on-one, interacting with the group. He missed all that shit, shit he had taken for granted some. Now he yearned for it, needed it, and desired it.

The morning meeting was going well, and then at the end of the meeting, the COD came out of Bobby's office and excused himself for interrupting the meeting and announced, "Family, Jaden is now off his seven-to-seven learning experience and has been assigned to the following job function. Everyone was silent, awaiting to hear the wisdom of the counselor; Jaden too. "Coordinator over orientation" was the new job function for Jaden, the COD announced and then excused himself from the announcement. As he went about his duties, he looked at Jaden and smiled. Jaden smiled back, an unspoken moment of understanding between friends.

Jaden now realized the reason and the purpose of the last ten days – well, most of it – acceptance, and he accepted without bitching and complaining. He trusted the counselors had a purpose and reason. He trusted in the process. He had learned to trust. Now he was given a great honor – the orientation coordinator, the one in charge of new brothers in gateway, the person who interacted with new brothers the most. He was honored. Jaden took his responsibility to heart, wanting to help the new brothers who came in get the program, understand it, realize the process, and accept it. He cared for the new brothers. He felt their nervousness and fear at one time and was able to overcome it. Jaden wanted and became a role model for the new guys – someone they could come to anytime for any reason.

Jaden was becoming a new person. He was receiving new positive feelings, feelings of hope, caring, trust, and empathy. These were new to him, but he liked it. He liked the new Jaden he was becoming. People wanted to talk to him, ask him his opinion on something, and share their pain with him, and this was much nicer than the alternative.

Bobby knew he made the right choice. He had seen Jaden take a moment of despair, a feeling of betrayal, and a dark hour, and Jaden had accepted life's unfair moments and continued on, utilizing all the tools Jaden had been given up to that point. Bobby was satisfied with the way Jaden carried himself for the ten days, doing the work without bitching and complaining, even smiling at times. He wondered what made Jaden smile, but he knew. He started his sobriety in gateway also, had done many seven-to-seven's, and even smiled while doing them at times.

Yep, Bobby knew, and he also knew the Jaden would become one of the strongest strengths gateway had ever produced, a strong asset to the program, a role model to new brothers. *That's it*, he thought. Coordinator over orientation – that was the right job for Jaden. It would benefit the new brothers as well as Jaden. Bobby was satisfied with the decision he had come to.

Chapter 24

THE TIME HAD come and Bobby called Jaden to his office. As Jaden arrived at the door, Bobby looked at Jaden. This was the house elder, the strongest strength in the unit. He was the role model and pace setter. Bobby just thought back to those days in the beginning when he tried the hypnosis sessions, had learned about the abuse the child Jaden had suffered, the murder at fourteen, and the other shit that won't be mentioned in this book. Bobby had made the decision to make Jaden house elder two months ago. He deserved the position in the unit and he got it. Bobby wasn't let down.

The main job of the house elder was to be the counselor when the counselor wasn't there and ensure the unit maintained its integrity, and Jaden had performed that function well and Bobby was pleased.

"Sit down, Jaden," Bobby said. "I have something I would like you to consider, but I want you to take your time to consider it," came Bobby's request. Jaden was perplexed, not sure what it could be. He listened. "I looked into your placement scores, the ones you received when you took your aptitude test upon coming to prison, and you maxed out at 12.9 across the board, so I was thinking . . ." – he paused, looking in deep thought – "I would like you to consider signing up for academic college classes here at Sheridan."

Before Jaden could reply, Bobby continued, "I feel as though you have a calling to help other addicts, a way about yourself. Something about you grabs the attention of others. You captivate them when you talk about your experience. You give them hope when you talk about the trials and tribulations you have met. They relate to you and feel your story. That is a gift, and if you should ever consider being a counselor, then education would be the first step." Bobby had planted the seed, the idea, an option, and then told Jaden to think about it and dismissed him from the office.

Jaden was flattered that Bobby held him in those regards – someone who could help others, but more importantly, Bobby had given Jaden a chance to do good and to do the right things – a chance to succeed in life. All his life, he had been told he was worthless, a piece of shit, not his father's son – all those negative things Jaden had bought into, leading him astray into a void of emptiness. Now, the past sixteen months has been the opposite; he was worth something, he was a good person who had done bad things and a human being with qualities that were admirable. The feeling he had now was of deep appreciation for those that cared for him, a warmth that burned within his heart, kinda overwhelming though, he could feel the tear forming in the corner of his eye, how do I repay what has been given to me he wondered ?

Jaden did as Bobby suggested; he spent the next thirty days talking to family members about his options and his fears concerning the option. This would be the first time a resident of gateway would be allowed to go to school or hold a job while being in the program, and that was a risk, a risk bobby was willing to take with Jaden. That's a big responsibility being placed on Jaden. He understood the dangers of the population. He would be interacting with the general population in a limited way, at the school building only, but still interacting.

The population was gang members and addicts still engulfed in their negative lifestyle. The peer pressure was very powerful out there. How would Jaden hold up? Then he understood the concept – the plan. Let Jaden have a small piece of freedom so to speak. If something goes wrong, he would still be in a controlled environment; they could still help. Kind of like a precursor to being released from prison. Bobby was giving Jaden a chance to experience what the future would be like. Jaden knew he would accept the challenge.

Jaden reported to Bobby's office after making the decision in his mind. He would let Bobby know that decision. Bobby was delighted that first, Jaden took the time to explore the option. Second, he was pleased that Jaden talked out his choices with the other family members and, third, that he had accepted the challenge. Bobby told Jaden he would make the arrangements and went to work, making it happen. Jaden was nervous, but he would be prepared – well, as prepared as he could be.

It has been a long time since Jaden was in a classroom, a place where he didn't feel comfortable in. He knew he was smart, but he just didn't like the work you had to put into to get good grades. Yep, he was lazy concerning that. It was something to work on. He wanted to work hard, get the best grades he could, be the best example of a person working the program . . . damn, he was nervous.

Bobby pulled some strings and got the plan approved, and in two weeks, Jaden was enrolled in college classes. The first class was Psychology 101. Jaden was very nervous.

Jaden liked school from the very start. It was real. It was more in depth than Grammar or high school. The teachers were involved, and boy oh boy, did he like psychology. He sucked up the information as though his mind was a sponge, thirsting for the dampness of knowledge. He applied himself 100 percent, studied every day, did the assignments, and did the extra credit, and once the class was over, he was rewarded with an A. That was his first A ever in life. He was so proud of his A. He told everyone – told them again and again and again. He got the hint when they told him to shut up, but in a good way.

He was like a child, earning his first shiny. This I say to put a smile on the face of Julie. Who is that? Don't worry, she will be all over the pages later in the book, but Julie was that girl he liked back when Jaden was eleven years old – the girl with the bright blue eyes, the good and pure heart, the one he didn't want to taint. Yep, she'll be back in his life soon, but for now, back to the shiny things. You're welcome, Julie.

Jaden was on a mission now. He liked school and was very good at it when he applied himself, and most of all, he liked the grade he received. He continued with his education, taking on the workload and meeting the challenges every day but still performing his responsibilities in gateway. That came first, and he reminded himself every day about that fact that if it wasn't for gateway, he wouldn't even be here.

There really wasn't any peer pressure at school. The inmates in college classes were trying to make changes in their lives also, and education was a positive direction. After some time, Jaden had sixty college credits, was holding a GPA of 3.30, and had only two classes left until he would graduate with an associate's degree, with honors. *Holy shit*, he thought, *where did the time go*. It zoomed past so fast.

Almost about to graduate and almost about to be released, he was feeling anxious. He needed to find a peaceful place and meditate, allowing everything to just settle and to clear in his mind. The time to face the world was coming fast, just right around the corner. He needed a plan. He needed a direction of focus. Shit, he needed his counselor. This time, however, Bobby told him no. He needed to work it out first, make plans and decisions on his own, and take charge of his life. Then he and Bobby would discuss it as friends, not as counselor and client.

Friends? Did he just say friends? Jaden looked at his "friend" and knew there was no chance in hell he would ever be able to repay Bobby for all he had done. Bobby had traveled to the darkest void within Jade's soul and reached out in his darkest hour and rescued him from himself. This man who stood before Jaden, this rescuer, this father figure – he was the one who saved Jaden, and Jaden would never forget that.

Jaden told Bobby to stand up and look at him. Bobby was surprised by the conviction in Jade's voice, but he stood up and faced him. Jaden was getting emotional inside. Feeling all choked up, he didn't speak, but instead, he walked up to Bobby and hugged him. The embrace held his deepest appreciation, his love, his trust, and his humanity, and Bobby felt his own tears falling now from his eyes. Jaden would be just fine.

"Okay, get outta here now," Bobby said. "I got work to do," and Jaden left the office. Bobby was touched very deeply at the show of honest affection Jaden showed him and then sat down and called his sponsor (the person one goes to for advice and direction or just to talk).

Jaden had the plan in his head. He would go to Lake Villa Treatment Center (gateway) and take the addictions counselor training course. He had decided to become a counselor – to follow in Bobby's footsteps. Bobby made the arrangements, and upon the day of Jade's release, he was going to Lake Villa, Illinois, to begin his new life. It seemed like so long ago, almost another lifetime, when Jaden first came through these gates – yes, another lifetime ago.

He spent the last night remembering his journey up to this point. Wanting his life to be fresh in his mind – all the pain, the struggling, the missed opportunities, the risky chances he took, the crimes, and everything else he had been through – to be fresh and there for a sort of rock for his foundation, a reminder of what awaited him should he fail. He had no clue what the future held for him, but for the first time in a long time, at least, he felt there was a future for him. He had some fear, maybe a healthy fear of what awaited him. Would he measure up? Would he be able to meet the challenge of the new life? He finally was able to sleep.

Chapter 25

THE DAY OF Jade's release from prison was here. He was ready. He had said his farewells and good-byes the night before, had his belongings packed up, and at the door, ready for an escort to take him to the processing building. He took one final look around the gateway unit, remembering the day he came, the struggles he had endured, and the battles he had won. The dayroom was empty; it was four thirty in the morning. He would be gone before any of the brothers would be let out of their rooms. A lot of time was spent here – a lot of changing. He would never forget any of it, but it was time to leave and time to continue his journey.

The processing out was fast, and he was transported to the train station and then arrived at downtown Chicago. He loved Chicago – the big city, the busy life of everyone passing him by, and the traffic in the streets. This was his city – his home. He needed to make it to the train that was going to Lake Villa and needed to get on that train. It was very important to get on that train! He could feel the temptation to not get on that train, felt the yearning within him to go home, to see his family, to show everyone the new Jaden. *Got to get on that fuckin' train. Dangerous to not get on that train.* Jaden stepped on to the train and took a seat. He was almost there.

The train departed and he felt safe, realizing just how strong the urges were and realizing just how much there still was to work on, but he was strong. He resisted this urge. He could resist the future ones, maybe.

He arrived in Lake Villa, a small village, like a town out of the sixties, couple of stores, and a few big chain names, but still very rural. He had an unpleasant feeling about this town, not to his liking – old habits, old feelings. In a town like this, everyone knows your business and you know theirs. Jaden preferred the anonymity the big city gave, being able to be invisible when so desired or desperately needed.

Old Jaden, he thought. He doesn't live by those needs anymore. He now can be in the public and can allow himself to be normal, open, and willing to share his life with others. There was a whole new world out there for him – no gangs, no drugs, and no need to always be on guard.

Jaden called the number for Lake Villa Gateway and was told they were expecting him and that his ride would be there in about twenty minutes. Sitting outside on the bench, he pulled out a cigarette and waited, wondering what tomorrow would bring. After getting to the center, Jaden realized the information was incorrect. The plan was mistaken. They were processing him as a new patient – a client. That wasn't the plan. He was supposed to stay there and start the training program – supposed to become a counselor and start saving people from their drug addiction, not be someone who needed saving. This was not what he wanted, not what he signed up for. This he wouldn't accept.

He called Bobby at Sheridan, explaining the situation, and Bobby's response was that his life was in his hands. The decision was his, either follow the path Lake Villa laid out or choose another path. The destination could remain the same – what the fuck. What kind of answer was that? Why couldn't Bobby just fix the mistake? Was this another learning experience? Jaden realized that every day would be a learning experience, wherever he was and wherever he lived. Every day would be about choices and consequences. Okay, he decided he would scratch this plan and design a new one. He informed the counselor at Lake Villa that he was leaving and called his mom for a ride. His mother was there in two hours and he left. What was the plan now? He had no idea.

Jaden found AA meetings in a lot of locations and started attending, also cocaine anonymous (CA). He knew the routine of the meetings and fitted in, making sober friends and hanging out with them. He found a job, working at a grocery store full time and that was his life for a while. Go to work, go to meetings, and socialize with sober people. He did as much as possible to remove the threats and the temptations from his life, all except one. Jaden's mom lived right smack-dab in the middle of the Royal's hood. He would see his old friends every day while waiting for the bus and while walking out or in his door. Going to the store or just stepping out the door for some fresh air, his past was in his face.

He told the Royals from the beginning that he was out, and that was it. He would not be a part of it – any of it. They accepted that; it really didn't matter what Jaden said. They knew if he lived there and was there, he would become involved once again. They had heard this story before from others, and all had failed to stay away. In their minds, there was no escaping this life – all were trapped.

Most of Jade's friends from the past were either dead, in prison, or had moved away to different parts of the city, still addicted to their drug of choice. The royals who were here now were the Royals of his brother's generation, the younger Royals. This one fact made it easy for Jaden to not get involved. They weren't here when he was. He had no history with them and no sense of loyalty to them.

Jaden was doing well with his sober life, having many friends and a busy life within the sober community. He was happy for the most part; he didn't have urges or desires to get high and didn't want or need to get fucked up. That part was easy for him. It was the other shit he struggled with. He had never formed a solid spiritual foundation in his recovery life and no real belief in a higher power, not for lack of trying though. No. Jaden lacked the partialness that others around him were enjoying, and he was sad about that. He had tried to believe, but it never took root within him. He knew there was something out there, just didn't know what it was. Maybe he never would. He figured he would just keep doing what he was doing, and everything should work out. For a while it did, and that was good enough to keep him sober.

There were instances in which his character defects were emerging, sneaking out here and there for moments of insanity and moments of freedom. Certain actions of his, coming to meetings late here and there, missing a meeting here and there, telling little lies about this and that – nothing big, nothing to worry about, so he thought. He forgot the lessons he had learned in gateway. "Fuck gateway. They lied to me," he reminded himself, sounding like the old Jaden, the addicted Jaden, the fucked-up Jaden. He brushed it off, not wanting to see or admit the resentment he was feeling and the sense of betrayal he felt.

Each day though, it became easier to miss a meeting, lie to his friends, and act out of his negative self, *What the fuck is going on with me?* he asked of himself. He didn't realize why he was digressing, even though it was slowly. He was digressing back to the old Jaden. He needed to work on something but what? It now has been three years since his release, and Jaden is now standing with one foot in sobriety and the other in bullshit. He is still socializing with sober people and has not used drugs or drank but is living dangerously, risking all that he has worked on. The changes he had made to become healed were now starting to unravel, and he knew why. He was spiritually lost. He had no real foundation to stand on, and he was sinking because of it. He needed help. But didn't know how. He just lingered in the thought and did nothing. He was stuck.

Julie was changing inside herself, becoming more determined to set some of her own goals as a priority in her life. Her children were doing well in school, socially, and emotionally. The both of them were very stable and maturing nicely. Well, there is all the dramatic acting that comes with being a teenager, but Julie was ahead of the game. She was a teenager once, you know. Julie decided long ago that she was the mother, not the friend of her children. If being a friend fit in, then that would be nice, but her children would have guidelines in growing up. They would have rules and would adhere to those rules, but for the most part, her children liked her, even when she denied them their wishes at times.

Julie's husband made a decent living, but they were not rich. They made the dollar stretch, and Julie did work part time at the woman's services program. Through her own experiences in life, which I won't share with you, it was working at her job where she encountered many women, women who had been through some of the most difficult times in life and shared their stories with Julie. Julie's job was helping the women to find resources to reestablish themselves as independent women, sometimes finding employment, food pantries, shelter, or other programs that could benefit the ones who needed it.

Each day at work was a fresh start at helping someone, and each day, Julie herself became more independent, more outgoing, and sure of herself. Being at work was a release for her. She loved her job but hated the situations these women were in. She desired to give her best effort at helping make their lives better in whatever way possible, and it was an escape from the reality of her own situation at home, with her marriage. She was no longer in love with her husband, but stayed in it nonetheless.

Chapter 26

THEN CAME THE day that his friend had offered Jaden and some others to go up to Wisconsin for the weekend. Jaden accepted. This would be a change for him, kinda like a getaway from his issues and problems – an escape

The ride was pleasant. The house they were staying in was very big, with a lot of rooms and that country feel to it. The house was a two-story A frame, had a large wraparound front porch, and sat on about two acres of wooded land.

The town was small, just a few stores, a family-owned one gas station, and a post office. Most of the area was wooded, not farming land, and the majority of the population were Native Americans. But it was not a reservation, just a community.

The couple of days they all spent there was fun, doing all kinds of shit and just hanging out with each other. Then Michael had asked everyone if they wanted to get their totems read by a shaman, totem being almost the same thing as a tarot card reading. Everyone said yes, and Jaden was intrigued by the idea. He always had an interest in other cultures, especially the Native American culture.

They all went with Michael to the shaman's house and made the introductions, and the shaman greeted and welcomed them all. He was Michael's uncle. Of course, he would do our totem. Jaden watched as the shaman started going through rituals and customs, burning sage to clear a path, meditating through humming to find the way to the spirits, asking the spirits to reveal the secrets they knew and held. Even if this wasn't the real deal, it sure as hell was entertaining. Jaden was mesmerized by the whole act. It held him captive, and he could feel the movement from his body to the humming of the shaman, as if he was riding along, going to meet the spirits.

The shaman had read most of the others' totem, and then it was Jade's turn. Something was wrong though as soon as the shaman started. Jaden could see and feel the change in the expression and demeanor of the old man, and he didn't like what it showed. It looked negative. It looked unfavorable. *Great! Why me? Why is everything about me always gotta be fucked up? Why can't I just be fuckin' normal like the rest of them. Watch this motherfucker tell me I'm the Devil or the Devil's son.* Jaden had said in his mind, angry and bitter, not liking the fact that the others had sensed it to. He hated the fact he had the past he had, and others had known about his past. Now they were seeing this shit, and it only increased the distance between them and himself.

The shaman looked into jade's eyes as if he could read Jade's thoughts, and Jaden felt embarrassed – guilty, sort of. The shaman asked everyone to leave – everyone except Jaden. Once they all were gone outside, the shaman spoke to Jaden, more like revealing to Jaden the purpose of being alone with him. He told Jaden the spirits were strong in Jaden's life, but there were different spirits, not all good, some bad. But *bad* is our word, our word for instincts, the instincts we find that is not pleasant.

The shaman revealed Jade's totem, and Jaden was not happy with the choice. Why couldn't he have a wolf, lion, or bear, maybe even an eagle. Those were cool and those that Jaden had liked, but no, it is not our choice which totem mirrors us. That's true because Jaden wouldn't have chosen the one he has, a fuckin' hyena. Who would choose a fuckin' hyena, a fuckin' scavenger. Jaden was pissed, but the shaman continued speaking. "I will show you your life, and you will see it through feelings, but what I show you must never be told." Jaden was shown and Jaden saw, not through his eyes but through his heart and his soul, and Jaden was terrified at what was revealed and the vision ended.

Jaden was dumfounded at all the shaman knew. It wasn't that the shaman knew Jade's past actions and violations toward humanity. It was that he had seen the deepest essence of his core, the bonding feelings that were hidden there, repressed since the beginning, from the first day he was traumatized and throughout his life, and now Jaden was allowed to feel the reality of that hurt, the hurt he suffered, and the hurt he caused. The shaman reached for Jade's hand and shared with Jaden the true path of a warrior, explaining that the path was a journey that a person makes and a warrior makes, not a warrior in the sense of a fighter on the battlefield but a warrior of life. The path had been revealed to Jaden – the chance of retribution for Jaden if he could accept the path of the warrior. Jaden chose the path.

The shaman explained to Jaden that the path would be about choices he would have to make and that the path would have alternate paths. Those would be where his choices would lead him, and each alternate path would and could lead back to the main path or have more alternate paths. Each choice would be Jade's alone. He did give Jaden one clue though; the hardest choice was usually the best choice. The shaman told Jaden his spirit was strong and that he had recognized this the moment he saw Jaden and wanted Jaden to know that the right choices in Jade's life would benefit many people, more than the amount that he hurt, but it would take a long time for this to be accomplished.

Everyone wanted to know what the shaman had told Jaden, but Jaden couldn't reveal it. He wasn't permitted to reveal it; this was not for the others, it was for Jaden. He explained it just like that, and they grudgingly accepted that. Michael understood more than the others. These things and the way they worked were not uncommon to him. He knew it was real, that it was important, and that it belonged to Jaden. Maybe that's what Jaden needed, a guide to follow. Maybe this would fill the emptiness he saw in Jaden. Who knows? Only time will reveal what is and what isn't. They would have to go blindly along with the ride, trusting in the process.

Jaden was very quiet during the rest of the trip; he had a lot to consider and a lot to prepare for. I wish I could tell you Jaden got on the path and everything worked out. Now he's a successful writer and lives the perfect life, but that isn't the way it goes, not in Jade's life. Life for Jaden became harder, more of a struggle – his burden to deal with knowing what he knew now. He had some success and some failures, and some progress and some setbacks, but he continued on the path. The path was not about being right or perfect. It was about meeting the challenges and facing them. Some challenges were harder than others. That was the type of challenge that Jaden failed that one day.

Jaden had always felt guilty about bringing his younger brother into the Royals, into the lifestyle – something he carried with him, never able to release that guilt, and it was that guilt that caused his downfall. Jaden's brother was dealing rock cocaine and using it also, hanging out late at night and selling the poison to whomever had the cash for it. One night, his brother wasn't paying attention to his surroundings and wasn't on guard, and it happened. His brother was run down by a carload of Latin Kings, dragged under the car for a distance of about one hundred feet, and on the edge of death. The paramedics had done everything they could on the way to the hospital. Now it was up to the surgeons and luck. Jaden's family were unable to reach him that night but finally did in the morning, and he was numb by the news. He felt guilty, responsible, dirty, and shameful. This was his fault.

He rushed to the hospital to see his brother – the wrong thing to do. He wasn't prepared for the sight he would see. His brother's body lay there in the critical care unit (ICU), limp and lifeless, machines connected to all parts of his body, keeping him alive. He eased over to see his brother's face to let him know he was there by his side and that he was not alone. His brothers eyes said everything – his fear and his pain – all visible and real in his eyes. Jaden couldn't hold the tears back, and he cried, cried for his brother's pain, cried for his guilt, cried for what was gonna happen next.

Someone else was gonna pay. The anger within him was growing very fast and out of control. All the tools he had learned in gateway were now broken. Whatever path he was on before was now gone. This was a different path. This was the road to revenge. This was his blood brother, not some pretend brother, not some friend he considered his brother. This was his baby brother, and the Kings were gonna be killed, a lesson would be taught to the Kings, the kind of lesson in which everyone else learns something by another's demise. This lesson would be loud and clear.

Jaden told his brother be strong, heal up, and that he had to leave but would visit every day. He had to go now, he had to become Lloki once more. Lloki was Jaden's street name as a Royal. Lloki was his alter personality, the one who lived and died by the sword. Lloki was resurrected, and Jaden was now dead. Anger, revenge, hate, resentment – these were the embodiment of Lloki, his core; terror, his shield; and death, his sword, and he was a force to be reckoned with. The battlefield was Chicago; the enemy was anyone in the path of his revenge. The rules were clear: Till the last one stands!

Lloki was the warrior, the one who knew battle and death, an expert on weapons and kill spots. Loki would track and kill his target and send a message to all others. This is my family, my blood. I protect them with death and terror. There will be no mercy. And so it began, Lloki was back, and the Royals stepped aside. All of them had heard the stories of this Royal; all had come to fear what he could do. He was not normal; he was insane. The Royals sent word to the other Royal sections throughout Chicago about what had happened to Lloki's brother, about Lloki being back, about the sinister look in Lloki's eyes, and the insane way about him. They were concerned this was above them – something they had never seen before. What should they do? they asked.

The other Royals, the older ones who knew Lloki, knew his reputation from before and knew there was no way to stop him unless they themselves kill him, and who the fuck would risk that? Any attempt to kill Lloki would be a risk to not only the one trying to kill him but to that person's whole family. Lloki didn't play fair; he was extremely unpredictable and equally violent. The chance one would fail at the attempt and be recognized was to great of a chance to take, especially when his brother lay in the hospital on a deathbed. No, this would be an opportunity for the Royals, a chance to launch a major strike upon the Latin Kings, the bitter enemies of the Royals, the object of Lloki's vendetta.

They all got together and coordinated a major plan of attack to hit four sections of Kings at once, while immobilizing the police in a trap. This was Lloki's plan, and it worked. The first phase started, the fires were lit at several bars the Kings frequented at night. The second step was once the cops got there, the fire trucks would come, blocking in the cop cars. The younger Royals moved trash dumpsters and nail strips around the fire trucks blocking them in. Next came the coordinated shootings at four different places. With precision and timing, the plan was a success, and Kings had died and a message was sent to all others, including the cops and all that took heed to the message.

What Lloki did that night, no one knew. His role was kept to himself, and the other Royals accepted that. Jaden didn't kill any Latin Kings that night, but instead he helped put the plan together and stepped back, out of the picture, allowing others to do the dirty work. Of course, everyone else thought he killed a King that night. It didn't matter if he did or didn't. They would think what they wanted. He had gained a reputation mostly from shit he never did. Isn't that something? At least the vendetta was satisfied in his mind.

The next morning, Jaden woke up, knowing the actions he did. He just sat there numb, realizing his failure. He allowed his old self (Lloki) to take control and act out and to be what he was, a killer, even if he himself didn't pull the trigger. He knew it was wrong, but his brother was fighting for his life and that justified his actions. No discussions and no debate, it was wrong in society's eyes, but society doesn't live by the code of the streets.

Jaden realized he was now a Royal again. No words need be spoken for his acceptance back. He never left as far as they were concerned. Jaden quit his job, quit going to meetings, and ended all ties to his once-sober life and friends. He didn't want them to be involved or become victims to this life. He was protecting them from that and from him.

Now it was time to get the show on the road. He was back, and he needed to make his mark. He decided to sell drugs, rock cocaine to be precise, calling an old number he never forgot. He arranged a buy. I know, everyone, this chapter is fucked up, probably angered and saddened at the choice Jaden made and the actions he took. Well, sometimes life is brutal, and we succumb to it. Some have to die so that others may live. Jaden was a survivor. He lived through the worst and managed to come out breathing, still fighting, however dismal it may sound. He was still on the path of the warrior, but this was a different type of warrior and a different path, one he had been on long ago.

Chapter 27

PUTTING THE NEW plan into action, Jaden broke down the large supply of rock cocaine, busting the mountains of dope into smaller rocks, dime-size pieces, and ten-dollar sizes and then bagged each piece individually. There was over eight thousand dollars in product sitting on the table, not bad for his two-thousand-dollar investment. The goal was not to become rich, just to pay the monthly bills and have some left over for odds and ends. Jaden didn't want to bring attention to himself and didn't want to become known as a drug dealer by the police. He needed to create a persona that was believable, without being stopped and searched when seen. The police in the Twenty-fourth District were new to him – all strange faces, something in his favor. He would try to remain in the shadows.

Jaden had secured a spot (location to sell drugs inside someone's home) and dealt only to people who were familiar to him. After a certain amount of sales, he would pay the person who lived their in product. That's always a great deal – no surveillance cameras to catch him on tape and no "only one way in and one way out." Jaden kept the .357 magnum revolver close to him, always within reach when he was there. You never knew when shit was gonna go down, and he had made up his mind that he wasn't going to jail again. They would be holding court in the streets, and the sentence would be swift. If he was going down, he was taking as many cops as possible with him.

The memories of his own addiction were clear in his mind; he didn't have the urges most addicts had, no need or desire to get high or drunk. No, his urge was to always sell and to obtain power from dealing drugs. This was his urge and his addiction, and he was in the full stages of relapse, but this was his life. The cards for which he was dealt, so he played the hand to the fullest extent. Jaden paid attention to the street vibe, when the streets had a drought, he stopped selling. He didn't want people to know he had the product. The Royals didn't know he had the product. His own kind would turn on him. They would want him to sell them some weight, but he couldn't. Cocaine in weight was a no-no, brought too much heat down from the law, and it was too easy for someone to get greedy, get stupid, and try to set him up. He acted like he felt the drought also.

New Year's Eve, all the Royals are at Lucky's apartment. There were about forty royals there and about twenty women. Everyone was drinking and having a good time, even Jaden. Jaden wasn't drinking, but he was having a good time. Jaden had met Lucky's sister, Victoria, and was attracted to her. Victoria was Puerto Rican, African American, and Polish; was skinny and had light colored skin, long black hair, and an outgoing personality. Yep, Jaden definitely had chosen her as his next woman, but he needed to get her to agree. That was why he was at the party. He knew she would be there and knew he would get a chance to holler at her. He also wanted to be discreet about it. He never liked anyone knowing his business; he always kept his life a mystery as much as possible. No one ever knew what he was thinking, ever.

Victoria was having the time of her life. She wasn't allowed to go to the hood where her brother hung out. There was too much trouble up there – too many thugs to try and fuck with her. That was her brother's rule. She wanted nothing more than to hang out, desiring the fun and the excitement the hood offered. She wanted to be a part of the scene. Well, at least everyone is here. She's drinking and having a good time, and he's here. She had met Jaden one day up in the hood on one of those special occasions when her mom sent her to relay a message to her brother. She ran to the hood, dying to get up there and dying to stand on the corner where everything happened, the place of the stories she overheard the Royals talking about.

She had heard many stories over the years, watched, and learned from her brother. She wasn't stupid, and she knew what she wanted, but was still young and naive to the streets. She craved action and adventure and knew the hood would supply plenty of both, so she ran at every chance she was given to get her hot little ass up there to be seen and to participate. It wasn't anything to do with the gangs though. She thought being in a gang was stupid, a waste of time and life. It was strictly the streets she desired.

The day she met Jaden, Victoria was on the corner of Greenleaf and Clark, with her two best friends, Carmen and Rosalie, and they were talking to Lucky. There were about six other Royals there. Jaden was across the street and had noticed the crowd. *Assholes*, he thought, *standing in a group like targets, easier for a shooter to hit someone on a drive-by*. Then she caught his eye, and without really thinking, he was on that same corner, being a target, all for pussy. Strange how pussy has such a control over a man's mind and makes him do stupid shit, act retarded even. So now Jaden is retarded, but he wanted to meet Victoria.

Lucky had made the introductions, unaware of the animal magnetism that existed between Jaden and Victoria – that instant attraction and that connection that is made within a moment's time. Jaden felt it, so did Victoria, but nothing would happen that day. The introduction had served its purpose. The hookup would come later. They both planned in their head, both unaware they both planned it. Jaden burned her image into his mind. She was hot, and he would be making sure he spent some time with her.

The New Year's party was coming to an end at Lucky's place, but the party wasn't over, just the location was, so they all decided to walk the twenty-two blocks to the hood. *Bad idea*, Jaden thought. First, if the cops saw the crowd, they were gonna break that shit up. Second, way too much attention and easy for an enemy to pick them off. Jaden went to the hood, but he went alone and took the alleys he knew, angry that Victoria wasn't coming. Well, tonight he would hook up with one of these bitches and release some of that energy he had. No relationships though; they were the last thing he needed or wanted.

Now they are deep in numbers on Clark Street; everyone is drunk and high. No one is paying attention to their safety, except one, Jaden. Standing away from the group, he positioned himself as the outsider and surveyed the scene as a shooter would. He found the weak spot, the access point, and the getaway route. He moved into position; he stood in the shadows close to the alley, the alley he would have used to get away, and waited, just in case. The main group was on Clark Street. He was on Estes.

He didn't have to wait long until he heard the gunshots and caught the movement of someone coming through the gangway behind the laundromat. Jaden took position for surprise and, at the right moment, jumped the shooter, but the shooter was so small and looked to be about fourteen. Jaden wasn't able to get a good hit on him, and the shooter was able to get about three feet distance from him and raised the large revolver at Jade's head. Jaden stopped dead in his tracks, staring at the barrel. He knew he was finished, waiting for the muzzel flash and the bullet to shatter his skull.

The little King fired. *Click*. Fired again. *Click, click, click, click, click.* "That's six, bitch," Jaden said as he pounced on the King. The King had no chance against Jaden. Jaden was a veteran at combat, and quickly had the King subdued, but that wasn't what Jaden wanted. He wanted the gun. As the other Royals ran up to them, Jaden tossed the King to them and grabbed the gun and tossed it into the bushes. That was his prize – his gun. The others could have the King.

The cops were on the scene within minutes of the shooting. The royals were thrown against the wall to be searched and questioned. The King had run away. The King had other concerns besides jail. He had lost the gun; no gang ever wants to lose a gun. About three days later, the cops found that little King dead. He was shot twice in the head and tossed in a dumpster. Gang life is this brutal – this real.

All the other shit that attracts young unsuspecting wannabe members is just the lure. Make no mistakes. Gang life leads to only two things: death or prison.

After the incident with the King and the gun, Jaden walked off to be alone, away from the group. He went to the local coffee shop and took a booth to think. Jaden was still alone. He still felt an emptiness in his heart. He tried hard not to think about the past, about his childhood. There were so many things he left unfinished, so many mistakes that he regretted.

When he thought about Judy, there was still a lingering pain there and the same for Jimmy. He thought about the women he had spent time with, the ones he had cared about and the ones he had used for the moment. Maybe it was because he thought he had stared death in the face again, maybe it was because, once again, something allowed him to continue on. He had heard others brag that they had stared death in the face and laughed. He himself had never laughed each time he came face-to-face with death. It was never a laughing moment for him. He knew the seriousness of each encounter and was always prepared to pay the final cost, not that he wanted to.

He always thought there was something out there for him – a destination he was meant to reach. Life and its purpose doesn't always make its intentions clear, and Jaden wasn't clear on his any more today than any other time before. She kept creeping back into his mind, and he could see her face, the first one, the very first girl he ever cared about, the one he sacrificed his desires for to keep safe from him – Julie. He wondered how she was, how she was doing, and where she was. He could see her young beautiful face when he closed his eyes. God, he wished his life was different, wished he would have been raised different, and maybe wished he had a chance to get to know Julie better. He pushed those thoughts away from him, nothing good ever comes from fairy-tale dreams.

Julie was taking lunch, sitting in her minivan, listening to music, not really the oldies but old enough for her to remember the songs from when she was much younger, when she was almost a totally different person. She was so shy and quiet back then, really never one to be bold and outspoken. Julie thought about her life through the years, but going backward, she thought about her friends and boyfriends. She thought about him – the one she wanted so bad to get to know, the one whose eyes had held so many secrets. She had seen the turmoil, the inner fight within him. She just never had a chance to know what that fight was. She smiled when she remembered how she had lied to her mom about going to the park for the activities, when she was really planning on meeting up with him.

Every time they met, they would talk. Well, he talked more, and she listened a lot. He always seemed reserved though, always seemed like he was holding back something. He was a bad boy, something she was never attracted to, but he was different. He was also so very sweet. She closed her eyes and remembered, seeing the visions of their talks by the park fence. Damn, he was so cute, and he was definitely a tough kid. Her heart was beating faster now, her body reacting to the thoughts of him, her mind trying to focus and trying to hold control of the visions, but the vision was only of his face, a face she longed to see again and a face she had loved, and his eyes were staring at her, and she looked away, breaking the concentration, ending the vision, and for the first time in a very, very long time, she whispered his name, "Jaden." She had a half smile on her face but also a half frown, such a bittersweet memory. So much was left unsaid between Jaden and her. Time to get back to work.

Chapter 28

JADEN WAS ABLE to meet up with Victoria several times once they were able to get each other's numbers. When he found out she was only sixteen, he decided he would wait. She was too young, and he wasn't ever gonna make that mistake again, but once she hit eighteen, she was fair game; she would be his. So they soon became cool with each other, kinda like friends. Jaden had talked to her about shit from his past, and she listened, never revealing what he told her. Jaden didn't tell her about crimes; he only told her the good stuff – the parties and the funny shit, and she ate it up.

These two had found some weird kind of companionship, which didn't involve sex, something new to the both of them. It seems Victoria wasn't a virgin. In fact, she had slept with some of her brother's friends already, something that she kept secret, knowing her brother would kill the Royals who violated her, betrayed him as it were. That's the fucked-up thing about the whole fake ass gang shit. There was no true loyalty. *Everyone was out for themselves, and there were no real bonds, nothing solid*, he thought.

Jaden's brother wanted out of the Royals. He had enough of this bullshit and asked Jaden to relate that to the others. "No problem." It was cool with Jaden. His brother wasn't like him and didn't have it in him to do what needs to be done. Most gang members don't. The other Royals didn't have a problem with it either, so it was done.

One less thing Jaden had to worry about was that the hood wasn't like it was in the old days. Now it consisted of maybe Estes, three blocks south to Lunt, and Ravenswood, two blocks east to Paulina. Holy shit, that's a big ass cut in territory, but the Royals didn't have the membership to protect anything larger, and none of them lived in the hood. The other gangs in Rogers Park were Vice Lords, Gangster Disciples, Ashland Vikings, and Latin Kings. Honestly, it was such a fucked-up boundary map that it's fair to say the whole fuckin' Rogers Park was up for grabs. Each gang was selling drugs wherever they wanted, and that was that. Some got caught with their guard down and then they would end up stankin.

The daily shit that happens on the street is a fuckin' soap opera. Actually it was very amusing, as long as you're not in the cast for the moment. Jaden would often find a place to chill out and watch the shit unfold. The racial balance of the area was simple, a fuckin melting pot – whites, blacks, Spanish, Oriental, and everyone else you can throw into the mix, a regular UN convention. The pimps and the hookers, the drunks and the addicts, and the bangers and the victims. Who needed cable?

It was during these moments Jaden reflected back to gateway, to all he had learned, and to Bobby. He felt the guilt and knew what he was doing was detrimental to his recovery, but what else could he do? No money to go to college, and he's a convicted felon, so a good job was out of the question, and his family needed the money. This was it, for now.

Try as hard as he could, he was unable to help being noticed by the cops. All it took was one time for them to stop and question him, run his name, and it was over. He would be watched from that day on. *Well, just gotta be more clever than them*, he thought. So began the cat-and-mouse game between them. Most times, he was aware of them, spotted their locations, and adjusted tactics, but sometimes he wasn't. This made him nervous. At any time, they could roll up on him and snag him. About the only thing in his favor was that his sister was dating one of the tact officers, something Jaden thought might come in handy, and it did. Being on parole – Jaden was still on parole – any violation would send him back to prison, unless he had a horseshoe up his ass, which the tact officer was, but he saved that for later.

About three months later, Jaden was now selling off of Greenleaf. His spot was no good anymore 'cause the hype (person who smokes cocaine) had moved away. This was riskier, and he was breaking his rules, slowly but surely. Not only was he out in the open with drugs, but he also had the gun on him, definitely a fucked-up situation if he got caught by the police by surprise. And he did, kinda. He had the gun stashed close by but had three dime bags of rock on him. When the tact officers came from the back side, he was caught before he even knew they were there. Luckily it was the cop his sister was fucking, and Jaden asked for a play. The cop said he needed a gun. Jaden gave up his; he was free to go.

Now I know many of you wonder about this practice between cops and criminals. You should see it for the true genius that it is. Instead of leaving a gun on the street, a gun that could be used to kill you one day, the cops rather let a drug dealer go for that gun. They are truly saving your life, and they know they will catch the drug dealer again. The cops are smart; the dealers are stupid, and that includes Jaden.

Jaden didn't take heed to the fact he got caught. He just ignored it and continued dealing, getting more reckless, taking chances he didn't need to. Now he was dealing in the daytime, selling to whomever, bringing a lot of product out with him. Nothing really makes much sense anyways. He thinks this is all there is to life, just a hustle – that's it.

Jaden didn't notice the other Royals that were dealing were getting jealous at his sales. He cut his product to be larger than others. He's taking the customers from them, and they were not liking the tactic. They can't complain out loud. Business is business. No, instead they will probably give him up to the law, he figures. Make as much as possible and what happens will be. The funny thing about that was that it came faster than he realized – two weeks later.

Jaden had woken up on a Saturday morning with no cigarettes and no money, and his mom wasn't home, so he couldn't bum a smoke from her. "Fuck it," he blurted out and grabbed fifteen dime bags and took his sister's car to the hood. The plan is simple: Sell some product fast and get some cigarettes. That's the plan, except for what happened next.

He sells to someone he had never seen before. The hype leaves and Jaden goes into the hallway out of sight. In the hallway, he grabbed the baggy out his ass and took three more rocks out. He might as well keep selling he figures. He walked back on to the sidewalk, and three unmarked cop cars pulled up on him. He swallowed the three bags and put his hands in the air, busted. The hype was an undercover narc, working with the citywide narc unit on dealer sweeps. Jaden is booked on manufacturing and distribution of a controlled substance. The crime is punishable six to thirty years. Motherfucker, still no cigarettes. Now he realizes just how bad smoking is.

Chapter 29

SITTING IN THE holding cell at Belmont and Western Police Station, Jaden does what he always did – lie on the concrete slab and go to sleep. He knows he's going down to the joint, just not how long. He tries to dream of something good and something relaxing, but no dreams come to him. Sleep will not allow him to escape the concern that is in the back of his mind. Everything is coming into view now. The time he spent in prison, the shit he pulled in Menard, not killing Jimmy's killer, gateway, going back to the streets, and now this.

Jaden thought the issues from the past were resolved and thought they wouldn't hinder him anymore, but here he was, back in the same fuckin' predicament as before. Why him? What does he keep doing stupid shit for? What the fuck is the answer to his problems? These are and always have been the questions he had. The cell door is unlocking. Guess it's that time for transfer to county.

Back in the county holding cells – remember this place, the foulest stench, and the forever waiting period, listening to the others tell their bullshit stories. On his last time there, he was only twenty years old. Now he was twenty eight, older but not smarter though. He had learned a great deal of things on his last journey but didn't use the knowledge he had gain, so he wasn't smarter, in fact, more of a dummy.

To know what he knew, to have the insight into his disease, and the map to change, he fuckin' took the road everyone travels. He caved in to the pressure, the false belief in his mind that he was expected to do the things he did. What a fuckin' joke. Jaden was not important to other people's lives. He wasn't the leading man in the movie; he was just one person trying to find his way and was distracted by the shiny things. Oh, those fuckin' shiny things – money, fame, notoriety, respect from losers, self-importance – all the wrong shiny shit.

He didn't have to avenge what happened to his brother; that wasn't his responsibility. He didn't need to sell drugs; he wasn't starving. It was something deeper, something about him that made him do this shit. Jaden's head hurt from trying to rack his brain for answers, he just found a spot to sit and sat; he was tired.

Once up on the deck, he went to his cell and went to sleep, unsure what the future held, but he knew there were only two options: Make some real changes or die. That night he dreamed, and the only thing he remembered of his dreams was the hyena. The path of the warrior shot into his mind. Everything the old shaman had said and didn't say came back to him, reminding him of a decision he had made back then. Jaden realized that to stay on that path required true strength, courage to remain focused, and a desire to want the truth. He thought long and hard for the next day or so about this, not talking to anyone really in the unit, staying to himself.

Finally one of the folks came up to him and said, "Hey, brother, I see you tatted up with Royals, you folks?"

"No," came the one word answer from Jaden. The answer came out before he had time to really think it through. "It was a long time ago, but not since I was younger," he continued.

"That's all good though. Since you was before, we can put you on count as aid and assist," the inmate said.

"No, I am not on count, and I'm not involved in any of it," Jaden retorted.

"Bet then, that's how it's gonna be," the motherfucker said, trying to put concern or fear into Jaden. Jaden just nodded back to him and walked away. The decision has been made again. Once again he was on the path, but he knew his weakness, his tender spot – he lacked a spiritual strength, not a religion. He kept confusing the two before. That was his fault. Jaden couldn't stand religion, any form of it. Spirituality was something different though, and he needed it if he was to live a meaningful life.

He knew he himself didn't have the strength to complete the change or to ward off the pressure from within. Only spiritual strength could do that. He remembered to see that strength in others at meetings, always jealous or envious of it, wanting it, and desiring it but never finding it. This time he would search for it; he would seek what felt honest and true within himself. This time he would succeed.

Jaden had to stay in the county for two months. There was a parole block on him getting a bond, but his parole was up now and the block was released. Now he had a bond, and his sister paid it. She had finished selling the rest of the product, sold it in large amounts to one of her connections, and took the money to bond her brother out of jail. Once out, he went home to his mother's apartment and told them what his plan was. They heard this shit from him many times but still wished him well.

Jaden started the next day with a fresh outlook and a renewed determination but no job. He needed to find a job. He called in a favor from the husband of one of his customers. The guy worked at a big-name car repair shop, and Jaden knew how to do minor repairs to cars, so he got him the job. It wasn't the greatest pay, but it was full-time work, and Jaden liked the work. He did basic repairs, maintenance shit really – oil changes, battery swaps, tire switch outs, brake work, shit like that.

Jaden was good and fast at his job, and his boss liked that. The other guys there took their time, always dragging their asses, but not Jaden. Jaden was on the money. A normal time to replace four tires on a car took the others about ninety minutes; Jaden took thirty. An oil change and lube took the others forty minutes; Jade's time was twenty. The other guys got a flat amount of pay per hour. Jaden was on shop rate. He got a certain amount of pay based on the job he did and based on the time the book says it takes to do the job.

The book says it takes ninety minutes to do a brake job. Jaden would be paid for ninety minutes, whether he finished sooner or later. Yes, Jaden liked the way that worked, and his goal was to always finish before the book time but still do the job right and well. Jaden was getting paid for eighty or ninety hours of work but only actually was at work forty hours a week. All he had to do was hustle his ass to fuck around at work, and he would get paid well. His boss loved this; he was moving cars in and out of the shop much faster now, generating a higher revenue than ever before, and he knew it was because of Jaden. Jaden was now his best friend.

The increase in revenue didn't go unnoticed by corporate headquarters that made it a point to inform him of a job well done. He told them thanks and informed them of his super star mechanic, Jaden. The corporate had noticed Jaden's numbers and awarded him certificates of achievement, letting him know they knew, and he liked that. Who doesn't like being noticed for doing a good job?

Away from work, Jaden was saving to get his own apartment, becoming self-sufficient. He was attending CA meetings again, sharing his experiences of relapse with the others. Jaden was a person who loved to read books, always allowing himself to be sucked into the world of the book, kinda like being there and witnessing the events unfolding but not being seen. One day, he was reading a book while on the train to work and something in the book grabbed his attention. He decided to check it out on his next day off.

Standing in the occult book store, a place Jaden had passed by many times in his life but never went in, always thinking the place was a scam, a sham to make money. He never saw a reason to go in. They did have cool shit like necklaces and charms in the window, but he never went in. Now he went in and searched for something, searched for the item that grabbed his attention. There it was, holy shit, he couldn't believe he had found a book on it, *The Book of Shadows*. He bought the book and hurried home, enthusiastic about reading it.

As he read, he was astonished at the revelations and the content, and he continued to read, soaking in what his soul was yearning for, a different way of life, a spiritual beginning, one that had no religious structure whatsoever. He once again had found hope.

Julie had made a decision to ask her husband for a separation, only for a while, to work some things out. He was confused but he agreed. They still lived together, the economy being what it was, but he stayed in the spare room. The separation allowed her to focus just on her and the children but not the marriage. With that responsibility put on hold, Julie decided to go back to college, one course at a time. She wanted to change the direction of her education goal and took a course in women's studies.

Working at the program had sparked an interest in her that she needed to explore. The course was wonderful, was very educational, and opened her eyes to certain circumstances that dealt strictly with women. She ate it up, taking the new information and building a sense of understanding about the dynamics of being a woman. The more she learned though seemed to raise in her a question. *Have I lived my life to my full potential?* she asked herself. Realizing she had not, she felt depressed. There was so much more she wanted to accomplish as an individual person. She always wanted to have a family, children, and be a homemaker, but there were other aspirations also, the ones that remained in the shadows, only whispering their wishes, but she had stopped listening to the whispers long ago. Now they were whispering again, and she listened.

Julie had sat her children down and explained the situation to her children, explained that sometimes, in life, people need a time out from certain things and need to be able to refocus on other avenues. She assured them all would be fine, and the children reassured her too. She wondered if they really understood. You know how teenagers are. She looked at her children with that loving stare and told them to get out of her face; she had studying to do.

The kids had seen the changes and were concerned, of course, but they liked the way their mom was doing things for herself. She seemed like she was happy. That's all that mattered to them.

Julie's friends had seen some changes also, noticing the take-charge attitude of her life lately and wondered what sparked it. They didn't ask her; they figured it was something she would share with them when Julie was ready. It didn't stop them from discussing it when Julie wasn't with the group, and they all put their own opinions out there as to what caused the change. One thought it was a midlife crisis. The other thought it was the marriage going bad. One even thought Julie was smoking pot, but whatever the cause, they all thought the change was inspirational and secretly wished they had the strength to follow her footsteps.

Monica, Julie's closest friend, was the only one who asked her about the change. Julie's only response was that it was time for her to find her. Monica understood and told Julie she liked the change and wished her success.

Where this road was taking Julie, she had no clue, but it was new. It was about her, and that she liked. Something she liked also was the separation. If only she could find a way to make it permanent.

Chapter 30

JADEN HAD READ that book every day until he completed it, but now he knew there was another book he needed, one that would help guide him along his journey. Back to the book store, searching, searching, searching, *found it*! This was called *The Way of the Shaman*, and it was exactly what he wanted. He dove into the readings with an anxiousness like a kid wakes up on Christmas morning at 5:00 a.m., running while half asleep to the Christmas tree, to the presents. That was his excitement.

The book had discussed the power of nature and how all living organisms share energy, and there were meditation exercises and other mystic tools that one could achieve. This was something Jaden could take hold of, something he felt a pulling toward. Jaden read and studied the book, practicing the meditation exercises, becoming more and more accustomed to the technique. Every day was about practice and improvement. Every day the world of the streets seemed farther and farther away, but not too far.

His court dates were getting closer and closer. Soon the time would come, and he knew he would once again surrender his freedom and give others control over him, his life, and his safety. There was nothing he could do about it. His attorney told him they had him good; the eyewitness was the buyer who was an undercover cop, and he got caught with marked money. All this Jaden knew to be true; he knew he would be found guilty if he went to trial. What he didn't know is how much time the state's attorney would offer him if he plea bargained.

The only positive thing was when they tested the cocaine, it came back less than what he thought and that lowered the crime to a class 1 felony, punishable four to fifteen years, much better than before. At the worse, he would do seven and a half years, go in at twenty-eight and come out thirty-five years old. *Damn, that's old*, he thought.

Well, he worked and he saved his money. He wanted to make sure he would have the funds he needed when he went to do his time. Again, he would buy the items that would make his stay as comfortable as possible, which isn't a lot. He also kept up with the shamanistic practices. The new ideas and ways were exciting to him. The peace he was feeling within was so real, so calming – something he had yearned for his whole life. He found himself not so angry anymore, not so quick to fall into negative thoughts or behavior, not that he didn't from time to time, but the episodes were not as severe – not so crippling. There was a new sense of freedom from himself that he felt, not being bound to his emotions, allowed to be human and enjoy life. This was what the others had felt and the thing he envied. Now he himself was part of that group.

The time went by so quickly, and he's coming up to his last court date. The thought of taking off and going on the run is in his mind, but he pushes it away. He doesn't want to go to prison, but doing so allows him to pay for his crime. That was his new direction now. He had committed a lot of crimes and had a lot of victims. He felt he owed a debt to society. There was a need to atone for the harm he had done, and he would. Slowly but surely he would atone. The best place to start is with the time he would serve for selling drugs.

The thing that sucked is that he had a lot of victims – shit that I didn't disclose in this story and shit that I couldn't. The list was long. It burned in his heart and mind. The journey would be a long one. There was one on the list he would save for last though, one special person who was so close to him, someone he felt he harmed most of all. That person he would save for his very last atonement. He had made the decision on how to atone to the last one. The answer came to him in a meditation period, when his mind was clearest – no cloudiness, no mixed emotions, just the answer. The journey starts soon, as soon as he goes to court.

On that day, the state's attorney offered him twelve years. He refused. His lawyer seemed concerned, but Jaden told him he had a plan. As the attorneys started their mumbo jumbo, Jaden asked the judge if he could speak. His lawyer advised him to remain quiet. Jaden hushed his attorney. The judge asked Jaden to make sure he wanted to say whatever he said. Jaden told the judge he wanted to enter a plea of guilty but speak about it. The judge agreed.

Jaden told the judge his story – his struggles, his accomplishments, and his failure. He informed the judge of his decision to atone for his wrongs and was taking full responsibility for his actions. The judge said that's nice and sentenced him to six years. Jaden thought fair enough and left the courtroom to the back holding cell. Now it begins.

He was definitely focused on what the journey would entail – the retribution he would pay. To those that were still alive, he would make amends. To those that weren't, his actions in life would make amends. He was gonna right his wrongs; he needed to and he wanted to. Start from the end and work backward – that was the plan. No more gang membership, no prison shanks, and no hustling in prison. That was the former Jaden. This time, he wouldn't let his decision be made out of fear. He would accept whatever came his way.

Jaden was sent back to Sheridan prison, the place he had paroled from, but this time it was different. He didn't sign in to gateway. He stayed in general population. He decided to go to the vocational school, signing up for automotive technology, something he knew about but never had training for. He figured it would be a good thing to fall back on. He had no trouble with the gangs; he didn't represent, so they paid no attention to him.

In all actuality, the prison system in Illinois had taken back control of the prisons, and things were more secure and restricted. The prison had built a supermax, and every inmate wanted nothing to do with that joint. In that joint, the inmate was locked down twenty-four hours a day, no movement at all. When it was time to shower the guards would roll a portable shower to each cell, one at a time, and the inmate would take a shower. All mail was read through a monitor that was rolled to the cell. The inmate was isolated and controlled completely. This was the worst place to be to do time because you didn't do time, time did you.

The prison was more relaxed. Very limited gang action took place, so it was actually nice to do your time without being in a gang. There were still altercations here and there, but nothing like before. There were no riots or massive gang wars, just one-on-one fights that were over almost as soon as they were started. Most inmates went to school now, trying to do something productive and trying to learn what they were unable to before.

Jaden enjoyed his class. He had an instructor that was very smart and had many years of experience dealing with inmates as students. Jaden took to him well and learned from him. The nice part about the class was that the students got to work on the cars that belonged to the staff and the guards – real-life experience, hands-on training. Jaden knew how to remove and replace parts – that was easy. It was the theory of how things worked that he needed to learn, allowing him to diagnose problems. There was a lot to learn, but he had two years to do it.

Even though he was sentenced to six years, he only had to do three. Then if he went to school, he could receive additional good time also, six months off for each year in school. Jaden would do two years in school and get one year off, serving a two-year sentence only. That's the way it works. He didn't qualify for additional good time. His cases were class X felonies, violent cases that couldn't receive shit for anything. He wasn't being slick; he was following the rules of the system, doing what was expected of him and being rewarded for it.

He would go to the prison library as often as possible, getting books that related to shamanism, but the selection was very minimal, but he knew the prison library was hooked up with the other library systems in the free library, the interlibrary loan program, and he utilized that service. The whole library system was at his fingertips, so he touched. Shamanism was not what his spirituality was, just a tool for him to learn to connect outside of himself. He had no name for what he believed, just knowing he believed in something worked for him. He knew it was real, knew how filled he felt within, and knew he was on the path.

Chapter 31

WHEN THERE WAS time for quietly relaxing and time to meditate, he would focus on the victims he could make amends to. The list was long, and his memory was not so good from all the years of drug abuse. He still managed to get the names or faces into view – so many though – not trying to focus on the length of the list, just the next one on top. Some of the people on the list he had an address for and wrote lengthy letters to, apologizing for the wrongs he committed against them, attempting to explain the why and the cause. He didn't explain the path he was on and informed them there was no need to write back, unless they wanted to. Many never wrote back, and he understood. He could only do his part; this was about his wrongs, nothing else.

In the course of two years, Jaden had wrote about thirty-two letters, maybe more or maybe less, but thirty-two seemed about in the middle so I'll use it. The more personal victims in his life were emotionally closer to him. Those he would make amends to, once paroled, in person. That would take a more personal approach. Mostly the list had family, close friends, and people from his past and also the ones who were dead or unreachable. For the ones who were dead and unreachable, he would have to allow the way he lived his life now to be his amends. He would help people just for the sake of helping, protect those whom he could protect, and harm no one else.

The last person on his list, the most important victim of all, that one was the hardest. He needed to take time to prepare himself for that. It would take a lot of years, a lot of amending with every single person on the list before he could attempt to even try to amend the last one. Damn that's a lot of amending, but when the time came, he would be ready. He would know when that time was at hand. Just thinking of the damage he caused to the last one was overwhelming. He hoped his offer would be sufficient. He hoped the path he was on would take him to that final person.

The time was here for Jaden to be released, and released he was. Same thing – the prison took him to the train station, train to downtown, train to the suburbs, and he was at his mom's house, home again. It felt good for him to be around his family he had missed them.

Both his sisters had children who were growing up, and so did his brother. His brother had two boys; his sisters each had one boy and one girl. He was gonna be in their lives in a good way and be the uncle he wasn't able to be before. A part of him always wanted to have children, someone he could love unconditionally with all his heart and soul, but that was not to be. He knew his life before was not healthy and realized what a good choice Judy had made the day she had an abortion. It still hurt though, but it wasn't crippling him, just painful.

Jaden never forgot Judy, thought about her a lot, and wondered what life could have been if he had changed, if they would have had their child, and if life was different for the both of them. The last he heard of Judy was that she married and was living out of state – good for her. Jaden knew the what-ifs were a waste of time. Life was different now for him, for her, and for everyone. Trying to relive the past was a fool's dream. He was tired of being a fool. Although thinking about his child wasn't a waste of time for him, he believed his child was a part of life, even though aborted. *Hurts too much to think about. Just let go for now*, he thought. Soon though the time would come, wrapping that thought around him like a security blanket, taking solace within himself.

Slowly his family started to realize the change within Jaden. Each day the trust was building once again, and his family was healing. His family was always very close, even when they fought among themselves. They would always be there for each other, always. Jaden had also reconnected with Victoria, and they started dating. The both of them spent a lot of time together, establishing their relationship. Victoria still was a partier, and Jaden wasn't. That seemed to work for them. Jaden didn't crowd her and never gave her static about her going out. That wasn't his way. He had lived his party life and didn't want to interfere with Victoria's experiences. She was still young and had a lot of fun still yet to have. Victoria was nineteen. Jaden was going on thirty. That's a big age difference, which does bring issues with it, but they would deal with that as it came. Why sweat it now?

Jaden's brother kept urging him to get a commercial drivers license (CDL) so he could drive trucks, a great way to make a living, and Jaden did. Jaden got a job driving where his brother worked, and it paid well – double digits, baby, yeah. It was good pay to him. He never made that kind of money honestly, and it felt good to earn it. He had a lot to learn about driving trucks – making turns, backing up, and following distances – but he caught on just fine.

He discovered another talent of his while driving trucks. He had excellent navigational skills, an uncanny sense of where he was, where he needed to go, and how to get there. He no longer thought of directions as right here, left there. Everything was now north, south, east, and west. He had become very accustomed inside the truck, comfortable as it were.

Oh, there were some instances that shocked him back into reality of the dangers of driving like the time he was driving in the snow for the first time. He was heading east on Lake Cook Road, just coming up to the crown of the overpass above the railroad tracks. He was a little too close to the car in front of him, maybe thirty feet, when the car ahead hit the brakes and started to skid, Jaden jammed the brakes also, which was a big fuckin' mistake. The back end of his truck was coming around his passenger side as the front was reversing also. He was now going sideways down the overpass. His fuckin' hands gripping the steering wheel, knuckles white, his asshole even tighter. The truck slid to a stop and he breathed, but he couldn't let go off the wheel, his hands had the death grip. It took about five minutes for him to get his hands to release. Then he checked his shorts.

There were a couple of near collisions. Some were because he wasn't paying attention; some other drivers weren't. All experiences he learned from, all which made him become a safer driver, a much safer driver. Jaden did a good job and was given a route to work. Route drivers had a much better job security than airport drivers. Anyone could work the airport for pickups and deliveries, but working a route required navigational skills, time management, and hustle. He had accomplished all three within a short time and was working the Northwest route: Cook, Kane, and McHenry counties. These were areas he never knew existed in Illinois, and he loved learning them and loved seeing the beauty of the land. So different than the city, so spacious and uncrowded.

The schools looked like college campuses; the homes were mansions to him. The streets were clean, with no gangs on the corner. With lakes and rivers to fish in, he wondered if the people who lived in these areas knew how lucky they were, lucky to not know what he knew, lucky to not experience what he had, and lucky to be wealthy. The grass is never greener on the other side, but what the fuck did he know? He assumed as always.

He had his job. He was in a relationship, and he had his path to follow, continuing to make amends. Sometimes time would pass before he was able to locate the next one on the list. As he found them, he would do his part and move on to the next. Such a long list still, still a long time to go to the last one on the list. His list was top priority, no matter what the journey will continue till the last one, no matter what else happens he would get to the last one, the most important one.

Jaden never revealed the complete plan to anyone. They wouldn't fully understand his mission. They didn't feel what he felt and didn't know the burdens he carried. This was his path, his way in life, and the only chance he had to set things right. A long time was spent hurting people, and it was gonna take a long time fixing it. After that, he would be able to rest, finally at peace with himself. The one thing he realized was that life was hard. There were no instructions, and a person had to do the best they could with what they had. It only took thirty years to get that lesson taught. Oh, the years he wasted – what a loss.

Julie was finishing up her classes, and the realization that it was time to make a decision about her marriage was at hand. She had decided to give it another chance to make sure the spark was fully extinguished before ending it. She could do that. She still cared for her husband, just wasn't too sure she was in love with him. There was a feeling she was having, not so much in her mind or even completely in her heart, but it was in all of her senses. Something was making itself known to her. She wasn't sure though what it was. There was a change coming, that much she knew, and a part of her desired the change, and the other was cautious.

Chapter 32

THAT WAS HOW it went Jaden worked on the list when opportunity presented itself to him to do so. He continued to drive a truck, although he did move from one company to the next a couple times, trying to find his niche. He liked driving but he wanted more; he wanted to get into the operational part of the transportation business. Being a driver was long hours, hours that were wearing him down.

The summer, spring, and even fall weather was okay, but the Chicago winters were brutal. The wind was starting to sear through his skin as he got older, touching the bone, chilling his whole body. Drivers just tough it out – no other choice. It reminded him of when he was about eleven years old, walking to school up Rogers Avenue, a nice-size hill at that age. That same wind, forcing him to go from one hallway of an apartment building to the next, slowly making it to school. That wind was terrible, and it blew an Arctic blast with each bellow.

It didn't take long for Jaden and Victoria to get an apartment with one another. They had decided to get one close to Victoria's job, out in the northwest suburbs. Victoria worked with Jade's mom, doing customer service, not a bad-paying job. Between them both, they made a decent living and chose a very nice apartment: two bedrooms, two baths, at a place that had a pool, clubhouse, workout room, and a tennis court – not a bad place at all.

Jaden's family lived only five minutes away, Victoria's lived about thirty minutes away. Everything was as it should be. Both were excelling at their jobs. They had a nice place to live, and they enjoyed their lives. Jaden loved the pool, spent a lot of time their swimming and thinking, always thinking about his list. Maybe he was meant to have a decent life, one without jails, death, or violence. It sure was that way now. He was starting to rethink the last person on the list, rethinking that part of the journey. Time will tell he's decided; it always does.

The year passed by so fast, and they looked forward to renewing their lease, but that was not gonna happen. They had received a letter in the mail one day from the leasing company, stating they would not be renewing the lease. They both wondered what the fuck had happened, unaware of any complaints there might have been. They went to the leasing office the next day and found out. It seems that someone who worked with Victoria, a person who had been fired from the job was spiteful and did some digging into Jaden's life and found the golden apple, so to speak. There it was – convicted sex offender. And she forwarded the information to the leasing company.

Jaden tried to explain the situation, but it didn't matter. It didn't matter that he had served his time for all the crimes he had been convicted of. The leasing company didn't want to be held responsible if something ever did happen. Jaden understood, but he was fuckin' pissed. Once again, he was the caged lion, being taunted by someone who knew he was caged, being bound by a desire to change his life, not wanting to be violent, not wanting to ever hurt someone ever again. There he was, now formulating the plan to kill the person who did this to him. It was so fuckin' easy for the thoughts to emerge, to formulate, and to try and control his path.

Jaden thought hard this time. He fought that urge and allowed it to play out in his head, but this time he allowed it to play all the way through to the part where he loses everything he built, all the hard work, all the changing, everything gone, with him in a cell or dead. He didn't like the ending of that. Nope, killing that bitch wouldn't make things better, only worse. He let it go and decided to move forward. Karma would get even for this, not Jaden.

It turned out some time later that they had discovered that the girl's life was in shambles. She had come back to Victoria's boss, begging for her job back but not getting it. She had become a drug addict and lost everything she had and now was homeless and desperate. That was the last they ever heard from about her. Victoria was satisfied with that. Jaden felt sad for her. He knew the hardship of addiction and the desolate feeling of despair and hopelessness. He didn't take satisfaction in her misfortunes, but he did feel she deserved it. Everyone owes for the harm they caused, but he was not the executioner. Karma was.

When the time came they had found another apartment, with all the same things as this one, but actually cheaper, that was nice. The new place was only about four blocks away, still close to Victoria's job. So it seemed like things worked out for them, but it still bothered Jaden knowing he would be held accountable for his past, even though he served his time and paid for his offenses. He knew the legal system was bullshit. There is no such thing as repaying your debt to society, well, not just by serving your time.

Repaying your debt to society involved a greater amount of payment than sitting in a cell and going to school. It demanded a change in attitude and behavior. Just staying out of trouble wasn't enough. It demanded getting involved in the community, becoming an asset to the community, taking a stand, and defending a community. This realization was smacking Jaden in the face, but it was true and it made sense to him. Just like the thought that he would always have that killer's instinct, always capable of violence. It was what he did that mattered and his behavior and actions that defined him, not the thoughts. Everyone has fucked-up thoughts, some worse than others. Some people think they want to kill someone for something, but they don't. Rational thinking takes over; Jaden was the same. He would be rational.

After driving a couple years for other companies, Jaden decided he wanted his own truck to be his own boss. Victoria's mom bought a used truck, and Jaden made payments to her. He signed on with a trucking company as an owner operator. Getting a percentage of the deliveries and pickups he did in his truck, he paid for the operating expenses for the truck though. Jaden loved it, loved being his own boss, but he soon discovered there is only one boss, the customer, and what a cruel boss they could be. They expected steak but wanted to pay for liver. The customers were very demanding and never paid the invoice on time. Jaden realized the game real fast.

The freight forwarders would use smaller companies for about six months, without paying the invoices, hoping the smaller guys would go out of business, thus not having to pay the invoices or at least being able to renegotiate the bill. Jaden wouldn't budge. Pay in full or we go to court. They eventually paid but never used his services again. The business world was brutal and corrupt and very unfair.

The shit he experienced and saw confused him about society. The rich cry foul when they are made to be the victim, but they victimize without fail when given the chance. Money made the rules, and money decided the outcome. No money to play meant you lose.

After about a year, Jade's truck broke down. He tried to fix it himself, buying the parts on credit cards. The credit card bill was running up and the income running down, a losing battle. He still owed about seventy-five hundred to Victoria's mom for the truck. He had talked to the owner of the trucking company he contracted with and they agreed to let him park his truck there, and he would drive their truck for 30 percent of the load. He made enough to pay the bills and still made payments to Victoria's mom.

About three months went by and the owner of the company was looking for a truck to buy. He asked Jaden what was wrong with his truck. Jaden said he didn't know. He told the owner how much he owed on it, and the owner offered to pay off the amount for ownership of the truck, Jaden agreed. Jaden knew how the owner operated, withholding work from owner operators, starving them of income, putting them in a bad financial situation, and then offering to take their truck off their hands for a steal. He was a slimy son of a bitch. He wrote Jaden a check for the amount and Jaden drove it to Victoria's mom, getting the title and bringing it back. He had told his girlfriend's mom to cash that check now. Do not wait, and she did that day. It was a done deal.

The owner had the truck towed to the repair shop, where it sat for two days and then came the problem. Jaden was asked to come into the owner's office. There sat the owner and Mario, the station manager. The owner told Jaden that the repair shop had informed him that there was extensive repairs needed, about fourteen thousand dollars worth. The owner explained to Jaden that if he would have known this, he would never have bought the truck and told Jaden he needed to get that check back because he wanted to rescind on the deal. Jaden told him he didn't have the check and that he had given the check to his girlfriend's mom. She was the owner of the truck, not him. That wasn't good. The owner wanted his money back; he was accustomed to taking advantage of others, not being taken advantage of.

The owner and Mario attempted to pressure Jaden about the money, almost in a threatening way. Jaden held in his laughter. He sized them both up, played out the scene as it would unfold. If they tried some stupid shit, he would fucking rip their throats out. He had nothing but discontent for the both of them. How many honest working men had they taken advantage of? Stole their trucks from, putting others in bad financial situations? And now the thief cries foul because he was stolen from. Fuck him and fuck Mario. Rot in hell, bastards.

Jaden reassured them he would go get the check. "I'll be right back," he told them and walked out the door and out of their lives. "Enjoy the truck, motherfuckers," he thought aloud. He was free from his obligation. He told them the truth. He didn't know what was wrong with the truck. He was honest, and they were greedy. Honesty won. Honesty is always the best policy.

Chapter 33

JADEN HAD A new job the next day. He was known in the trucking circles as a good driver, one who could get the job done, so it didn't take long to find work. He found a great job. He became a union driver, making the most money per hour he ever made. He worked Monday through Friday, from 7:00 a.m. to 3:30 p.m., had great union benefits, and didn't have to work like a slave. The work was physical, handling underground water pipes, fire hydrants, and other piping, large valves, and accessories. But he liked that too. He wasn't afraid to put his back into it and to get dirty.

Jaden was doing well, and he and Victoria decided to buy a condo. The mortgage would be damn near as much as the rent they paid. Why not own it? They took about seven weeks and finally found a place, a two-bedroom condo, with one bath, completely remodeled. The price was in their range, so they decided to buy. The mortgage was a little higher than the rent they had paid, but they could afford it.

The new job, the new condo, his new life – for the first time Jaden was doing it the right way, and good things were coming his way. He was happy. Jaden had decided to run for the position of board of directors within six months of buying, and he got elected. He had seen some bad elements on the condo property, something that concerned him and wanted to deal with it before it got out of control. Now he was a board member. He set about gathering the information he needed to attack the problem.

He worked at his job for almost two years until the economy started its recession. The work was getting slow, the orders were not coming in as much, and he was the low man on the seniority list. Jaden was laid off. He went to the unemployment office and applied for benefits and then went about looking for a new job. No one was hiring. Work was slow everywhere. So he just sat on unemployment, collecting a check, which provided him with a lot of free time, enough time to sink his teeth in the existing problems on the condo property. Jaden studied the rules and regulations of the property, and he found major violations. He put a plan together and started his new mission.

The first thing Jaden attacked was the parking situation. There were cars there that shouldn't be there – cars that didn't have parking stickers and cars that did that shouldn't. The whole parking situation was in chaos, and Jaden took charge. He contacted the tow truck company and met with the supervisor, discussed his plan, and they coordinated together. On the first night of the plan, Jaden had thirty-two cars towed off the parking lot; the next night, seventeen; and the night after that, twelve. Jaden came in like gangbusters and surprised everyone. Everyone was scrambling to make sure their car was safe. At the same time Jaden instructed the management company they hired to send out a letter informing all owners and renters that there would be zero tolerance on parking lot rules. Within thirty days, every car was legit. Everyone parked in their assigned space.

The next order of business: Hire a security guard company and go after the gang members and drug dealings. Jaden trained the guards the way he wanted them to observe, report, and take action. Every night the police were called, whether it was for loitering, gang activity, and drug activity. Even for loud music the police were called, and their presence was felt on the property, and so was Jade's.

Jaden had instructed the guards to inform residents to keep their hats straight, being turned left or right on the property was considered gang activity and the police were to be called. Some of the gang members tested the guards and Jaden, but they stood strong, an unbreakable wall. The gang members lost the fight. The drug dealers lost the fight.

Jaden had spent countless hours collecting vital proof of drug dealing and, one day, went to the police station to speak to the tactical officers. He introduce himself, informed them about his complete past, and his role in life now. He presented the police with the evidence, his phone number, and a master key to get into every hallway on the property. He signed a letter of consent allowing the police to come onto the property to conduct searches and seizures and to conduct investigations. Jaden had given power to the police. Now ain't that a motherfuckin' trip? Jaden working with the cops. No one would believe it. The next few months was very active with arrest and evictions. The owners who rented were getting violations for rule infractions and the fines that came with that. Jaden wasn't playing; he was serious, and he was gonna win.

A couple times, individual gang members thought they could intimidate him – no chance. He would die protecting his investment and die protecting the people who were afraid. Jaden would put his life on the line. Would the assholes be willing to also? Nope. He knew it. Don't ever bluff with a man or woman willing to risk it all. The bluff never works.

Within a year and a half, the property was beautiful – no gang members, no drug dealing that could be seen, all cars where they should be, no loitering in the parking lot, and no crimes being committed. Jaden could see the change that took place, but it was most evident when he started noticing children playing in the courtyard without their parents watching them and when he saw people coming out of their units to walk around the property for a late-night stroll. *A job well done*, Jaden thought. The property was clean and safe but needed to be maintained this way every day. He knew it could go back to the old way in a matter of a month. Jaden was the guard dog.

He was also now well known in the nationhood, on the property and off. On the property, he was the guy who cared and who helped people out. Off the property, he was the guy who didn't play any games and kept a tight leash on the going-ons of the property. Jaden had full control of the property, something he wouldn't relinquish until the day he would sell his unit, and that wouldn't be for a long time he thought.

There were new people who would move in from time to time, trying to set up a drug store or trying to gangbang there, and Jaden was on them. It didn't take long at all for Jaden to sniff them out, and when he did, he was all in their shit. Every time they looked left, he was standing to the left; every time they looked to the right, he was there. He was their nemesis, and he didn't back down.

There were landlords who didn't care who they put in their units, just wanting the rent. Jaden served their asses too. The violations added up, and Jaden instructed the management company to send the info to the lawyer and bring the landlord to court. They won their case, and the association would evict the tenants and take over the control of the landlord's unit to collect rent for the purpose of paying off the fines. Jaden knew if he attacked the pocketbooks, they would get in line, and they did. Some fought harder and longer than the others, but in the end they all fell in line.

Jaden was paying his debt to society, and he felt good about it. He understood now why it took a lot of work to pay it, and he knew he would be repaying it for the rest of his life. He was given another chance at life, and he would show his appreciation every day.

The property now had a reputation as a safe place to live. The police rarely came on the property to patrol. Guess they felt Jaden had control of that. He would call if he needed them.

Jaden had also formed a cleaning company, to take over the cleaning of the property. It wasn't being done to satisfaction, and he was able to do it at a lower price, thus saving the association money. He had hired his sister to do the cleaning inside the buildings and his various people to do the outside cleaning. The outside cleaning was easy, just sweep up and liter, clean around the garbage bins, change the dog waste station garbage bags, and minor stuff like that, usually took about an hour a day, Monday through Friday. Everyone Jaden knew wanted that job, but he gave it to who needed it, switching people from time to time.

Truthfully, he liked being on unemployment. It gave him a chance to walk the property every day, talk to owners and tenants, and be aware of what the property needed and the goin'-ons. He liked the feeling of facing the criminal element and winning and understood the concern others had of doing so themselves. He thought this must be the reason he went through the life he did – to strengthen him for this challenge, to meet the fear and danger and not waiver, to remain steadfast in his pursuit for a better property. He knew it would take someone like him to get rid of people like him; his experience counted for something.

His whole life he can remember his dad attacking his character and his self-esteem, damaging Jaden every night with both physical and emotional abuse, the feelings of shame of being so poor, and the embarrassment that he did without simple things others had. Jaden remembered all of that shit, all the negative feelings he felt toward himself, and they had taken its toll. He remembered the people he had harmed in his life, both physically and emotionally, the stealing he had done to family and friends, the girls he had working as escorts, the fights, the shootings, and the stabbings. He remembered every single evil fuckin' thing he did, and it played in his heart and mind.

Hopelessness was something he felt for a long time also, but now he had hope. Now he had people stopping him on the sidewalks of the property, thanking him for his hard work. Even the cops had showed him respect, knowing his past didn't matter. They were judging him on his actions now. Jaden was feeling like a member of his community, like a part of something good, and it warmed his heart. All the board members and management company knew some of his past. He disclosed it to them when he became a board member. The residents also knew. He didn't try to hide it and didn't want to have some secret he kept from them. It was out in the open, and nobody was ever gonna use his past against him, ever again.

Chapter 34

AFTER SOME TIME of being on unemployment, Jaden went back to work. This time he took the only job he could at a remodeling center, making deliveries, at a much lower pay rate. It did feel good to get back to work, and he had a very cool boss, probably the best boss he had ever had. Jaden busted his ass for his boss. The boss knew it and was appreciative of that. They had developed a good working relationship and also a friendship. Jaden did whatever was asked of him, even the shitty stuff, the back-breaking shit . . . oh my god, did that shit hurt!

Three thousand pounds of tile is no fuckin' joke. To be lifting those boxes off the truck and carrying them into someone's garage was very hard. The pain that comes is harsh. Most of the deliveries were to the rich people's houses in the north suburbs, places like Highland Park, Wilmette, Skokie, and other places where us common people don't find ourselves driving home each night.

One thing he learned about rich people is that they don't appreciate very much. They expect very much. Never any thank-yous and never any tips, just a "Bye now. Thanks for breaking your back, and please don't ever come back unless I need a pyramid built." Yep, I got some resentment there too. I'll work on that later when I'm on my yacht that I bought with the money I make from the book sales.

Well, wouldn't ya know that Jaden went to do a delivery one Tuesday morning with a four-hundred-pound cast iron bathtub held on a wooden pallet by a plastic strap? Jaden went to do this delivery alone, as usual, and was able to get it off the truck. The customer refused the delivery because the saleslady, who was also the district manager's wife, figured that they ordered the wrong tub, something she did a lot, every day, but that seemed to never be brought to the light of management.

Well, Jaden had to get it back into the truck, and while lifting it, the plastic banding broke, causing the weight to shift, falling on Jaden and sending him to the hard concrete floor of the customer's garage. He had heard the plastic snap and felt the sudden weight shift, but all he could do was turn his body so that his broad, thick shoulders would take most of the impact, well, most of it. Once on the ground, he only felt major fuckin' pain. His back and neck were in excruciating pain, and he screamed out, tears streaming down his face, the pain not stopping, not relenting, only an agonizing sharpness tearing at his consciousness. He was immobilized, unable to move.

When the owner came out to the garage and saw the horrific sight, he screamed for his teenage son. Jaden could hear the father telling his son to help him to get the tub off the driver, and they were able to, but Jaden couldn't move, still numbed from the constant pain that had taken hold of his body. The father was on the phone to 911, almost panicking as he described the situation and gave the address. Once off the phone, he could hear the owner trying to reassure him that the paramedics would be there very fast. Just hold on, but he was slipping in and out and getting weaker by each second, only each shot of pain waking him up from the emptiness, recalling him back, demanding he feel what needed to be felt.

The owner waited about fifteen seconds before he called the paramedics back, yelling at them and telling them he thinks the driver is dying, and then he heard the sirens in the distance, getting louder very fast, until they were there at jade's side. "Are you allergic to any medication," asked a voice. "Nnnooo," Jaden whimpered. It was very hard for him to speak, to even mutter a single word. He felt a prick in his arm, and then he felt nothing soon after.

He was in and out of consciousness, awakened each time he felt the bumps in the road, but there was no pain anymore, but he couldn't think clear and couldn't focus. It was much easier to sleep, just wanting to sleep. Why won't they let him sleep? The bumps Jaden felt were not the road conditions. It was the paramedic shaking him, keeping him from blacking out or even into a coma. He just didn't want him to close his eyes. Almost at the hospital. Gotta keep this guy awake was his main concern.

Silently he was rushing his partner to hurry the fuck up. He knew time was of the essence. He saw the size of the tub and felt the weight of it as he and his partner moved it out of the way for the stretcher. "Fuck, this thing is heavy," he blurted out as they moved it. He couldn't even imagine the pain that would come if this fuckin' tub fell on him. Finally, they arrived and the ER team was fast and efficient. Within forty-five seconds, Jaden was in the ER being attended to.

The doctors were asking him questions, but he couldn't focus and couldn't put the words together; he was numb. The doctors were talking to each other, going over procedures, examining Jaden, trying to determine the extent of his injuries. They prodded, poked, pushed, felt him like a piece of fruit in the farmers' market.

The doctors ordered x-rays to be done and scheduled the MRI also, just to be safe. The orderly came to take Jaden to the x-ray department, Jaden unaware of anything except he was moving.

The customer had called Jade's job once the paramedics had left, explaining what had happened to their driver. Jaden's boss flew out the door of the store and sped away to the hospital, scared for his driver and scared for his friend. He felt guilty, knowing he should have sent two guys to do that delivery and knowing how heavy the tub was. He had sent Jaden before many times to do these deliveries, always by himself. He never had a problem, never once. That was one of the reasons he sent him today; he knew he could do it. He hadn't noticed the skid was secured by a plastic strap, no one had. If he had paid attention to it he would have sent two guys. He cursed the owner of the store, always complaining about employee hours, always cutting their time, leaving the delivery crew short of drivers but not deliveries.

Jaden was a fast worker and handled twice the delivery load than any driver. It was because of Jaden that the store was able to handle the workload, and he never complained. He said a prayer for his friend and pressed down even farther on the accelerator.

The morphine was wearing off. The pain was coming back, and the x-ray technician was moving him about to get him into the position he needed to get the proper x-ray shots, and each time it was hurting more and more. About thirty minutes later, the pain was back, just as strong as it was in the beginning, but not so much in his back, mostly in the neck, which Jaden told the doctors. They ordered some more morphine, lesser amount this time but enough to help with the pain. Jaden was fully conscious, aware of the doctors talking to one another, examining the x-rays and waiting for Jaden to go to the MRI room.

The doctors had informed Jaden there were no broken bones – a good thing – but Jaden could have told them that. Not that he ever had a broken bone, but he was sure from what he heard about it that he would know. Time for the MRI. That was slow and painless, all done in twenty-five minutes. The end result was three bulges in the neck.

What's a bulge? I'm glad you asked. In between each vertebra, there is a sack that has fluid. The purpose of this sack is to be a big pillow, stopping cartilage from touching each other when compressed. When fluid leaks out, it causes a bulge in that area, and does not perform its function completely. When pressure is applied there is pain. The cartilage sometimes hits the nerves, and then you hit the fuckin ground in major excruciating pain. Believe me. I know this shit from firsthand experience.

Jaden's boss was in the ER room and asked Jaden how he felt. They talked and Jaden explained what happened or at the parts he remembered. Eventually it was time to go, and Jaden was checked out. His boss gave him a ride home. This time he drove slow, trying to make the ride as painless for Jaden as possible. Jaden thanked his boss and went into his condo and then called a workman's comp attorney. He wanted to make sure he was protected and that he wasn't railroaded by the owner of the company.

The attorney came to his condo the next day. Jaden signed the papers, and the attorney went to work. Jaden went to see a doctor his attorney recommended, and the slow, painful process of rehab started. Jaden would be off of work for a total of five months. His days were spent going to rehab and resting. After three months of this, the pain was still there, so they scheduled the steroid shots into the neck, not as painful as he was led to believe. The first shot was in December; it didn't help at all, but the next shot in February did help a great deal.

After that Jaden was allowed to go back to work, but they had decided to lay him off. They said business was slow. Bullshit, Jaden hired another lawyer and sued their ass for discrimination against the American with disabilities. He won the suit and went on unemployment. He didn't fully recover. The bulges would be there forever, but it wasn't too bad. He could still work. He looked for work, but nothing was out there. He decided to take advantage of a program designed for people on unemployment to get training in specific fields. He had a CDL but they offered him to a chance to go to school and upgrade his class to an A.

CDLs are divided into three classes: C is for any single vehicle under sixteen thousand pounds total weight, B is for any single vehicle above sixteen thousand pounds, and A is for a combination vehicle (tractor trailer). Jaden took the classes for four weeks, and once he finished, he had a class A CDL, but he had additional endorsements on there. He could drive tractor trailers, double and triple trailers, and tankers and carry hazardous materials. He had the full CDL

Now with his new license, he went looking for work, sure he would find something, but he was wrong. Every place he went to either didn't accept felony convictions or wanted at least two years' experience. He was fucked, but he still had unemployment benefits and that helped. Every day he filled out applications. Every day he waited for a reply. Every day nothing.

He had bought a computer, a laptop, and had installed the Internet, mostly to have for informational purposes. That's what everyone says to justify it, I bet. Eventually Jaden learned about Myspace. He first got on to play a game called Mobsters. He loved it. It was fun and interactive with other players on Myspace. Then all of a sudden, he was getting these messages. "Is that you, Jaden?" is how they always started. Holy shit, people from his past were finding him and contacting him.

The first was his ex-wife's sister. She was cool, and they chatted for a bit, but Jade's girlfriend was mad about it and insecure about it, so Jaden quit communicating with her. He felt like torn about that decision. He wasn't doing anything wrong, but it was a problem. He wanted to keep chatting, but he understood how his girlfriend felt. He took the easy choice and hated that he did. He felt like a coward for doing that and resented that decision, a decision he would never make again.

Julie was making some scones and relaxing in the kitchen, drinking her coffee. She was back to the old routine and unhappy. The love was gone; there was no mistaking that, but she felt she had made a decision and was gonna stick with it, regardless of her feelings. There were some differences though in the marriage – less time spent together, more time for Julie, and doing what Julie liked to do. She spent a lot of time being involved in her kids after school activities. Those were her moments of true happiness. She just loved her children to death. The other great love was cooking and baking. She was chef Julie to everyone who knew her.

She kept having that weird dream again, walking along the Chicago Lakefront in late July. The air was very hot, but the breeze from the lake made it bearable. She was eleven years old in the dream and wearing her white jacket, the one she loved very much. Off in the distance, she could see him, a young boy about her age, trying to walk toward her, reaching his hand out as he got closer. Her heart started beating faster; she felt a sudden urge to close the gap and to grab hold of this boy's hand. She couldn't see his face clearly though. He was still too far away, but he was familiar. He was someone she knew long ago; she was sure of that. Just wanting to get closer she started to run toward him, almost close enough to see his face and to see his eyes, and then she would wake up.

Standing at her kitchen counter, she was trying to remember his face. If she could recall something from the dream, the boy was always a little too far away. She felt that feeling of change more often now, and it was getting stronger each day. She wished she could know what it is. She didn't even know how to imagine it. Maybe it would be something small or maybe a big change. She had no idea, but she knew it was coming. She wondered if it had something to do with the boy in her dreams. She wished she could recognize him; he was so familiar.

Chapter 35

THIS WAS THE first time Jaden had really explored the Internet – a lot of things at his fingertips and a lot of time passes by when you're on the Internet, hours go by in a blink of an eye. Jaden was researching all kinds of things that peaked his interest, but something he really was concerned about was the economy. He looked up every bit of information he could imagine, followed the links and followed the money. He was learning much about the way the world functions, how interlinked each society had become with each other, and how dependant.

The world market was something that was unpredictable. At least Jaden was out of his debt. He was only able to understand one major concept. The world economy had grown fast, much too fast to stay stable, something he was concerned about. He saw problems with the system and figured out the breakdown. With medical technology and medicine, the world population was increasing, and so were the demands on natural resources.

The very wealthy played the market on a very large scale. They were the true providers of the economy, the risk takers, but they would not gamble their fortunes, not risk their survival. When they got nervous, they would pull their money out. The banks would follow that trend and put a halt to the lending, drying the funds up for millions of small businesses. The end result is this: When money gets tight, people get nervous. They stop spending. When people stop spending, businesses stop making money and workers are laid off. Bills stop getting paid, and more workers are laid off. There becomes a sudden increase in unemployment; soon that money dries up.

With no jobs, the unemployed go on public assistance programs. That sudden increase becomes a burden on funding, funding that isn't there because the tax revenue has decreased from the lack of taxes collected. Soon the funding will be nonexistent. Can you see the problem here? No money and no jobs, but people still need water, food, and shelter. People will be filled with fear, people with families, how do they survive? The scenario will not be pretty. Human nature will resort to instinctual needs and those needs being fulfilled, no matter the cost. Jaden knew what was to come if the economy didn't fix itself. He decided it was time to make a plan, a plan to survive.

The thought of the economy didn't consume him, but he did prepare. He did his research, looking for all the variables he could think of, and the plan became well formed and very plausible. It would be a harder life, but it would be a life. The plan was for his family and his friends. He put it together and designed some indicators to watch for – signals that would show him that the time has come, and once those signals showed themselves, he would forward instructions on what to do and how to do it to everyone he had on his list. Jaden would not be going though; his path had a different direction.

His amended his list was getting very short. There were four people left on his list, and with the Internet, he was finding the others and making his amends, except for the last one on the list. That would be different, the final amends, the end of his journey. Jaden had written his list to follow his life in reverse; he would work it backward, ending in his child hood, getting closer to the source of what destroyed his innocence, the source of what changed him, which made him take the path in life that he walked.

He was not born into this world as a hurtful person; he was conditioned that way from the years of abuse at the hands of his parents and from the others who were fucked up also. All of this made him a violent person, a scared kid trying to protect himself, trying to protect his feelings, his heart, and his soul. He tried to keep what little he had left. These thoughts and feelings still so fresh in his mind and still so fresh in his heart. It hurt so very much to feel, never relenting and never healing completely, but he was getting closer to the beginning of that hurt. There the final amends will take place.

Jaden's head hurt, all the planning in his mind, all the directing and trying to arrange all the pieces, putting it all together, took its toll on him. He has spent a long time following and adjusting to stay on his path. He looked forward to the destination. He looked forward to resting. Soon he thought, hopefully it will be soon.

Life was tough, with the complex arrangement of others in a person's life, it was difficult to manage. First, a person is an individual having goals and dreams that are desired. Trying to obtain and reach those things are difficult in itself, and then when you add family members and their personalities and attitudes, complications arise. Dealing with family shit is very trying on a person. We all try to get along but everyone knows that family arguments and fights occur a lot. Well, in Jade's family it does. Trying to work those issues out and still deal with one's own life is hard.

Then if you add friends in your life. Well, the whole thing becomes much harder, way more complicated. Then add people from work, school, and neighbors, and a person's life has just become a lot to manage, trying to navigate the circle without creating problems almost impossible. What if you had children to the circle? Life is hard but rewarding when we manage it successfully, when we are taught the right tools to use. Those tools are simple: love, compassion, unselfishness, sharing, morals, values, empathy, and self-esteem. Remove one of the tools and the job gets harder. The more tools you remove, the harder it gets. Jaden's tools were removed, replaced by mistrust, suspicion, fear, and a whole bunch more of broken tools. That's what he had to build with; he built a prison for his soul.

So Jaden look forward to the rest that waited for him, the peace of mind at the end of the journey. He wanted to complete the list and end the journey. He wanted to be healed, no longer wanting what hurt him to hurt anymore, to be able to be healed from the poison that surged through his veins, burning his soul, keeping him incarcerated to those emotions. Freedom was not far away, within reach, but there were four left. He desperately wanted to find the three. He knew where the last one was. The last person on Jaden's list was never very far away. He had always kept tabs on the last one, always knew the whereabouts, always watching.

Four to go. That was his thought, *Almost done.* This was his journey, and he would stay on it. The path was clear to him, and he was focused. The only thing that bothered him was those crazy dreams he was having. It started out with him walking along the Chicago lakefront. In the dream though he was eleven years old and the lakefront looked as it did back then. As he walked, he felt he was in some kinda of spiritual place. The movements of the birds, people, and even the air was slower, almost slow motion. As he walked, he spotted a little girl off a ways, unable to take his eyes off her, his heart starting to beat faster, his body flushed with an excitement he hasn't felt in a very long time. *Who is she?*, he wondered. She looks familiar, but who?

He started walking faster in the little girl's direction, but the distance didn't seem to be closing as if he was walking in place. He started to run toward her, reaching out his hand, trying to reach her, his mind and heart telling him to get to her, reach her, hug her, and never let her go. He was starting to feel the urgency so much that was near panic. He had to get to her. This was his last chance, but he wasn't getting any closer. There was something that obstructed him from getting closer, but he couldn't see it. It was something invisible. Damn! Why can't he get to her? Then he wakes up. Covered in sweat, heart still racing, he tries to remember what her face looked like. Who was she?

Jaden had gone with his girlfriend and her best friend to her best friend's family reunion. He hated these things, but this one he wanted to go to. Victoria's best friend's half sisters were with a girl Jaden had known back when he was sixteen. The two had hung out together, and partied together. *They were cool. It would be nice to see her after all these years,* Jaden thought. So he went, and it was good. He had seen her, they had talked, and the reunion was over – no big deal.

He didn't stay long. He never stayed long at any get-together or event. He would go, mingle, and leave, never leaving a bad impression, always being welcomed back. His girlfriend stayed. She was gonna go party. This was their routine. They would show together then go different ways. He never suffocated her, always respected her space, but not always the case for him. Victoria was jealous and insecure. She always kept a watchful eye on Jaden. She knew his past and knew he was sneaky and a flirt. Yep, she was always all up in his shit. Normally that didn't bother him. What did bother him were the accusations and the insinuations. It's one thing to be accused when you are guilty of something, but when innocent, it hurts to be accused.

Jaden knew Victoria didn't trust him, even though he had been faithful to her since the beginning, something he had decided he wanted to do. He wanted to be in at least one relationship in which he didn't cheat. Once in his life, he didn't want to betray a woman's trust, even if the woman didn't trust him. This was very hard at times. There were situations where he had to run away, actually run away. He had kept his word though. He hadn't betrayed her or himself. He liked the fact that he had at least this accomplishment. This one thing no one could take from him. At the same time, he knew their relationship was coming to an end. He had that feeling again – that feeling he had felt one time before in his life, the only time he had recognized it.

He made the hardest decision in his life then but knew he must follow the course. Following the course had broken his heart and had taken something he had loved from him. He now felt that feeling again, and because of the past feeling, he was unsure if he wanted to follow, but life sometimes makes it impossible for you to ignore its plan for you, so he knew it was gonna end, just wasn't sure when and how. He told himself he would remain faithful to the day it ended; he owed that much to himself and Victoria.

Jaden reconnected with people from his past. He was trying to find the ones on the list. He didn't have many friends, maybe three at the most. He didn't let people into his life. He knew a lot of people, but to be friends required something more than casual conversation each day. Jaden's idea of friendship was about knowing one another, not just habits or daily things, not only birthdays and likes and dislikes; it was much more. It required trust and a risk of being vulnerable. There is where the problem lay for Jaden, being vulnerable to someone new. He never felt like he could trust completely, so he feared being vulnerable to being hurt. Remember that prison he built with those broken tools? Well, this is where it gets in the way of a person's life, well one of the ways.

Like I said, Jaden didn't have friends. He had acquaintances – that was it. He didn't truly know how people from his past had remembered him, either in a positive way or a negative. He figured negative though; he wasn't a nice person back then. He still sent friend requests though to the people he remembered, and he got a lot of friend requests back – a whole lot. Maybe he wasn't such an asshole after all, he thought, not believing all the people who had sent requests.

This is misleading though. Jaden was new to the site, didn't realize that people were in unspoken contests to have as many friends as possible on the site, kinda like a prestige thing. *Oh my god, are you fuckin' serious?* He laughed his ass off. Well, it was more like, "OMG, LMAO ru fkg sra, cnt bel it. Hahaha, LOL." Just thought I would put that in there. That's communication now, a bunch of letters and smiley faces. Mail is done without a stamp. This shit was new to Jaden. He didn't understand most of the abbreviations, and he didn't give a fuck. He would type each word, but he did use the LOL, LMAO, and the yellow faces; it was strictly peer pressure you see.

He realized quick that of his sixty-eight friends, he only talked to about sixteen. Half of them were his family; the other half were friends. Jaden would search his friends' pages for their friends. He was looking for the people on his list, but there was someone else he wanted to find, not sure who it was, but thinking he would know when he found the person.

Each day, he searched, something inside him was driving him, motivating him to continue. Then he saw her name and, without a moment's hesitation, clicked the button and sent a friend request to her. She was the one; he knew it in his heart and soul, and soon everything was starting to make sense to him. His journey through life was clearer than it ever had been. He never forgot her; he remembered her name, her look, and her smile. He remembered a lot of details about her; it was Julie.

He thought back to the time when he was eleven years old, in the classroom, to seeing Julie. The memories came rushing back. She was pretty. Jaden was attracted to her, feeling something in his gut, making him nervous all of a sudden. *What the fuck is going on with me?* he asked himself. His palms were sweaty. He wanted to talk to her but felt unsure of himself, lacking confidence, having a huge lump in his throat. She looked at him. He caught her and knew something was there, but what is something? At eleven years old, Jaden was discovering that feeling, a longing for the attention of a girl, not the sexual part, but the emotional part of it. The heart beating fast, the constant staring at one another – you remember, don't ya?

The classroom was like this. Most of the kids knew each other, and there were the popular kids and then there were the smaller cliques, maybe three hanging together, usually just two. Most of the kids knew each other from the area, from hanging out in the summertime. Jaden knew just two kids, the other peewee Royals. The school had Royals there. Most of the Royals were in eighth grade. Jaden was in fifth grade. The fact that he knew eighth graders was a plus for him. He wasn't alone.

Julie had friends at school, mostly her age and her grade, but her sister was older and in the higher grade. I believe she knew the Royals, maybe even made friends with some, which was cool for Julie. Julie was different than Jaden. She did her schoolwork and completed her homework assignments. She applied herself toward her education, not Jaden. Jaden didn't do homework, never did, and his grades suffered for it. He was not stupid; he passed all his exams, he just didn't do homework.

Back to the good stuff, well, some of it are good, but it didn't work out well. Remember those broken tools of Jaden's? Eventually they talked, Jaden and Julie, and they liked each other. Julie didn't say much though, kinda quiet and reserved, but her eyes and smile said everything. She had these bright blue eyes that could light up a room, fill it with warmth and softness, and a smile that invited you in, welcomed you, putting you at ease. Her hair was brownish blond. Well, that's the color Jaden remembers, and he's not gonna argue the point, and it flowed below her shoulders, with it parted to one side of her face.

She was definitely very pretty, and something else? Something he couldn't quite put his finger on. Something about her attracted him to her in a different way, in a way that was something new to him. Damn, he didn't know what it was, but he liked it. The broken tools though were all he had to work with though, and insecurity and low self-esteem were building shame.

Jaden looked at his life – drunk father, addicted mother, poor family, violent home. He was ashamed of his life and his parents. He also knew his life and the direction he was going wasn't right for her. She was good, she was pure, and she was innocent. He knew he could never ask Julie to come over and hang out, never allow here to see his home life, for Christ's sakes. His family could be drunk and start beating the shit out of him in front of her, or worse. This fuckin' scared the shit out of him. What could he do? Nothing he realized, so the friendship never went further, but instead he pulled away, resenting his situation even more, killin' his soul a little bit more than before.

They still talked here and there, but he had to guard himself from being hurt, but more than that, Julie was so good and pure, compared to him. She was something he would never be and he didn't want to taint that goodness. He wasn't good enough for her. With the life he had, he felt like garbage, like trash that gets discarded every day. There was no hope for him, and thankfully, he had not yet reached the point where he didn't care for others yet. Thankfully he had enough humanity in him to push Julie to a safe distance, out of reach of the poison that flowed in him, but Jaden was sad.

Chapter 36

THAT WAS HIS memory, his feelings, and his despair at the time. At eleven years old, he was able to feel the burdens of a destructive life that awaited him. How the hell can a child process that type of shit and remain normal? To have a chance in this world? Life is hard by itself. To add broken tools to the mix only removes the hope for something good to come. Jaden hadn't ever expected good to come to his life growing up. He expected the worse, and it came.

Now as an adult, he acted the part, playing a role, surviving as it were, but the agony of the past never vanished, always with him, buried deep within his being, a constant reminder of where he came from and what he had been through. The gunshot wounds, the knife marks, and the stitches were the physical scars he bore on the outside. The emotional scars were the ones that he carried on the inside. Those were the scars that never healed and never stopped bleeding.

Then came the day he found her. Right there on his computer screen, in the list of friends of one of his friends, he saw her name, Julie. Anxiety, nervousness, and curiosity had him all at the same time. He saw the box on the screen, "Send friend request," and he thought for a moment, wondering if she would remember him. He clicked the button, and there was no turning back. Jaden thought about it all day and even the next day and decided he would wait and see. Julie didn't get back to him right away, probably one of them people who barely ever checked her page, he thought.

He continued to talk to some of his friends on the site, just catching up on time, rehashing old glory days of hanging out when he got the message that she had accepted the friendship, so far so good. He was curious to see how life had been to her, where she had gone, what she had done with her life. Jaden was always curious about people from his past. He wondered if they had traveled a road similar to his or if life was kinder to them. The one thing he did learn was that the more fucked-up someone's childhood was, the more similar their road had been to his.

As soon as he got the chance, he sent Julie a message and she replied. Then another message and then another reply. Soon they were chatting just about every day. The theme was kind of like a get to know you all over again. Jaden was cautious not to share too much. He didn't want to weird her out, as some before. He eased into the parts of his past that were colorful, to say the least. He enjoyed all of it – learning about her with each chat session and her learning about his.

Julie definitely had a great sense of humor. She was a wise ass like Jaden; he appreciated that. He hated chatting with someone who couldn't smile or laugh and couldn't find the humor in things. And she could conversate well. The topics were deep and meaningful, another thing he appreciated. Too many times, people talked about surface things – all shallow bullshit, generally a waste of time, never contributing to the friendship anything more than a quick hello, none of the others would do.

With Julie, Jaden was comfortable, able to say what he felt and thought, able to reveal things he normally wouldn't, and he could be honest. Jaden was tired of not being able to be completely honest with people; he will give them some but withold the rest. He knew they could not deal with him much more. Julie, on the other hand, was dealing with all of it and not judging him and not holding him in contempt. Jaden had revealed some of the things from his past, and Julie would tell him that was wrong. She didn't like what he had done, but she did not hate him for it and wouldn't push him away for it. Now Jaden was building a friendship, one built out of honest and respect. This is what he wanted out of a friend. This is what he would return also. He wouldn't lie to her about his past, or if asked a question about his life, he may not answer the question, but he wouldn't lie.

What did concern Jaden was the fact that Julie had seen the pain he felt as a child and saw it through his eyes. *How could she understand what she saw at that age?* he wondered. Was she the only one who could see it, or were there others? He hadn't remembered anyone else ever saying that to him, not even close to it. He decided to ask her the next time they chatted what exactly she saw. "You were being torn by something" was her reply. Jaden was floored by that response. She could see the struggle within him and the constant battles he fought every day. Julie didn't know exactly what those battles were, but she knew they existed. Jaden realized that Julie was very intuitive about people. She was able to read things about them, a natural talent. Maybe she would be the one, the one who was strong enough for him to reveal everything to.

Jaden had searched from the day he made his list for one person from his past who could handle what he needed to reveal, a complete accounting f himself, a washing of the soul. The person needs to be able to understand what he shared and be able to process the information and still not judge him. He needed to know what her boundaries were and what limitations she had. There was much to learn about Julie. He didn't feel like he was using her or that he lied. He honestly wanted to establish a friendship with her, one that would be strong and healthy. So each time they talked, he shared some of himself with her, and she shared with him.

He looked at the photos she posted of her life. Wow, she was beautiful and definitely in shape. She was married and had two children, one son and one daughter. Their names won't be in the book. They have a right to their privacy. Jaden recognized Julie's sister; he remembered her from school. He remembered being afraid of her; she always looked like she wanted to beat Jaden up. He kept his distance. That thought put a smile on his face, such a long time ago. Jaden realized by now that Julie had what it would take to be the *you* he would give his final confession to. She would be the second to the last person he would make his amends to then he would finish the journey. The last person on the list was himself. He would apologize to her for using her for such a thing, but he needed her.

She was in his mind and heart – the perfect person from his past to share his secrets, for her to know and realize the monster he sees himself as. This would be no easy task for Julie. She is so against any type of violence. It sickens her heart to know of these things, and the final violent act that Jaden would commit would test her resolve, maybe even her sanity. She would be the only one he will reveal his plan to, but he couldn't just tell her. He needed a way to do it where she wouldn't run away, afraid to take on the role destiny has chosen for her. If she would have known what his plan was and where his journey ended, she would end all contact with him, not because she was angry but because she would try to stop the final outcome. He loved her for that.

Jaden decided to start the revealing process in the disguise of a book he would write, tell the tale, and reveal the truth, allowing her to read the book while in its beginning phase. He would send her chapters as they were written, slowly giving her the truth about his life, the crimes he had committed, the monster at the other end of the computer screen, a safe distance from her and those beautiful bright blue eyes, the eyes that could melt the hardness within him. They could make him to feel guilty about his final amends, tempt him to not finish his journey.

Jaden knew now what he didn't know back when he first met Julie. He had fallen in love. She was and will always be his first love, a love he never was able to experience, a love he searched for his entire life, only to find mere imitations, but not the real thing. Julie was the real thing, the one who made his heart beat faster, his palms sweaty, commanding his gaze upon her if she was present in the room. He knew with all his experience and knowledge that the first day he saw her she would forever remain in his heart, and he had yearned for her his whole life, but always came away empty and alone.

Judy looked kinda like Julie. She had certain qualities that Julie had, and Jaden found familiarity in them. He was attracted to those qualities, to Judy, because she reminded him of Julie, but he didn't know that then. The thing he knows now is that if you want something and know the real thing, then the fake one will never do. If a man proposes to a woman, does he give her a cubic zirconia for an engagement ring? No. He gives her a diamond. Jaden wanted his diamond. But that's not what his destiny was. His life wouldn't follow that path.

He had nothing but broken tools. Everything about him was fucked up, no matter how hard he tried to succeed in life, he was still Jaden. He would try to act the part of a good man, but truly he wasn't. He knew himself better than anyone. He knew it would only be a matter of time that he would be able to keep up the charade he played. Sooner or later, the life he built would crash down, fall apart around him, and once again those instincts would kick in and he would be the monster. You cannot build a solid foundation with broken tools, and that's what Jaden had to work with. He was unable to fix the tools.

He started the book, and the words came out so fast, as if the barricades were opened, allowing the pressure of confinement to finally break, releasing the pain and agony he had held for so long. Each word had pierced his soul, each sentence a shattered shard of reality, and each paragraph a reminder of the truth, the truth of what had happened to him as a child, the brutality he had experienced from his father, the abandonment of love and trust, the destruction of his self-esteem, the constant daily beatings hurting him and terrorizing him, the shame that surrounded his being, his existence. Jaden was reliving the past as he wrote, and the emotional wave had crested and he was crying.

Each time he wrote he cried, these were not just words on the screen or ink on a paper. This was Jaden – all he was inside and all he had done in his life, not a story but a chronicle, a confession. He cried over the pain he felt and the pain he caused. Suddenly he was more resolved at finishing his journey. He needed to complete it to finally rest. Just to finally let the secrets be known was a relief to him, having spent the past forty-three years protecting the monster's damaging chaos, the sickness that controlled his every move and every decision in life. Without any restraints, nothing holding him back, he was letting everything go, and the overwhelming release of the emotions had him on edge, but determined to get the confession finished, determined to reach the point where he could rest, an eternity of peace was at the end of this road, and the road was narrowing.

Chapter 37

JULIE COULDN'T BELIEVE she had received a friend request from Jaden. It must have been thirty-two years ago since she had seen him. She had to sit back and remember, trying to recall the memories from her mind, packed away far in the depth of childhood times. She was around eleven years old when she saw him walk into the classroom. She couldn't take her eyes off him. Jaden had dark brown hair, about two inches below his shoulders, parted in the middle, and wavy. His facial features were actually pretty well proportioned to his head, nothing that someone could make fun of or laugh at, not that anyone would.

He stood there with a bad-boy look, an attitude that said he wasn't gonna take any of that new-kid bullshit. All of that didn't matter to her. What did make a difference was his eyes. Jaden's eyes were a very light brown, almost a hint of orange, almost. To look into his eyes was like looking into his soul. She couldn't look away. There was something she saw but couldn't put her finger on it. She was definitely attracted to him. He was cute.

Julie remembered some of Jade's mannerisms, the way he talked and behaved in class. Yep, he was a bad boy. That was for sure. Jaden may have been new to the school, but he was from one of the hoods. She had noticed he was friends already with two other kids in the class – trouble makers – and she noticed he knew a lot of older kids in school, the ones that were in a gang called the Royals. She didn't know if he was a Royal but felt he was. Her instincts were usually right when it came to people. She was interested in Jaden, and it seemed he was interested in her. *But what does that mean?* she wondered.

The both of them had met and talked her and there, and every chance she got, she would just stare into his eyes, those soft, troubled eyes. What was it that they held? Why did he look like he was torn by something? She wanted to get to know him better and wanted to be close to him. There was something strange happening to her every time she was near him, every time they talked. Her heart beating faster and her palms sweaty, she would feel hot in her body, not burning but just heated, something she never felt before. She was sure it had something to do with Jaden. The dreams – he had to be the boy in the dreams she was having. Holy shit, that was so weird. The dreams had come first and then his friend request. Something was happening. There was a change coming. Would Jaden be a part of that change?

There were a couple times they would meet after school, talking about different things, but the topic never mattered. They were both only interested in spending time with each other, not really knowing why. What do you expect of two eleven-year-olds? They had no clue they had both felt their first hint of love and attraction with the opposite sex. Julie would travel to Pot Park, a pretty good distance from her house, but never able to stay long, wanting to stay forever, wanting to be next to Jaden as long as possible. She had felt they were getting along well, getting close, until he started to pull away, eventually ending the meetings altogether. She didn't understand why, but she knew he was fighting something inside him, being torn in different directions. She was hurt when he stopped wanting to be around her, but she was more hurt in not knowing why.

"Wow, that was so long ago," Julie said aloud. Nobody was home, her husband at work and the kids still at school. Julie had the day off from work, deciding to upload some pictures to her page. That's when she noticed the friend request from Jaden, her heart starting to beat to an old familiar pace. She was ecstatic that he requested the friendship and had questions for him, wanting to know what ever happened to him and how his life was now. She accepted the request, and the chat sessions started almost immediately. She had crossed into a territory she had no clue of its direction, but she didn't care. Jaden was back in her life.

The two of them started talking and the conversation just flowed, no real awkward moments, almost like they knew each other without ever separating. She loved the way he used words, putting things together in a refreshing way, so unlike the other people she chatted with. He was honest with his answers to her questions – honest with his humbleness. She liked that about him, wondering about his eyes. Oh, he was a flirt and very good at it, putting a smile on her face with the things he said, never being disrespectful, just a flirt.

There was something about him though. She couldn't quite place her finger on it, but she knew there was something. He seemed like he had an experience about him, but which experience, she didn't know. Their conversations were pretty interesting. Jaden had shared some of his life with her, but with some reservation, maybe a little concerned that she would somehow judge him. *That's silly*, she thought. That was not her way. Julie felt like she was pretty open-minded about life. She was not naive about what happens in the world, and she conveyed this to Jaden. Actually she found what little he had shared so far to be interesting.

One day, when she was on her page, she had become curious as to how Jaden looked after so long of not seeing him. She went to his page and clicked on his photos. Within a second of seeing his photo, she had caught his eyes, and those old feelings had resurfaced. His eyes were the same as they were all those years ago, still very mesmerizing, sexy, and still torn. He had gained some weight and had his head shaved bald. He was definitely a thick man, big boned. He looked like he had a presence about him. The pictures were of Jaden and Victoria in Fort Lauderdale, Florida, on vacation with Victoria's two best friends. Julie studied the pictures, memorizing every detail she could of Jaden and then pushing those feelings back down, out of her thoughts, somewhere where they couldn't do no harm.

Sitting on her couch, she finished her coffee and scones, smiling at the warm thoughts she had of Jaden, smiling at the what-ifs, unable to push the feelings away just yet, wanting to play with them and wanting to imagine what could have been – those school yard crushes, innocent fantasies of a preteen girl. Julie wasn't a preteen girl anymore; she was a woman. She had grown up and out. She was healthy and athletic, had a very nice athletic figure, and was well endowed in the upper area. Standing about five feet five, she was very attractive and had that sex appeal about her.

Not being conceited, just realistic and honest, she liked the way she looked and knew Jaden liked it too. He had said so in a couple different chat sessions. He said she was hot! That always makes a woman smile, why wouldn't it? *Shit, what am I doing?* she questioned herself. *I'm married with children.* The reply came to fast, almost as a defensive answer from a guilty person. Was she guilty of something? Jaden had no doubt awakened something in her, something she felt for a very long time but didn't want to deal with. Hoping what she kept bottled up would just change or disappear, but it never did.

Wow, Jaden is gonna write a book. She thought that was a cool idea, especially after he gave her a small look into some of his life. She wondered how that would come out. She did think he could write. He showed that much in his chatting text. She hoped it would be good reading. She hoped she would be pulled into the story. She had no idea.

The writing started, and he had finished three chapters already and sent them to her via e-mail, and she pored right into the story. "*Holy shit, he is a good writer.* She was captivated by his flow of the story, loving the way he expressed his thoughts and didn't stray from the topic. She was finished within a matter of minutes. Reading had always been one of her strengths, a passion of hers. When she finished the chapters, she got on the computer right away, wanting to encourage Jaden to keep the writing going. She was getting the full story of his childhood memories, the life he experienced growing up in his home. The shit he went through devastated her though. The abuse he suffered in his home was terrible, not right, something that made her angry. They had shared some similarities as children. She had seen some abuse also, not toward her, but toward her mom. She felt a kinship with Jaden, wanting to wrap her arms around him and protect him, protect them both. She always knew there was something behind the sad torn look in his eyes, and now she had the answer; now she understood his pain.

Chapter 38

JADEN WISHED HE could watch as Julie read his story. He wanted to see her expressions as she read the different pieces of his past and wanted to know how it touched her – her reactions to everything he revealed. All he knew is what she told him she felt. He trusted that, but there are things people do with their expression that tell so much more than words. They reveal the other stuff. That's what he wanted.

It is December first. He just finished chapter 25 and sent it to Julie. He knew there would only be thirty chapters and had constructed the whole plan in his head, from beginning to end. Chapters 26 through 30 he would withold from Julie until the time was right. He would send her the rest after Christmas. He didn't want to fuck that up for her. He knew once she discovered the truth, what his plan was, her whole life was gonna change. At the moment, she realized this was no book, just a confession. She would understand what the final act was gonna be. He was trying to explain to her in the end chapters that this is what he wanted, something he had to do, hoping she would understand over time.

Jaden had already picked the date, January 1, 2001, very symbolic: 1-1-11, the symbolic meaning of one being the start of something, something without Jaden. He was ready. He had prepared for this over the past months. He had written out a last will and testament, leaving a little something of himself with his family. Jaden decided long ago that the person last on the list would be him. He himself had harmed him in ways that were terrible and permanent. He had been his own worst enemy, the monster he feared. Now the road was coming to an end. He would take his own life. His last final murder would be of himself. He wanted to end the pain and agony he had lived with for so long, quiet the beast within him, and lay to rest the unhappiness he felt. Life was not what he wanted; he wanted death.

He didn't believe in heaven and hell, so there was no controlling fear that what he would do would send him to some make-believe lake of fire. He knew exactly what would happen. His body would die, and his energy would be absorbed by the energy that was all around us. Some of that energy was Jimmies, some of it was his unborn child, and some was his dad. Jaden knew that in his death, he would have closure and would finally be healed from his pain and sickness. He was tired of using the broken tools to work with; it's time to throw those tools away.

He knew his girlfriend, Victoria, would be going out that night to celebrate New Year's Eve. He would be alone. He decided he would go to Indian Boundary Park, a place from his childhood memories, a place he always felt happy at. His final look upon this planet would be of a pleasant place. He had picked up the gun about six months ago from an old connection of his. He put the gun away, keeping it hidden from Victoria.

Now he had the gun in his hand. He had disassembled it and was oiling it up, making sure the weapon would be fully functional for the task at hand. Jaden had played his part perfectly, not one person in his life knew of what was coming. He acted like his life was moving forward, even taking a promotion at work, acting excited about it, revealing nothing otherwise. There was no reason for anyone to suspect his intentions. To them Jaden was doing very well and happy. Suicide is the farthest thing from their minds. Whoever knows when a person is contemplating suicide? Don't they always act like nothing is wrong until you find them afterward?

Okay, the plan is to leave out at about 9:00 p.m. and head to Indian Boundary Park and wait for the moment the clock strikes twelve midnight. If he planned it well, and he was sure he did, Julie should be finishing the book around ten thirty. That's when all hell breaks loose in her head. He should eventually get that call from her at about eleven fifteen. He smiled. He had tried to call her phone once, but she didn't answer. She later had told him she didn't need complications like that in her life. He never called her again. Funny, she would be calling him now. *Hmmmm, should I answer?* he thought with a smile, knowing he would.

He would like to talk to her during his final moments. She was after all his first love. He knew how the situation would play out; he had predicted the whole scenario in his mind. He only hoped the timing was right, hoping she would read the chapters as soon as she got them. He had built up the suspension of what was in the book to Julie, taunting her with the unknown, driving her crazy to find out what he wrote. Julie had a curious nature about her; he played into that nature. He was almost positive she would read the book as soon as he sent it to her. He would send it at 9:00 p.m. on December 31.

He still needed to finish now the final two chapters. The last two were descriptions of what was to come, what was happening, and the final amends. Jaden hated the fact that Julie's life would change after January first, but he knew she was strong enough to come to terms with it. It wasn't like she was in love with him, not like there was a chance of the two of them ever being together. He threw that chance away, protecting her from him. *That is so fucked up*, he thought. *I walked away from her when I was eleven so I wouldn't hurt her, and now I'm gonna end up hurting her anyways. damned if ya do and damned if ya don't.*

He had attempted to see if he could pick up on any type of feelings she would have for him during the chat sessions, but she had been reserved, not hinting even a little of what she felt. She had told him though that she was unhappy in her marriage, feeling like her husband and her were not meant to be together. That's because she was meant to be with Jaden, he wanted to say, but held his tongue, remaining silent. He wanted to reach through the miles of space that separated the both of them, to pull her into his embrace, to feel her body pressed against his, and to inhale the smells of her hair, her lotions, her essence. He longed to hold her and comfort her, to comfort himself, to have the one thing he wanted for the longest of time, to love unconditionally, and to be loved that way. For Jaden it wasn't about the sex; it was all emotional and all spiritual, but he knew it would never come to be. Julie didn't have those feelings for him. He was not the one she wanted.

He continued to bring the book up to the present time, to have it complete and ready for her. The time was passing, and he typed with a feverish pace. The finish line was in sight. He had but a small distance to close, just about done with chapter 28 and was gonna start chapter 29 and begin the emotional roller coaster. He went over all the details in his head, tweaking the flaws or little things he left out. He had written out all his personal information pertaining to his bank accounts, basically all his passwords. He wanted Victoria to have access to whatever funds he had left. She would need them to pay the bills.

Leaving Victoria wasn't something he didn't think much about. She was his girlfriend for the past ten years. They had shared their lives together, and there were some really great memories, but he was gonna finish the journey, and she was still young enough to move on with her life. He figured she would be okay. Leaving her was not something that caused him any sorrow; he just didn't feel it. He wished he had but there was no regret in him for leaving Victoria this way, part of the reason he had to finish his journey, to destroy the monster that had no empathy for others.

He had his birthday coming up, December tenth. His youngest sister's birthday was on the ninth. They would spend it together with their family. This would be his last birthday celebration, his best celebration. He would not argue with any of his family. He was gonna enjoy the party and play Monopoly. He normally never took many pictures of himself, the reason why was never clear to him. He just didn't was all he knew, but this time he would take many pictures, something for his family. He was proud of his family. All of them had made changes in their life, faced many struggles, and came through safe. Their story is just that, their story. Maybe one day they will write a book and make some money, so I won't tell their story.

The birthday party was great. Everyone came, and there was not one argument. The food was plentiful and good. The company was even better. The whole family was playing board games and having fun. The first game was Cranium. That was about acting out clues, drawing clues on paper with eyes shut, or making clues out of clay – very fun game. The next game was Monopoly. Did I ever tell you that Monopoly was my favorite game? No, I don't think I did.

That game has been our family game since the dawn of time. I can remember my parents playing that game with my dad's brother and wife when I was very little. We would all go over to my uncle's house and the adults would drink beer and play Monopoly. The kids had their own Monopoly game, the standard edition, but my uncle had the special edition, the deluxe package – nicer board, better design on the pieces. All the pieces were shiny; I always liked the shiny pieces better. That was for you, Julie. At least I could do for what you will go through very soon.

Always watching the adults play created a sense of that was the big game, the real deal. All four of the adults were Monopoly experts. They knew the game and knew the rules without fail. It was always an intense game, especially with the amount of drinking they did. When the kids would play it was exciting, but nothing would be as exciting as to play with the pros who sat at the kitchen table. Everyone of us kids was excellent at Monopoly. We all had a love for the game like no other. Maybe it was us trying to measure up to our parents, giving them bragging rights and making them proud.

The only problem with the adults playing Monopoly was the game never would have a winner. Something would happen while they played to cause a big fight, and the board would sail into the air, the pieces flying into different directions, searching for a hiding place. That was our cue; all the children were experienced at this point. We knew what was coming, and we ran for a hiding place, praying we wouldn't be found, and that some drunk motherfucker wouldn't take it out on us. Jaden and his cousins had shared similar childhoods. They too had been beaten on many occasions by their drunk father. All the kids shared in that bond.

Jaden sat at the table now with his five-year-old nephew, who desperately wanted to be a part of what the adults were doing. Jaden looked at him and then smiled and told him to pull up a chair and play. The look of excitement his nephew had warmed Jade's heart. He wanted his nephew to experience the game for the first time, the right way – no violence and no fear, just simple pure enjoyment of the game and the interaction with his family.

His nephew's mom would make all the decisions regarding property trades, except when it came to trading with her. Then the rest of the players would vote. Majority would win. Jaden would manage his nephew's property, make the decisions on what to build and how many to build when it came to houses and hotels. The rest would be up to his nephew and the throw of the dice. His nephew won the first game, and Jaden couldn't have been happier for him. His nephew ran through Jade's condo, telling all his family members he won, he won. Jaden hated the thought of leaving his nephew's life come January first, but the decision was made.

Jaden looked at his family, watching them all get along, talking, and discussing all kinds of things. He loved them all. The vicious cycle was breaking. He was sure of that. Maybe one or two more generations and his family will have erased the poison that been spread among them. He hoped they would be able to move on after his death. He had written his final letters to them all – his last good-byes.

He had shared bits and pieces of his life experiences with the older nieces and nephews, even the horrible shit he did. He wanted them to know him and the things he had done, but he had watered it down for them. He wanted them to know that there were dangers in the world and not to be naive. He also wanted them to know that there were consequences for every decision they would make whether good or bad, and that bad decisions carried many heartaches and pains that would last for years, not only affecting them but others as well.

He spent as much time with them, being an uncle and also being a friend. His oldest niece was eighteen. He had given her a car for her birthday, knowing she would need it for her last year of high school. He was proud of her; she was becoming an adult, dating boys and working for the things she wanted in life. Her whole life was before her. He hoped she would enjoy it. He wiped the tear away for his eye. There would be no signs to his family of what was to come; he had to finish his journey.

Chapter 39

Finishing Chapter 25, Julie was feeling something special. Jaden had put her in his book, in the beginning and now in the later chapters. He was so loving – the way he wrote of her. She could feel he had strong feelings for her, possibly a lingering love from their childhood, but was it real now? Was it something reignited from the conversations they had? She thought about it, and she just didn't know.

She herself was trying to come to terms of what exactly she felt for him. She cared about him without a doubt and was attracted to him, and there was the way she felt when she looked for a inbox message from him every day. Julie had strong convictions though about cheating and betrayal. She could never do that to her husband and to her family, but she knew she had strong feelings for Jaden, very strong feelings.

How though? She has not verbally talked to him, hasn't actually seen him in over thirty-two years. How could she feel the way she does? How could something that she felt as a little girl still survive after all these years? Was it a school yard crush, or was it something stronger, something more deeper than that? She was racking her brain, trying to understand what she was feeling and why.

Now she gets an e-mail from him, saying he won't send any more chapters until it's done. "What the fuck," she blurts out, getting curious looks from her family, who by the way thinks she spends way too much time on the computer – way too much time. She's always chatting with people, always laughing or talking to the computer when she is on. The last chapter left her yearning for more. He built it up and left her dangling. *What a smart-ass*, she thought of Jaden. Well he better get to finishing that book and be quick about it. She smiled, realizing her demand fell on deaf ears.

She was staring at her children; they were the love of her life. She was so involved in all they did and so supportive of their decisions. She made sure they would have the proper tools in life to build something they could be proud of and have stability in life. Julie was a terrific mother, and her kids loved her too. Of course, she had her doubts about things from time to time but all mothers do. Moms always question themselves about those little things: Did they do this right? Did they do that right? – always hoping the right choice was made.

When the choice is made out of love, it is always the right choice, Julie. Without a doubt, he knows every choice Julie made concerning her children was made out of love; she knows no other way. This is not flattery. This is what he believes, and it does not come from whatever affection he may have for her. It comes from what he sees and know about her.

Well, Christmas is close now, so many preparations to make and so many things to get ready. Life gets real busy around Julie's house at this time of year, and Julie goes crazy with her lists that she makes. Most people have about seven to ten things on their daily list, not Julie. Julie has about thirty. The pure energy this girl has is unbelievable. Jaden gets sleepy just thinking of all that running around and work to do. This is normal for Julie. Every year, she kicks into overdrive and gets it done. This year, she doesn't know will be different. Christmas will be the same, spent with family and friends, gifts exchanged and smiling faces.

New Year's though will not go according to the plan. Her list will be out the window, and she will have a grave undertaking guiding her night. She suspects nothing out of the ordinary. Jaden has done well to conceal it.

With so much to do, they get very little chat time in, their own lives almost pulling them away from each other, but still they yearn for each other's communication. Julie is busy with her errands and list; and Jaden, with his new position as second-shift operations manager. The both of them are busy. Time is taken up with each thing that requires their attention. Time is passing by, and destiny once again will keep them apart.

Jaden realizes how close the final day is getting. Julie thinks there is plenty of time to share her life with Jaden and to allow their friendship to grow. She looks forward to the next time she can get to Chicago. She would love to hang out with Jaden and spend some time just talking. Is that what she wants, just to hang out and talk? She questions her motives and wonders what she really wants to find out. Maybe she wants to see if there's something there between them. Maybe there could be a future for them together. She is definitely not happy in the marriage, and Jaden has expressed his decision to end his relationship with Victoria. Maybe something's there? She just needed to see him and to look into his eyes. She needed answers.

Every preparation Jaden could make was done. He was relaxing now, knowing all there was to do was wait and finish the book. He had completed his letter to Julie – his final farewell and his amends for what he was gonna put her through. He had asked her a favor though. Once she was able to move on after his death, if she ever felt the desire to have his story published, if ever there was a profit from the book, could she donate some of that profit to an organization that helped woman and children? Jaden wanted no profit for himself. This was to make amends not a get-rich scheme. If by some chance this story could make money, he would love for those people who had nothing to profit from it – a way to make amends to those he couldn't do so himself. For those he harmed and didn't know he had, it was a final act of sincere apologies.

He finished the letter with "I'm sorry," and for her to understand his pain, his sorrow, and his burdens that were too much for him, he needed to lay it down and needed to finish his journey. And he told her that she was his very first love, and she ended being his last love.

The time was at hand, only seven days to go; he was ready. The only concerns he had was if Julie would read the chapters when he thought she would and would he be able to arrive at Indian Boundary Park with the gun, without any police interference. That would suck to be stopped by the police and arrested for possession of a firearm by a felon. He would go back to prison, and everything he planned would be wasted. He hoped for a clear path to his resting place and to his place of forgiveness and salvation. *Please, whatever power that is, allow me to finish my road, allow me to end the pain and agony I feel.* He closed his eyes and repeated this prayer.

Christmas was wonderful. The time spent with families, the laughter and sharing, the food, and the singing of Christmas carols were amazing, and both of them were happy. Both Jaden and Julie had a great time with their families. Jaden had sent a quick e-mail to Julie wishing her a Merry Christmas, and she had done the same.

Jaden also informed her the book was just about done, but he requested a special favor of her, "Anything if I can," she told him. "Promise me you will read the chapters at 9:00 p.m. on December thirty first," he asked her in chat. Easy enough to do, so she promised. He was more serious now. "Remember, Julie, you promised, and I will hold you to that promise," he typed on the key board. "I will, I will," she typed back. "Why so important for that date and time?" she asked him. "Because you will see how it is tied into the book. It's something special just for you. I hope you find it very pleasant," he misled her, hoping he sparked her curiosity to the limits, almost as if she had no control over her curiosity. No matter what, she was gonna read that book at that date and time, no matter what.

He wanted her to finish the book and have time to call him, he wanted to hear her voice before he died and wanted to tell her he loved her from the moment he saw here to this very moment now. He had searched his whole life for that love, but only to find imitations, at best carbon copies, never the real thing. His life had no more purpose for him; he was ready. He spent the last days playing in his mind over and over every single horrific crime he had committed; this strengthen his resolve to kill the beast within him and end his agonizing pain once and for all.

After they had finished chatting, Julie had a strange feeling about the conversation. Why did he make it a point for her to promise what she did? He seemed kinda reserved this time, kinda like something was settled, and he was at peace with it. What though, she didn't know, but she had an uneasy feeling something wasn't right – something bad was gonna happen, and she was concerned. She decided to reread the chapters, look for a hint in the words. What was it he said between the lines? Look between the lines. She kept looking. What was it though she was looking for? Feeling a sense of urgency she read faster. With every word she read something was clicking in her mind, something was connecting the dots and crossing the Ts.

This book was not just a book, she thought. It's something else, something she couldn't put together exactly, but she knew now that Jaden had decided on something, and he was telling her through these chapters. What the fuck is he trying to say? She tried to contact him, sending him an e-mail saying they needed to talk, but he didn't respond. Was he ignoring her? What was he hiding? What was the decision he made? She needed answers and didn't want to wait, but she knew he would make her wait, he would reveal everything on December thirty-first at 9:00 p.m. to the dot.

Chapter 40

THE FINAL CHAPTER is done. The stage has been set, the actors are all in their place, and the director is Jaden. He now calls action and the play begins. Today is December thirty-first. It is 6:00 a.m. and Jaden wakes up and pretends to feel sick. He calls his boss at work and tells him he won't be able to come in. His boss says okay and hopes he feels better. They hang up. No fucking way Jaden is gonna work on his last day alive. You can believe that. He goes back to his room and climbs into bed, sleep comes within moments.

There was the same dream again, at the lakefront, but this time he isn't running toward Julie. This time he is walking slowly, and she is walking toward him, but they are not children anymore in the dream. Now they are as they are, adults, older. The both of them are now face-to-face, and Jaden is staring into her eyes. He is captured by her beauty, held in the moment, taking in all that is pure and innocent of Julie. He feels his heart pounding, the sweaty palms, and the warmth in his heart. Now he knows that feeling. Now there is no unknown. He is in love with her and always has been from the moment they first met. He reaches for Julie's hand, and she gives it to him. Standing there, he is caressing her soft gentle hand and revealing his love for her through his eyes. Julie holds his eyes with her own, and she is feeling his love and returning hers also. She no longer has questions for him. She knows the answer to the only question she ever truly had, and his eyes answered her and she was at peace with the answer.

He heard the voice in the dream, that voice from many years ago, which stopped him from killing Jimmy's killer, and the voice was so sweet to his ears now, so calming and soothing, and the voice said to Jaden, "Love her with all your heart, and she will always love you." Jaden woke up from the dream, confused by the message of the voice, confused about his final day today. Why would he get that message? Was he getting his path confused? What the fuck, why can't life be clear and easy to understand? *It was just a dream,* he told himself. *More like a wish,* he admitted in his head.

Julie is up very early. There's only one thing on her mind. She is gonna let Jaden have it for refusing to answer her e-mails. What kind of friend does that? Doesn't he know he hurt her by doing that shit? Fuck, fifteen hours to go till he sends the rest of the chapters. Today was gonna be a on the edge day for her. She desperately wanted to read the chapters, find out what the fuck was going on, and what he was planning. She decided to call in sick at work today. She wanted to go back over the other chapters and try searching again for something that would give her a clue. She finished brewing her coffee and sat on the sofa. She had printed the chapters out, easier for her to read and go through, with some pens next to her, she would underline and make notes of anything she found to be a clue.

Jaden kept telling her in their chat sessions, "Don't panic. Remember, it's just a book. Was she panicking for no reason? Was she reading more into it than she should? She just didn't know for sure; he had seen to that. He said he would take the truth and his imagination and braid it together, but for her not to worry and for her to remember it's just a book. He was fucking with her, and she realized he was the master at this game, he had established his expertise at creating confusion and doubt. She was unsure about everything, except that she knew at that 9:00 p.m. exactly, she would have the remaining chapters. What the fuck was happening to her? What was she feeling? She was worried about her friend. That was evident, but there was something more, a sense of sudden desperation she would lose him. Lose him? He wasn't hers to lose, was he?

She was getting a headache trying to sort everything out, trying to understand her feelings, the emotions that were building inside her. She was scared this was real and not a book and that she would never hear from Jaden again. The last time he thought he would hurt her, he walked out of her life. Would he do it again? Why would he think he was going to hurt her? Everything was a question. The answers were more questions. Damn, he was hard to read right now.

She imagined what he must have been like when he was on the streets, doing the terrible things he did. She knew he must have been a force to reckon with, the way his mind works, able to create the idea, build the setting, and put everything into motion, manipulating the characters, creating confusion and doubt, hiding the intent of whatever it was he had wanted to accomplish. He was definitely skilled at this game. She was truly understanding just what kind of fucked-up person it would take to create this shit. She was starting to realize how bad his childhood really was for him, and the toll it took. She just wanted to chat with him, talk to him, see how he was doing, she just needed, needed what Julie, can you say it, can you allow yourself to feel and acknowledge what is there? She asked herself these questions, and she knew the answer.

She realized now what she felt and when she had first felt it. Thirty-two years ago, Julie had laid her eyes on Jaden and had fallen in love. She was too young to understand it then, but it was clear now. He was here first love. The relief of finally being able to understand that, to acknowledge it, to know what she felt. She was still in love with him, and she realized that feeling never left. It only slept within her, never showing itself. It's now 3:00 p.m., and she is going crazy waiting. *Oh, he was gonna get an earful for this*, she smiled. That would explain the feelings she had when he contacted her again, when she chatted with him, and when she read his story, his confession, *his confession*! Holy shit, that was it. He was confessing his crimes to her.

Jumping up from the sofa, spilling her coffee, she went back to every single e-mail she saved, read the text, and found the clue she was looking for. He kept saying he was tired and his journey on this path was almost over. Oh, sweet Jesus, no. She now understood what the fuck he meant, and she was in a full-blown panic. *Oh my god, oh my god*. She started reading the confession, reading it with her eyes wide open. Now she saw the words. Now they spoke the truth to her. "Damn you, Jaden, you lied," she hollered out. He lied to her when he told her not to panic – it was only a fuckin' book.

Bullshit, she knew what the fuck he was planning, or close enough to it, and she knew it was tonight. Sometime after nine. She was getting hysterical, trying to think what to do, jumping back onto the computer, she sent him an e-mail: "Jaden, I know what your gonna do. Please write me. I need to talk to you. Don't do anything till we talk." *Click*. she sent it, hoping he would reply. What to do if he doesn't? She was thinking very fast. Thoughts didn't come clear, and she was starting to cry, starting to realize she might not be able to stop him. There was no doubt that he would do it. "Goddamn you, Jaden!" she screamed, feeling that sickening feeling in the pit of her stomach and that painful stab at her heart. She fell to her knees, having trouble breathing, catching the air she needed, trying to calm herself down.

Three in the afternoon and Victoria has left for her mom's house; she was gonna meet up with her brother and her friends there. They have a whole night of drinking to do, and they all couldn't wait. Jaden was sick, so she understood why he didn't go to work and he never went out for New Year's Eve, nothing out of the ordinary. She never had a clue. Jaden's family would have many questions for her after tonight, but she would have no answers. He knew he had succeeded at alarming no one. His only concern was getting the final chapters to Julie and getting to the park, and hopefully, she would call before the time comes for the journey to end. He hoped she would call.

He laid his clothes out on the bed. Never one to iron his clothes before, he did it now. He had a nice pair of beige kakis and a darker beige pullover long-sleeved shirt. His shoes also matched, and he would wear his leather trench jacket. He went to the computer and deleted his social page and then turned off the computer. He decided he had some time and decided to shave his face and head and then take a shower. He had put all the letters to his family on the dining room table, and the sheet that had all his passwords that Victoria would need. He was feeling very calm and very relaxed as he went into the bathroom.

Julie, on the other hand, had pieced together everything – all her intuition and love of reading. Her skills at research and comprehension had put it all together. Jaden was gonna kill himself some time tonight. She didn't have much time; he wasn't answering his e-mails, and he wasn't online now. She needed to contact him – contact someone. Wait, both his sisters were on his page as friends. She could contact them. She ran to her computer and navigated to her site and then attempted to go to his site. What the fuck, his site was gone. He had deleted everything. There was no way she could contact anyone from his end. Jaden was tying up all loose ends, shutting down his life, and Julie was feeling helpless, not knowing what to do. She grabbed on to his lie that it's just a book and told herself it's just a book over and over again as she was crying, knowing it was something else, not a book.

Jaden went to the computer, turned it on, and went to his e-mail page, clicked her name, and attached the whole book and sent it. He then petted his cats and walked out the door, driving to Indian Boundary Park. The time was close at hand, and he was ready. Julie was on her computer at 8:30 p.m., waiting impatiently for the inbox to light up, staring at the screen and the time on the bottom right-hand corner. Fuck, that clock moved slow. She was gonna get a hold of him, one way or another. If she couldn't, she had determined she would call the cops and give whatever information she had. He may be mad at her for it, but at least he would be alive, and that's all that mattered at this point.

Her family was home now; they were watching something on the TV in the living room, and she was in the kitchen. She told her family she was taking care of something very important and did not want to be disturbed; they understood. There it was. She clicked the box, and the words were in front of her eyes. She started reading the chapters he wrote, and with each word, her gut was twisting. She realized she was right. He was gonna kill himself, and he planned to do it at 12:00 a.m. She read that he would have his phone with him, and he hoped she would call. He wanted to talk to her before he finished his journey. She ran from the computer to her phone, not finishing the final chapter.

Where the fuck is his number? It wasn't on her phone. Shit, she had deleted it when he had called that time, not wanting any problems should her husband see the number. Was that the reason Jaden called, so she would have his number for tonight? Fuck, she realized she was playing catch-up and that Jaden was way ahead of her. He had months to plan this; she had only today to figure it out.

Her mind racing, she was confused on what to do. She was breathing fast. She ran back to her computer, went to the phone companies Web site, attempting to search the phone record archives to see if the number was there. No such luck.

"Goddamn you, Jaden, why like this?" she said out loud, unaware her family was watching her run around the house hysterical, searching for something, but for what, they didn't know.

She tried going to other people's sites, seeing if they were friends with any of Jaden's family. She covered about fifteen sites till she found one. There she was, Ivy, Jaden's younger sister. She clicked her page, came to her site, and sent a message: "Your brother is in great danger. I need his number. Matter of life and death. Send someone to Indian Boundary Park." *Click*, the message sent.

She was shaking now, not knowing how long it would take for his sister to respond. The page said she was online, but sometimes people leave their pages up but are away from their computers. She couldn't wait. She needed to contact more people. Time was moving fuckin' way too quick. She was losing her fuckin' mind. It had been a long time since Julie had prayed. It wasn't something she really believed in, but tonight, she said a silent prayer, her eyes closed, wet from the tears pouring down her eyes.

She went back to her computer and decided to finish the last chapter, hoping this was just a book and that at the end, there would be a message giving her some form of hope. There was a message; it was his phone number and a short little message for her that read: "Thought you might have deleted the number, so here it is again. Jaden." Her fingers had the number dialed before she could count to one, and the phone rang. "Pick it up," she said aloud. "Please, for god's sake, pick it up." Jaden was on the other end of the phone, sitting on the park bench, just smoking a cigarette, when the phone rang. He looked at the number – long distance. She must have finished the book early. He answered the phone.

"Hello, this is Jaden," he said.

"Where are you?" Julie frantically asked him.

"Right where I said I would be. I'm at Indian Boundary Park," came his reply.

"Jaden, what are you planning on doing? – no, don't answer that," she didn't want him to say it – didn't want him to confirm or reaffirm any twisted purpose he felt he had. "Just listen, I know I didn't tell you this before but I want to talk to you to tell you things I've felt but couldn't admit to before," she started saying. "I just don't want to do it under these circumstances. Can you leave the park, maybe go home or somewhere else?" The question was a tactic. She knew he was a romantic. He would need to carry out the plan at the park. Nowhere else would do for him. She needed to get him away from the park.

"Julie, time is short. Maybe you should tell me what you're feeling," he answered her.

"Jaden, I know you feel this is the only way, but it's not. Everything you've been through has been terrible, but if you do this, then you will still be hurting your family, creating more victims. Your journey won't be over 'cause there would be no amends to your family," she told him, trying to confuse him, trying to use whatever she could to stall him, and praying to God his sister will show up, but did she even get the message?

Ivy had finished painting the second room and decided to take a break, make some tea, and check her messages. It was 9:30 p.m. and she was tired. She had a message from some girl named Julie. The name was familiar, but where did she know it from? Oh yeah, she was one of Jaden's old friends from school. She clicked the message that read: "Your brother is in great danger. I need his number. Matter of life and death. Send someone to Indian Boundary Park." *What the fuck?* She reread it and sent a message back to Julie: "What do you mean?" but no reply came back. She thought about the message and then decided to call her other brother. She told him about the message, and they decided to take a chance and drive to Indian Boundary Park. First, she would call her brother though and see if Jaden would answer the phone. No answer. She was getting concerned. Her brother arrived, and they took off. She filled him in on what she knew.

"I have written them letters explaining things, Julie, but I don't want to talk about them, only about you and I," he told her.

"No, first promise me you won't do what you said," she told him.

"What's gonna happen is gonna happen. This journey needs to end" was his reply.

With no other thought that could help and no other tactic, she told him the truth, "I love you, Jaden," and she was quiet.

Jaden's sister and brother were about thirty minutes away from the park. They decided to call their other sister and mom, telling them what they knew so far, which was hardly anything. They only knew their older brother was in some sort of trouble, and they were going to help. They didn't know what to expect.

Jaden was listening, waiting for Julie to continue, and then he could hear her breathe and say, "I have always been in love with you, but you walked out of my life so long ago, and now your gonna do it again. Why?" she asked.

"This isn't about walking away from you. It's about ending the suffering and pain I feel. It's about making sure the vicious cycle doesn't continue. It's about protecting you."

"Don't you fucking say that," she interrupted him. "This isn't about none of that. It's about you taking the easy way out," she informed him. She wasn't thinking about stalling him. This was an issue she wanted to resolve with him and make him understand that there are other ways to deal with what he felt and what he was going through. She asked him to tell her about the pain and describe it.

He began slowly, going through the emotional turmoil as it felt inside of him, relating the exact way it numbed him and crippled him. She was listening, trying to feel his pain as he continued to tell her. She noticed his breathing getting more rapid, sensing a change in the way he was speaking. She continued to listen. Jaden gave her everything he had inside him – the foulest of the deeds he had done and the most shameful of the guilt the frightened child that lived within Jaden was now experiencing. He was crying, reliving his childhood over again, and Julie was witnessing, her gut twisting and turning from the terrible sound that came from the other end.

Jaden was in horrific pain; he sounded like he was dying. She could hear the familiar sound of uncontrollable crying. He wasn't talking now. She just heard his agony, sitting there, staring into the nothingness, tears rolling down her cheeks. She could see the vision in her mind – the trees, the park, the bench – and could envision him balled up on the bench or ground in agony, slowly unraveling his life and reliving those memories, and she realized there was nothing she could do. This was out of her control. She was powerless.

Jaden was completely gone now. He was in the moment of the past, being beaten by his dad, taking those horrific blows, each hit more destructive than the last. The pain was jumping around so fast, each memory taking turns at attacking him. Now he was feeling the agony of Jimmy's death again, unable to control what came to him next, only able to feel, feel everything the memories brought, surrendering to the onslaught, unable to defend himself, just feeling the agony and allowing the tears to flow. Now he was feeling the hurt of when his child was aborted, and that in itself brought on another surge of guilt, remorse, and anger. He couldn't move; he was held in place by his agonizing restraints. As he lay there immobilized, each event from his life had resurfaced, forcing him to feel the moment. There was no escaping this. There was no defense mechanism strong enough to stop the torture he felt.

Julie was listening and thought Jaden was slowly starting to lessen the agonizing sounds, not crying as much, but he wasn't talking, and she was getting nervous, "Jaden, Jaden," she was calling his name on the phone. There was no reply, but she could hear he had stopped crying and those painful sounds were over with – the calm before the storm. She continued to yell his name on the phone, "Jaden, Jaden. Goddamn it, answer me, Jaden!" Then she heard it – that one loud bang vibrating through the phone, through her ears, straight through to her heart. It was a gunshot, and she could no longer hold her pain in. She screamed in agony, "Nooooooooooooooooooo . . . oh god, whyyyyyyyyyyyyy!"

CPSIA information can be obtained at www.ICGtesting.com
Printed in the USA
238319LV00002B/3/P